# 杜立德医生在月球

[美]休·罗夫丁 著
盛正茂(Zhengmao Sheng) 译

文匯出版社

# 目　录
## Contents

**月球狂想曲**
——译《杜立德医生在月球》有感（代自序）
**Rhapsody of the Moon**
——On *Doctor Dolittle on the Moon*（Introduction）

第 一 章　登陆新世界 / 001

第 二 章　色彩与芬芳之地 / 007

第 三 章　渴啊渴 / 013

第 四 章　英雄吱吱 / 021

第 五 章　高原之上 / 027

第 六 章　月亮湖 / 034

第 七 章　巨人的踪迹 / 042

第 八 章　会唱歌的树 / 048

第 九 章　植物语言的研究／053

第 十 章　月球上的麦哲伦／058

第十一章　点火／064

第十二章　爱漂亮的百合花／069

第十三章　有多种气味的花／074

第十四章　送给百合花几面镜子／080

第十五章　穿上新衣／085

第十六章　月亮的传说／091

第十七章　我们听说了"理事会"／098

第十八章　管事的／105

第十九章　月亮巨人／113

第二十章　医生和巨人／120

第二十一章　奥托·布劳奇来到月亮上的故事／127

第二十二章　月球上的伙计听说了医生／134

第二十三章　一位王／141

第二十四章　杜立德医生在月亮上做手术／149

第二十五章　又见帕德尔比／157

## DOCTOR DOLITTLE ON THE MOON

1. WE LAND UPON A NEW WORLD / 172
2. THE LAND OF COLOURS AND PERFUMES / 179
3. THIRST! / 185
4. CHEE-CHEE THE HERO / 193
5. ON THE PLATEAU / 198
6. THE MOON LAKE / 204
7. TRACKS OF A GIANT / 212
8. THE SINGING TREES / 218
9. THE STUDY OF PLANT LANGUAGES / 224
10. THE MAGELLAN OF THE MOON / 230
11. WE PREPARE TO CIRCLE THE MOON / 235
12. THE VANITY LILIES / 241
13. THE FLOWER OF MANY SCENTS / 247
14. MIRRORS FOR FLOWERS / 253
15. MAKING NEW CLOTHES / 260

16. MONKEY MEMORIES OF THE MOON / 267

17. WE HEAR OF "THE COUNCIL" / 275

18. THE PRESIDENT / 283

19. THE MOON MAN / 291

20. THE DOCTOR AND THE GIANT / 300

21. HOW OTHO BLUDGE CAME TO THE MOON / 308

22. HOW THE MOON FOLK HEARD OF DOCTOR DOLITTLE / 317

23. THE MAN WHO MADE HIMSELF A KING / 325

24. DOCTOR DOLITTLE OPENS HIS SURGERY ON THE MOON / 333

25. PUDDLEBY ONCE MORE / 341

后记 / 356

AFTERWORD / 359

# 月球狂想曲
## ——译《杜立德医生在月球》有感
### （代自序）

正如大家所知，这本《杜立德医生在月球》，与其他"杜立德医生"系列的作品一般，对于故事中的动物角色们进行了拟人化的描写。虽然这种写作手法自格林童话始已被世人所熟知，而且还有着刘易斯·卡罗尔笔下的白兔先生和安徒生笔下的丑小鸭等大名鼎鼎的角色争锋，但是休·罗夫丁所创造的动物们仍然能够凭借其独特的风格脱颖而出。因为罗夫丁笔下的动物们尽管拥有了人类的情感、思维和智慧，却依然保持着属于自己的语言，并没有像绝大多数童话作品里的动物们一样开口说人话。热爱动物的杜立德医生则在博学多才的鹦鹉波莉尼西娅的指导下慢慢学会了动物们的语言，从而获知了动物们的心事和烦恼，并且竭尽所能帮助他们。在本书中，杜立德医生更是学会了昆虫和植物的语言而得以和他们进行良好的沟通与交流。这种独特的写作手法深刻地体现了作者身为人类对于动物的尊重和地球万物平等的思想。

本书以杜立德医生的少年助手托马斯·斯塔宾斯的视角记录了和医生一同四处探险的经历，这样的叙事角度比起第三人称叙事或者以杜立德医生作为第一人称叙事，更让少年读者们能够感同身受：少年托马斯所惊叹所好奇所疑惑的，也正是少年读者们所惊叹所好奇所疑惑的，这样的切入点，使文章显得更亲切更有说服力。

虽然本书是一本童话作品，描写了医生和动物们在月球上发生的种种探险趣事，但是看似荒诞不经的表面，背后却是作者借书中角色之口表达了他对于当时人类社会所发生的一些问题的看法。事实上，在其他的几本同系列小说中，休·罗夫丁已经批评了宠物商店和马戏团主为了赚钱对动物进行的虐待，而在本书中，休·罗夫丁则将评论的中心转移到了政治和宗教上。你看，书中的月球是被一个"理事会"所治理的，这个组织由月球上各种不同种类的动植物们推荐的代表所组成，目的是为了"保障月球的和平，防止争斗和战乱"。这很明显是对于当时新建立的国际联盟的借鉴。在作者笔下，这个理事会的存在保证了月球上的生物之间不会由于争夺资源而爆发战争，也很好地保证了外来物种不会对他们造成威胁。而在作者写作的几年时间里，国际联盟也成功地避免了意大利、希腊和芬兰等地发生的冲突。休·罗夫丁在书中对理事会的褒扬不能不说是对国际联盟的认可和期望，也是曾经在一战中作为英国爱尔兰卫队一员的作者对于世界和平的向往。

除此以外，作者亦借用书中猴子一族中流传的古老神话为引子，提起了宗教话题，表达了他本人温和宽容的宗教理念。在传说中，远古人类由于"那些老派的太阳崇拜者们认为月亮是太阳的妻子或者女儿，所以把她视为女神。而另一些人认为既然月亮曾经是地球的一部分，那么只有地球才有资格和太阳一起被视为神，而不是月亮"的缘故经常爆发部族争斗。杜立德医生对此发出了感叹：只要活得开心，做一个真诚友善的人，那么邻居家的信仰又有什么要紧呢？是啊，为了这样一个渺小可笑的争论而爆发了残酷的战争，人类真是多么愚蠢可笑！可惜，从古至今人类为了宗教的原因而爆发的战争真是不计其数，而且至今仍没有停止。

此外，虽然在休·罗夫丁写作本书的时代人类对于地球之外的世界所知甚少，但是他却能在书中精确地描绘月球上的重力特征、崎岖地理和真空地带，即书中所说的"死亡带"，甚至先主流科学界十余年暗示了月球的起源并非因为"离心力",而是一场大碰撞的结果。我想,除了天马行空的想象力以外,这很大程度上应该归功于作者在麻省理工学院所接受过的教育。

可惜这样一本好书也并非完美无瑕:整本书的情节略微显得有些拖沓,特别某些章节对于月球地貌和风光的描写都显得有些单调、冗长和重复。不过,瑕不掩瑜,这本《杜立德医生在月球》仍不失为一篇儿童文学佳作。

盛正茂

2017 年 3 月

# Rhapsody of the Moon
―――On *Doctor Dolittle on the Moon*

**(Introduction)**

As many readers might have known, this *Doctor Dolittle on the Moon*, just like any other Doctor Dolittle books, personifies the animal characters in it. Though personification has been a literary element long applied by novels and fairy tales and was made famous by Mr. Rabbit of Lewis Carroll and the Ugly Duckling by Christian Anderson, the animals in Hugh Lofting's books still stand out. It is because even when they possess human feelings, mind and wisdom, the animals continue to speak their own languages instead of human tongues. Instead, Doctor Dolittle, being an animal lover and more importantly, a human being, is the one who learns animal languages from the wise old parrot Polynesia, thus being able to understand their problems and concerns, and to assist them better. In this book, he goes even further, mastering the languages of alien plants and insects. These rather unique imaginations clearly exhibit the author's respect to other creatures and the philosophy of equality among all beings.

This book is delivered from the perspective of Doctor Dolittle's young assistant Thomas Stabbins, who accompanies the doctor through many of his adventures. Compared to a third-person perspective or Doctor's own perspective, the author's scheme could best relate to the readers, many of which are as young, or curious as Stabbins. What amuses him also amuses the readers; what delights him also delights them; what confuses him appears to be the aim of their curiosity. Such a perspective makes the plots more "familiar" and persuasive.

At first glance, this book appears to be a description of an exploration with novelty and a childlike sense of humor. However, laid in its plots are the author's comments on some social problems met by his contemporary society. In previous books Lofting had already criticized the circuses and pet shops for exploiting animals, while in this book the focus shifts to politics and religion. Behold, the Moon is ruled by a Council, consisting of representatives of lunar species, responsible for keeping peace and preventing conflicts. This is an apparent reference to the League of Nations, which had successfully put ends to violence and controversies in multiple regions, including Italy, Greece and Finland. Praising the organization and efficiency of the Council, Hugh Lofting, a former member of the Irish Guards in British Army during the First World War, shows his recognition of the League of Nations and hope for world peace.

Furthermore, using the myths of monkey tribes as a lead, Lofting mentions the religious topic, expressing his moderate nature. According to the monkey myths, ancient humans had an argument on if the Moon, or the Earth, has the privilege of being worshipped along with the Sun, leading to a bloody tribal war. After recording this story, Doctor Dolittle exclaims "Just as though it mattered to any one what his neighbour believed so long as he himself led a sincere and useful life and was happy!" Indeed that is true; however, religious warfare has been a phenomenon regularly repeated in human history, and could be seen at many places around the world today.

Even though we human race only knew little about the world above atmosphere in the 1920s, Hugh Lofting accurately describes the gravity and landscapes on the Moon, as well as the oxygen-free vacuum in space. He even preceded the mainstream science community, suggesting that the creation of the Moon was not a result of centrifugal force, but of a great collision. All these speculations are not only mere imaginations of the author, but also the gifts of his MIT education.

However, such a great novel is not without flaws: the plots are slightly sluggish, and in several chapters there appear repetitive depictions of lunar sceneries — yet these minor defects could not overshadow its greatness, this *Doctor Dolittle on the Moon* is still worth compliments and bearing the name of an outstanding child literature.

**Zhengmao Sheng**
In March 2017

# 第一章
# 登陆新世界

我，托马斯·斯塔宾斯，医学博士约翰·杜立德的助手（也是"沼泽上的帕德尔比"镇上的鞋匠雅各·斯塔宾斯的儿子），一直想着有一天能记录下我和医生在月球上的探险经历，可惜总是觉得无从下笔。毕竟要想回忆起那几周中的分分秒秒可不是个简单的活计。虽然我做了厚厚的几大本笔记，但是它们基本上都是学术性的资料和数据，而我则想把这个故事分享给除了科学家以外的其他人，所以我对此总是感到纠结不已。

人们总想知道我们旅途中的各种见闻。我一开始打算寻求叽喽的帮助，我把我完成的前几章读给他听，让他提些意见。不过他的兴趣主要放在了"月球上有没有老鼠"这个问题上。我想这个问题有些难以回答，我不记得在那儿曾经见到老鼠的踪迹，不过我十分确定月球上肯定有这些小动物的存在，至少，肯定有和老鼠差不多的生物存在。

然后我又去问了咕咕,他很好奇我们在月球上能吃到什么蔬菜(拍拍对这个问题嗤之以鼻,还说询问咕咕是我能想到的最糟糕的主意)。我接着又去问了母亲,她想知道我们带的内衣裤如何换洗,还有其他诸如此类的琐碎问题,而这些细枝末节我已经记不太清了。我最后去找了马修·马格,他的问题比我母亲的或叽噗的还要糟:月球上有商店吗?那儿的猫猫狗狗长什么样?看样子,这个好心肠的、卖猫食的男人把月球想象成了一个和帕德尔比或伦敦东区差不多的地方。

我终于意识到尝试写下大家所感兴趣的一切是行不通的。这不禁让我想起了头一次去杜立德医生家里时亲爱的老波莉尼西娅问我的一个问题:你善于观察吗?我一直以为自己是个不错的观察家,但现在我可不敢再这么说了,毕竟我发现我已经记不清那些大家都感兴趣的细节了。

这主要还是因为我的注意力太过分散。打个比方,如果把一个人的注意力比作黄油,那么面包就代表着吸引人注意力的事物,而如果有太多"面包"的话,"黄油"肯定就不够了。而毫无疑问,在月球上吸引我的奇观实在太多了,所以我对它们都几乎没有什么清晰的记忆。

如果说真的有谁能对我的写作起到最大的帮助,那自然就是那只带着我们飞往月球的巨蛾——杰马洛·巴伯利了。但鉴于他现在不在我身边，我想我还是先抛开其他人的意见，用自己的方式来讲述这个故事好了。我的叙述不可能是绝对准确的，也可能有所遗漏，但不管怎样，请跟着我的回忆一起走进那段冒险之旅——

巨蛾载着我和杜立德医生在月球那反射着太阳光的地表上空盘旋，我们尽可能地把身子贴在巨蛾的背上，欣赏着周围的风景。很明显，巨蛾对这个神秘国度的地形了如指掌。他庞大的身躯慢慢地向着一个四周都是小山

"我们乘着巨蛾登上月球啦"

丘的谷地中央降落下去,我甚至已经可以看到下方那平整干燥的沙地了。

这些低矮的小山丘和远处的高山(更远处的山峰掩藏在稍近一些的山脊之后,被淡淡的暗绿色光晕所笼罩)都有着杯口一样的峰顶,看起来像被切掉了一块似的。后来医生告诉我那些是死火山。这些冰冷的山峰也曾经喷出岩浆和火焰,但经过长时间的风化和侵蚀就变成了现在这种奇特的形状,它们中的一些甚至已经被流沙所淹没,看不出原来的样子了。这让我想起了蛛猴岛上名为"低语的岩石"的山峰,虽然这两个地方的其他景观大不相同,但任何一个人都能看出这两个火山口之间的相似之处。

我们在下方长长的狭窄峡谷中没有发现任何生命迹象——没有动物,也没有植被覆盖,但我们并没有因此而垂头丧气——至少杜立德医生没有。因为医生说他在巨蛾飞越月球表面的时候看到了一棵树,这就意味着月球上有水和生物的存在。

当巨蛾下降到离地大约二十英尺时,他张开了翅膀,像个大风筝一样轻巧地降落在地上,稍稍弹跳了一下,又滑行了一段,终于停了下来。

我们登上了月球!

现在我们终于要开始习惯这里全新的大气了。但在我们正式"登陆"之前,医生让那只巨蛾先在原地停留一会儿,让我们花些时间来适应这儿的新环境。

巨蛾非常乐意接受这个建议。事实上,我猜这只可怜的大昆虫本来也想休息一会儿了。医生又从上衣口袋里掏出一些途中省下来的食物分给我们,我们几个便一边嚼着巧克力,一边环顾四周,打量着月球上的新奇景象。

月球上的天光总是会突然变化,这种现象在我看来和地球上的极光有些相像。前一秒你看到的粉色的山脉在下一秒就变成了绿色,而它们像紫罗兰一般颜色的阴影一眨眼的工夫就变成了玫瑰色。

在月球上呼吸有点儿困难,于是我们只好尽可能握紧手里的"月铃花"。这种橙色花儿散发出的香气让我们在路上成功穿越了地球和月球之间的无空气带。如果我们不通过这些花呼吸的话便会咳嗽个不停,不过好在月球表面的情况比起外太空要好上一点儿,所以我们呼吸起来并没有那么困难。

这儿的重力状况也令人费解。我们如果要调整一下走路的姿势或者快跑上几步几乎都不会费什么力气,但肺部的压力却不小。最让我惊奇的是在这里我只要摆摆手臂就能像在水里游泳一样漂浮起来。我心情舒畅地哼着歌(虽然因为嘴里塞满了巧克力而含混不清),满心期待着能赶快越过山丘,翻过峡谷,去探索那全新的世界。

当然啦,首先我们得把带来的行李卸下来。虽然我们带了不少大件儿,但在这个星球上我们只要轻轻一蹬就能从二十五英尺高的巨蛾背上跳下来。随着"啪"的一声,我们轻轻松松地着陆了,行走在了月球那柔软的沙地上。

在月球上行走比在地球上轻松许多

## 第二章
# 色彩与芬芳之地

不管怎么说,作为一支新世界的探险队,我们的四位队员都是非同凡响的,而且我们之间配合默契、天衣无缝。首先是波莉尼西娅:她好像从不惧怕任何恶劣的环境,无论面对干旱、洪水、烈火还是大雾,她都面不改色。好吧,也许我这话说得有些幼稚,不过时至今日我也想象不出有什么困难能让这只非凡的鸟儿后退一步。而且她似乎每周只要吃上几颗种子(不管什么种类都行),再喝上两三口水就能保持一副活力充沛的样子。接下来是吱吱,虽然他对食物的要求并不低,但他总能找到自己想要的一切东西。同时,他还是我见过的最棒的食物采集者,当大家都饥肠辘辘的时候,他可以在一片陌生的森林里仅仅凭嗅觉就告诉我们森林中有哪些水果或坚果可以果腹。这种绝活连医生都无法理解——事实上,就连吱吱自己也不知道他是怎么做到的。

然后就轮到我自己了,虽然我并没有太多的科学素

波莉尼西娅每周只要吃几粒种子就行了

养,但我知道如何在探险时干好助手该干的活,另外,我也非常熟悉杜立德医生的行事方式。

最后该谈谈我们这个队伍里的核心人物——杜立德医生了。很少有科学家能拥有像他这样的品质,他从不认为自己知道一切。对于他所不知道的,他总是表现出孩童般的好奇,这不仅能让他更快地学到新的知识,还能让其他人更乐意传授他们的经验。

**吱吱是我见过的最棒的食物采集者**

没错,这的确是个罕见的组合,而且我毫不怀疑大多数的科学家都会嘲笑这样的一支探险队,但正是我们,完成了这次史无前例的远征。

就像以前很多次探险之旅一样,医生并没有在前期准备上花太多的时间。他可不像有些冒险家那样,每到一处都要插上旗帜再高唱国歌。在确定我们都已经准备完毕之后,医生就决定出发了。于是我和吱吱,当然还有蹲在我肩上的波莉尼西娅，便跟在医生身后，踏上了这段旅程。

我得说在月球上探索最初的几个小时就像在做梦一样。那里前所未见的景象和奇特的失重带来的浮空的感觉，总让我怀疑是否下一秒就会有人把我从床上叫醒。所以我尽量不停地和医生、吱吱及波莉尼西娅说话，尽管有时候我也没什么想说的，但我喉咙里发出的声响至少能让我清醒一点。好在我们慢慢地开始习惯这种感觉

**医生带的指南针一直疯狂地转**

了。因为我们很快就发现，除了不断变化的地表和天空的颜色外，视线范围里已经没什么太多新奇的玩意儿了。医生随身带了一个指南针，但是它一直在疯狂地转，怎么也停不下来。

最后医生只好放弃用指南针来导航的想法，转而使用月球图和目视来确认方位。后来，他向远方一处山脊的尽头——也就是当初巨蛾在月球表面盘旋时医生看到的那棵树所在的方向走去。但是，这片区域中的山脉从外表看起来都十分相像，我们能够勉强在月球图上辨认出身后的几座山峰，但是图上面却找不到我们面前几座山脉的影子。这使得我们更加确定，我们正走向从未被人类观测到的月亮的背面。"我想我的推测是正确的，斯塔宾斯。"当我们缓缓走过沙地时，医生对我说："水一定只存在于从地球上观测不到的月亮背面，所以天文学家们总是声称水不存在于月球上。"

在此期间，我一直专注于月球上奇异的景色而忽略了对气候的感受。之前，医生总是担心月球上的天气要么热得让人难以忍受，要么就比北极还要寒冷。事实上，除了空气有点稀薄之外，这儿的气候十分舒适宜人，甚至偶尔还能感到有阵阵微风吹过。

我们几个一直在努力寻找生命的迹象——虽然我们并不确定会遇上什么样的生物，可是脚下松软的泥土不可能留下什么动物的印迹,对此,就连经验丰富的追踪专家吱吱也一筹莫展。

月球上的空气中弥漫着一些奇异的气味——它们大部分都是芬芳好闻的,但偶尔也会有些令人不愉快的气味混杂其中。不过,除了巨蛾带来的"月铃花"的香气之外,我们辨认不出其他任何一种。

我们继续赶路,翻过一座又一座山脉,可是仍然没有发现那棵树的踪迹。在连续徒步行走两个半小时后,我们感到有些筋疲力尽。毕竟虽说在月球上行走比在地球上轻松许多,但是把那些行李一路搬到这儿还是耗费了我们不少力气。波莉尼西娅说她可以飞到前面去探查一下,可是医生希望我们四个能待在一起。

又走了半个多小时,在仍然一无所获的情况下,医生终于同意了波莉尼西娅的请求,于是那只鸟儿飞到前头去了。

## 第三章
## 渴啊渴

波莉尼西娅离开后,我们几个便坐在几大捆行李上休息,她像一只老鹰般朝空中飞去,在一千多英尺的高空中盘旋了一会儿,又慢悠悠地飞了回来。看她飞得这么慢,连医生都有些不耐烦了。不过她给我们带来了个好消息。她说她看见了那棵树,不过距离我们还是很远。医生忍不住问她为什么过了那么长时间才回来,她认真地说她必须保证飞回来的路线正确,才能给我们带路。的确,波莉尼西娅的认路本领这会儿能给我们帮上大忙,而且那么长的距离会让任何最细小的路线偏差变成巨大的错误。于是,我们又信心满满地跟在波莉尼西娅身后上路了。

当那棵树终于出现在视野中时,我们都估计那棵树离得不太远,但之后我们才发现实际距离和我们的猜想大相径庭。这可能有两个原因:一是透过月球上的稀薄空气和光线的折射,远方的景物看起来都被拉近了;二是

**波莉尼西娅有认路的本领**

这棵树的体型巨大得难以想象。我想我永远也不会忘记这棵树,毕竟它是我们在月球上见到的第一个生命啊。当我们在这棵树下站定时,"黑暗"已经慢慢出现在天边。我说的"黑暗"是指月球上黄昏时那奇怪的暮光,看样子这就是月球上的夜晚。在我看来,这棵树的高度至少有三百英尺,树干最粗的地方直径估计也有四五十英尺。它的奇特外形不同于我所见过的任何一棵树,但它也不像其他任何一种植物。我不知道应该怎么描述它,它好像是——活着的。可怜的吱吱吓坏了,脖子上的毛发根根直竖。我和医生花了好一会儿才说服他帮忙在这棵树下扎帐篷。

奇特的大树

入夜之后,风仍然一如既往轻轻地吹着,我们还可以隐约看到地球的轮廓,不过由于没有光线的反射所以看不太清楚。当我们几个躲进了帐篷,拿出巧克力当晚饭吃时,医生还一直坐在外面,抬头盯着那棵树上奇形怪状的枝条。

在微风的吹拂下,那些枝条也在摆动着,但奇怪的是,虽然风吹得十分平缓,但这些枝条却在剧烈地摆动,看起来就像一只被铁链拴着的动物一样在不停挣扎。另外一个奇怪的现象就是,这棵树发出的声响也不是普通的风吹树叶发出的沙沙声,因为即使没有晚风吹过,树枝仍然会吱呀作响。我能够看出即使是老练的旅行家波莉尼西娅也对这棵树抱有戒心,因为鸟儿对于树和风的感觉比人类要灵敏得多。我原本希望她会飞到树上去查看一番,但她并没有这么做。至于吱吱,虽然他是一名在非洲丛林里整天和树木打交道的原住民,我也实在没有什么把握说服瑟瑟发抖的他去帮我解开这个谜团。

吃过晚饭,我们几个又忙活了起来。我花了几个小时帮医生记笔记,我发现在一个新世界里度过的第一天有着不少新鲜事物可以记录。我们测量了气温、风向、风力、登陆的大概位置,还有气压什么的(医生随身携带着一个气压计),这些数据在大部分人眼里枯燥无味,但对于科学家来说却是十分重要的资料。

我一直希望我能回忆起我在月球上的第一个早晨是如何从睡梦中醒过来的。前一晚我们在兴奋和疲惫中酣然入睡,第二天早上睁开眼睛后,我足足花了十分钟才反应过来自己并不是待在熟悉的帕德尔比。要不是看见医生在对面的沙地上整理仪器和书籍,我甚至不敢相信我真的在月球上。

现在我们最需要的东西就是食物了,我们带来的储备已经快要见底了。医生开始后悔自己和巨蛾分别得太过仓促:自从离开巨蛾,直到在树下扎营这段时间,我们都没有见到任何可能的食物来源。现在想要再回去找他

我们带来的储备快见底了

问问这周边的状况也不太可能了,毕竟路途遥远,而且他也不会等我们那么长时间。但不管怎么样,寻找食物这事可耽搁不得。于是我们赶紧打包好行李,准备继续前进。不过,要往哪个方向走呢?既然我们已经找到了这棵树,那么这周围肯定有着其他的植物或者水源。我们远眺四周,除了裸露的岩石和沙丘外一无所获。这回不等医生下令,波莉尼西娅就振翅飞去找寻生命的痕迹了。

波莉尼西娅去找寻生命的迹象

过了一会儿,鸟儿回来报告说:"好吧,我压根没看到任何树的影子,这鬼地方简直和撒哈拉大沙漠一样。不过,看到那儿的山脉没有?那儿有座山峰长得像顶帽子。看到了吗?"

"看到了。"医生说,"怎么了?"

"那儿的地平线轮廓和其他地方的不太一样。我不敢说那里肯定有绿洲,但一定不会只有茫茫沙海。我想我们还是赶快动身的好,走到那儿可不轻松。"这段路程的确不轻松,看起来这几乎成了我们和饥饿之间的一场赛跑。没吃早餐对我而言不算什么,我们以前在地球上不知错过了多少顿早餐,但几个小时的长途跋涉之后,那片山脉似乎仍远在天边,这就让我有些垂头丧气了。

与我正相反,那段时间里医生看起来却干劲十足。我知道他其实和我们一样又饿又渴,心里也一定十分焦急,但是他仍然努力地打起精神和我们讲一些他以前遇到的种种趣事,来振作队伍的士气。医生后来告诉我,他年轻时曾经受雇于多支探险队——不是因为他的知识,而是因为他风趣幽默的性格使队伍中的其他人受益匪浅。

说真的,这一路上如果没有医生的话,我是绝对撑不下来的。我以前还从未体验过如此口干舌燥的感觉,我感觉我努力走出的每一步都会是最后一步。

我迷迷糊糊地强撑着跟上队伍,不知过了多久,我好像听见波莉尼西娅大叫:"快看!前头有森林!"在我最终晕过去之前只记得吱吱把一个用树叶卷成的杯子放在我嘴边,然后我的嘴唇上瞬间感到了一股沁人心脾的清凉。

吱吱用一个树叶卷成杯子给我喝水

## 第四章
# 英雄吱吱

当我从昏迷中清醒过来时觉得有点难为情：我真是一个不称职的探险队员。看见我醒了，医生立刻朝我这儿走了过来，他看出了我在想什么，安慰我说不必对自己的行为感到惭愧，他又解释说吱吱和波莉尼西娅早就习惯了在这样炎热干旱的地方旅行了，所以这种环境对于他们而言并没有太大影响。

"不管怎么说，"医生接着说道，"斯塔宾斯，你做得很棒，你走完了全程。我认识许多经验丰富的探险家，换作他们，表现也不会比你更好了。这趟旅程可不轻松——你干得很不错！起来吧，该吃早餐了——感谢上帝，我们终于找到吃的了。"

我摇摇晃晃地坐了起来，很快，一堆奇奇怪怪的东西——后来我才知道那些是不同的水果——就被摆在了我们面前。吱吱虽然还对这种会动的树和低语的风声心有余悸，却仍然尽职地挑拣着可以食用的野果。我和医

医生表扬我："斯塔宾斯，你做得很棒，你走完了全程。"

生都从未见过这些水果，但如果吱吱说它们是安全的，那我们就没什么好担心的。

吱吱找来的野果中有些如同一截树干那么大，有些又只有一粒核桃那么小，但是对于饥肠辘辘的我们来说，它们奇特的外形一点也不重要。我们关心的只是不停往嘴里塞更多的食物。吱吱还把找到的水装在巨大的坚果壳里和用树叶卷成的杯子里给我们喝。我觉得这些不知名的水果真是我平生吃过的最好的一顿早餐。

第四章 英雄吱吱 023

吱吱找来野果充饥

吱吱，你克服了恐惧，自愿深入丛林为筋疲力尽的我们找来食物。对于这个世界上的其他人而言，你可能只是一只曾经在街头卖艺的普普通通的猴子，但对于我们而言，你克服恐惧拯救我们于饥饿的壮举能让你的名字永远和历史上的伟大人物并列。感谢上帝让你和我们在一起！如果没有你的勇气和令人惊异的丛林生存技能，我们也许早就倒在了月球的沙地里了。

好吧，言归正传，我一边吃着水果，一边观察着四周的情况。在我们前面是一片高原,高原上生长着一片郁郁葱葱的森林,高地边缘的山坡上则长了几丛灌木和几棵孤独的小树。我们很好奇这些小树是如何在这些偏离森林——也就是偏离这片森林赖以生存的水源——的地方存活下来的,但我们提出的假设没有一个能完美解释这种情况。医生得出的最让人信服的解释是这里有一个地下泉眼,它不仅给高原上的大片植被提供水源,其支流也同样滋润着这些边缘上的植被。毫无疑问,要让一片

医生得出最让人信服的解释——有一个地下泉眼

丛林长成现在这种规模需要几百年甚至上千年的时间。这里有座繁茂的森林对我们而言是件好事，否则我们这次探险几乎是一次彻底的失败。

吃完了这顿新奇的早餐，我和医生便开始询问吱吱是如何在森林中找到这些水果的。

"其实我也不太清楚我是怎么做到的。"吱吱答道，"我被吓坏了，一直闭着眼睛。我穿过参天大树、丛丛灌木、下垂的藤蔓，还有低矮的树根——老天，我那时真是饿慌了，使劲地闻啊闻，当然，我很快就闻到了水果的味道。于是我爬上了一棵树——一半的时间都闭着眼睛。老天！我看到了那片巨大丛林的全貌——和任何一只猴子所看到过的任何一片丛林都不一样。那儿的果子闻起来都棒极了。我爬上爬下，闻来闻去，摘了一大堆水果。在路上，我还找到了一种植物的根部，闻起来有点像生姜，不过味道更好。我吃了个饱，又带上几块这种树根，一路跑了回来，然后，我正站在这儿给你们讲故事呢。"

好吧，亲爱的吱吱在故事里描述了许多他自己的英雄事迹，但这些描述并不能告诉我们太多关于面前这片森林的具体情况。不过，我们几个已经整装待发，准备好亲自去一探究竟了。我们把从登陆之后就一直随身携带的大件行李卸了下来，找个地方放好，然后就向着离我们大约四英里远的高原之上的森林走去。我们现在可以轻松找到回营地的路,不必担心会迷失在月球上。

这次的攀登还是挺轻松的,脚下的沙地非常坚实。我们在这陡峭斜坡上踏出的每一步都让我觉得离某些伟大的发现又近了一点——我们终于开始了解月球上的生态环境了。

我们终于开始了解月球上的生态环境了

# 第五章
# 高原之上

我们在月球上与大片树木的首次相遇实在是一次奇妙的经历,当时的场景至今还历历在目。我们几个在登上高原的那一刹那就看到了几英里外的一堵由丛林组成的绿色之墙。那儿的树木虽然种类不多,但任何一种都和我们在地球上见过的品种截然不同。

比方说,有一整块几平方英里大的地方全被笼罩在一棵像蕨类植物一样的树下。另一棵树则使我想起了地球上一种有着小白花的显花植物(它的名字我一时想不起来了),月球上有种树和这种植物长得一模一样,花朵一堆堆地铺在枝条末端,茎秆呈现出泛白的绿色,只不过它的体型恐怕有地球上那种植物的一千倍大。这种树的树冠非常浓密,我们后来发现即使雨水也无法穿透它的树叶。正因如此,我和医生后来将其命名为"伞树"。总而言之,森林里的树没有一种是我们曾经见过的。

花朵一堆堆地铺在枝条末端

还有一件事也一直困扰着我们——我们几个一直都能听到一种奇怪的声响。我们已经知道,在月球上,哪怕是极细小的声音,也能传出去很远,但这仍然无法解释这种怪声音的来源。我们刚爬上高原就听到了这种声音,这是一种乐音,但又不像是单一乐器发出的,而像是一整支管弦乐队正在轻柔地演奏着。这着实给我和医生带来了不小的震撼。

在离森林还有一英里左右的地方,我们停下来稍作休整。我发现在月球上，不同地貌之间总是有着很清晰的分界，就连那些小小的景观之间也有着明显的边界。我们现在身处的地方就有力地印证了这一点：在我们站着的高原边缘是一整片不断延伸的坚硬的沙地，表面光滑得如同一面镜子。再往前就突然出现了那片郁郁葱葱的森林。我很好奇在远处这片丛林是否也会突然被另一种地形取而代之。

现在我们的首要目标是去找到一处稳定的水源。我

吱吱追踪昨晚留下的记号

们让吱吱做向导,他一路沿着自己昨晚留下的足迹跑进了丛林。对于我和医生来说,穿越面前开阔的高原地带不算什么,但到了丛林边缘之后继续前进就不容易了。吱吱在丛林里穿行大多靠的是在树枝间跳跃,但我们可不行。于是,吱吱让我们几个在丛林边等待,他自己则前去追踪昨晚留下的记号。

过了一小会儿,医生问我:"斯塔宾斯,你昨晚半夜有没有被吵醒过?"

"没有。"我告诉他,"我实在太累了。怎么了?"

"你呢,波莉尼西娅?"医生没有理我。

"醒了几次。"波莉尼西娅回答。

"那你有没有听到,或者看到什么……呃……奇怪的东西?"

"有。"她说,"我并不是百分百确定,但我总觉得好像有什么东西在营地周围窜来窜去看着我们。"

"嗯哼。"医生咕哝了一句,"我也感觉到了。"

然后他便一言不发,陷入了思考之中。

我百无聊赖地等着吱吱回来,环顾周围的月球地形,又发现了一件奇怪的事。由于月球比地球小得多,我所能看见的距离也短得多。虽然远看那些多山的地区没有什么不同,但朝平原方向看去时的景象却与地球上的地平线景象截然不同。在这里,地平线的弯曲清晰可见。

举个例子说吧,我们现在站在高原上向远处眺望,最多也只能看到七八英里外的景色,再过去的一切就都在地平线之下了,这使得那些远方的高山只露出了它们的峰顶,因而我们一直错误地低估了它们的海拔高度。

远方的高山只露出峰顶

吱吱终于回来了。他告诉我们他找到了昨晚留下的记号,并且已经准备好带我们一同前去。不过他看起来一副萎靡不振的样子。医生问他发生了什么,吱吱好像自己也说不出个所以然。

"医生，一切都还好。"他说，"至少看上去是这样。我不太确定这儿的生物找你过来干什么，但自从我们几个离开那只巨蛾之后我就连一只动物也没见着。可是这儿的环境很适合动物居住啊。这个问题总是困扰着我，在地球上，动物们找你帮忙时可不会慢吞吞的。"

"可不是嘛！"波莉尼西亚嘟囔道，"我们可都见识过他们在手术室外头吵吵嚷嚷的样子。"

"可不是嘛！"波莉尼西娅嘟囔道。

"嗯哼。"医生咕哝了一句,"我也注意到了。不过我也不知道他们为什么这么做,看样子他们不是很喜欢我们来拜访……好吧,不管怎么说,我希望这儿的动物能尽快现身。现在这种情形实在是……呃……我想尽量表现得乐观一点儿……令人沮丧啊。

## 第六章
# 月亮湖

于是我们便跟着吱吱前往那处水源。森林外头原本还算明亮的光线在丛林里几乎完全被遮天蔽日的枝叶所阻挡。我在这之前仅有的一次丛林探险经历是在蛛猴岛,而那里的景色也和这里很不一样。

通过观察这里树木的外貌与体型,医生认为它们的年龄已经很大了。我对此完全同意,它们威严高大的样子的确给人一种从宇宙之初就一直存在于此的感觉。而且令我们感到惊奇的是,这儿很少看到腐烂的植物,地上只有稀疏的枝条与树叶,而不是像在地球上的森林里那样随处可见倒下的树木。这儿的树木上也没有乱糟糟的枝条,每棵树看起来都好像在这儿无忧无虑地生长了几个世纪一般。

终于,在走了很长一段路后——在这段路程中我们可谓是举步维艰,因为那些有我腿一般粗的藤蔓总是会拦住我们的路——我们来到了一片空地,那儿有一个水面如镜的湖泊,湖泊最宽的地方有至少五英里。湖泊的尽头是一座风景秀美的瀑布,围绕着湖泊的是长满了好几平方英里的巨型芦笋林。看起来这些有着庞大体型的芦笋完全占据了湖泊边所有的生长空间和养分,因此这儿完全没有藤蔓的踪影。这些几百英尺高的芦笋的顶端看起来很好吃,不过我很怀疑我们爬上去之后会发现它其实比橡树的树干还要坚硬。

那儿有一座水面如镜的湖泊

医生、我和吱吱一起走下沙滩去湖边查看水质,发现湖水十分清凉解渴。这时,约翰·杜立德医生又发话了:"我打算乘船到湖心去探索一番。吱吱,你觉得这附近有什么木材能用来做成独木舟或者木筏吗?"

"我想是有的。"吱吱说,"等我一下,我去周围看看。"

于是,我们又开始跟着吱吱沿着湖边搜寻适合用来造船的材料。但正如我之前提到过的那样,由于这儿几乎找不到什么干枯倒地的树木,我们一筹莫展,而且那些树棵棵高大挺拔,看起来就十分沉重,还会分泌树脂,也不是造船的理想材料。再说了,我们手头仅有的工具只有医生别在腰间的一把短柄小斧,它和那些大树比起来简直小得可怜。

不过,在我们继续向前走了差不多一英里的时候,事情似乎出现了转机。我看到吱吱朝树林深处瞥了一眼,回头朝我们做了个"快点儿"的手势,然后就消失在了丛林中。我们赶紧跟了上去,发现他正在剥掉某样东西上覆盖着的爬藤和苔藓。这个物体躺在树林之中,距离湖边不会超过一百英尺。

我们急忙上前帮忙,不过没人知道我们究竟发现了什么。这个东西长得几乎看不到尽头。我认为它是一棵枯树——我们在月球上看到的第一棵枯树,或者是类似的什么东西。

第六章 月亮湖 037

"吱吱,你觉得这个东西是什么?"医生问道。

"是一艘船。"吱吱十分肯定地说,"绝对是一艘船——一艘手工制成的独木舟。非洲人用的就是这种船。"

"是一艘船。"吱吱十分肯定地说。

医生显然不敢相信这种说法,他喊道:"可是——吱吱,看看这玩意儿有多长!这可是一棵成年的'大芦笋'啊!我们已经清理了差不多一百英尺了,可是还是看不到船头啊!"

"这我就没办法了。"吱吱说,"但它肯定是一艘手工打造的独木舟。医生,你得爬到它底下去看看,我会指给你看工具和火烧留下的痕迹。这艘船被翻过来了。"

在吱吱的指引下,医生爬到这个奇怪物件的底下去了。过了一会儿,当医生出来时,他一脸困惑:"好吧,吱吱,这些的确有可能是工具留下的痕迹,不过也有可能不是。至于火烧的迹象嘛……虽然十分清晰,但也可以说是意外。毕竟如果这里发生过一场火灾那么就说得通了——"

"在我的非洲老家那儿,"吱吱打断了医生的话,"那儿的土著人就是这么做的。他们会先用火烧掉树干的中心部分,然后再用原始的工具在木头上凿刻——就和这儿一样。医生,我能肯定这是一艘很长时间没有用过的独木舟,你该看看它的船头——是被削尖的。"

"我注意到了。"医生说,"可是芦笋本来就有一个尖头啊。"

"是啊。"波莉尼西娅也说道,"还有,我说吱吱,到底是什么样的人能划动这艘船啊?我是说,你瞧,这玩意儿足足有一艘战列舰那么长!"

紧随其后的是一场以医生和波莉尼西娅为一方,吱吱为另一方的长达半个多小时的争论。不过在我看来,这不过是一段普普通通的木头,只不过在一侧有着开口罢了。至于它是不是人工制成的,我可没什么头绪。

不过很明显,这玩意儿如果真的是艘船的话,对我们来说太过庞大,绝对无法使用。于是我立刻打断了他们的辩论,建议说走远点去继续找合适的木材才是正事。

看样子医生也很高兴这场并没有多大意义的争辩总算画上了句号。我们几个又沿着岸边走了一英里多,终于找到了一片稀疏一点儿的树林。这里没有高大的芦笋,只有一些更加低矮、枝干也更加纤细的小树,所以医生很快就用那把小斧砍下了足够的木材。我们把树皮剥成一条条的,用它们把木材捆在一起,很快就造好了一个足以承受我们四个加上所有行李重量的木筏。在浅水区时,我们用一根长长的篙子撑船,而到了深水区之后,我们手头的工具就换成了一支用斧头削成的船桨。

医生一上船就开始让我不停地记笔记。我们在行李中携带了一面制作精良的渔网,医生用这面渔网来搜索月亮湖里可能存在的生命迹象。

"斯塔宾斯,"医生向我解释说,"研究这儿的鱼类是一件非常重要的事,因为在进化过程中鱼类是很重要的一环。"

"进化?"吱吱问道,"什么是进化?"

于是我便尝试着向他解释这个词的意思,不过很快

我们用一根长长的篙子撑船

医生又把我叫去记笔记了——我有点如释重负的感觉，毕竟解释这么一个复杂的专业术语的确是一项枯燥冗长的工作。不过波莉尼西娅接过了话茬，三下五除二地解答了吱吱的疑问。

"进化嘛，吱吱，"她说，"就是关于为什么斯塔宾斯身上没有长你身上那条尾巴的故事——因为他不再需要它了——也是关于你为什么现在还需要这条尾巴的故事……进化,不过是学究们用的词罢了——不过是把一件简单的事情变复杂罢了。"

而与此同时,我们对湖泊的探索却既无聊又无趣。我们捞上来了一些水蝇和它们大得出奇的幼虫,但却没有发现丝毫鱼类的踪影。奇怪的是,这儿的水生植物倒有不少。

我们在湖里划了几个小时船之后,医生终于发话了:"好吧,毫无疑问这儿的植物王国比动物王国繁荣得多——这儿的动物好像也只有昆虫。不管怎么说,我们还是先去湖岸边上扎营吧,说不定之后会有什么大发现呢。"

于是我们回到了出发的地方,把小船固定好,然后在干净的沙滩上搭起了帐篷。

我想我永远也不会忘记那古怪的一晚。我们四个都没有睡好。在黑暗中我们听见有些巨大的物体在帐篷周围行动。虽然我们什么也看不见,但我们很确定一定有什么东西在观察着我们。就连勇敢的波莉尼西娅也睡不着。现在看来,在月球上的确有着不少动物,只不过他们似乎还不打算对我们露出真容。这种时刻被窥视着的感觉真不好受,更别提我们还处在这么一个陌生的环境中了。

# 第七章
# 巨人的踪迹

那天晚上,另外一件扰人的事情就是月球上那连续不断的奇怪乐声了。不过由于当时发生的怪事实在不少,再加上我们几个心里隐约存在的焦虑,我们很难把所有的曲调都一一记住。第二天早上,吃完了前一天剩下的水果之后,我们又继续开始打包准备上路了。当我和医生在整理最后几个包裹时,吱吱和波莉尼西娅自告奋勇前去探路。他们俩可是很擅长这种工作。

当我和医生互相帮忙背上行囊时,吱吱急匆匆地跑了回来。"医生,你猜怎么着?"他因为太过慌张而显得有些结结巴巴,"我们在那儿发现了一些足迹,是一个人的足迹……不过大极了,你绝对想不到有多大。快跟上来——我会指给你看。"医生抬起头看了看吓坏了的吱吱,顿了顿,一言不发地背上了行囊。我们走之前,还最后看了一眼露营地,以确保没有落下什么重要的东西。

第七章 巨人的踪迹 043

我们在那儿发现了一些足迹

吱吱探查的路线并不是直接穿过湖中央,而是沿着湖右侧——我们曾经探索过的方向前进,途中还要穿过一片低洼地。我们紧跟在吱吱身后,很好奇接下来迎接我们的会是什么。我们顺着河流走了差不多一英里,随着河面逐渐变宽,离河岸也越来越远,终于走上了干净坚实的沙地。我们远远看到了在河岸边等着我们的波莉尼西娅。走近后,我们才看到波莉尼西娅身边有一个巨大的脚印,无论怎么看都与人类的足迹一模一样,只不过尺寸庞大得令人难以置信,它足足有四米多长。而且这样的印迹还不止一处,在岸边排列着一整串类似的脚印,好像是一个巨人在沿河行走。

一个巨大的脚印

波莉尼西娅和吱吱一直用询问的眼神看着医生,希望能获得一个合理的解释。"嚯!"过了一会儿,医生小声自言自语道,"看样子月球上住着个人类——或是像个人类的什么物种。老天爷!要什么样的怪物才能长到那么大啊!我们还是跟着脚印去看看为好。"

吱吱显然被医生的计划吓了一大跳,他和波莉尼西娅都认为最好是离这脚印的主人越远越好。他们两人的眼中都露出了惊慌的神色,但并没有能阻止医生的计划。我们跟着这些巨大的脚印慢慢前行,满脑子都是童话里巨人的故事。在走过了大约一英里之后,脚印转进了一侧的树林,然后消失在了苔藓和落叶之中,很难再找出什么痕迹。我们只好重新回到了岸边。吱吱在医生的要求下花了不少时间尝试着在森林里寻找巨人留下的蛛丝马迹,比如折断的树枝或者泥地上的压痕之类的,可惜我们没能找到任何有用的证据,而且看样子巨人重新回到湖边的可能性实在是微乎其微。于是我们只得放弃追踪,回到原定的探险路线上来。

随着我们一行人向世人从未见过的月球背面继续深入,这些树林变得越来越神秘。那些树看起来精力都十分旺盛,它们那些粗大的树枝像人的手臂,而枝条末端的分叉则像人的手指,在轻柔的微风中剧烈地摆动着,看起来古怪极了。

一路走来,医生都没怎么和我们说话,偶尔开口,也总是在重复一个话题,那就是月球上少见的腐烂状况。

"斯塔宾斯,我真是对此毫无头绪。"一次,他在休息时难得地多说了几句,"为什么……为什么这儿的落叶这么少?""这个细节很重要吗?"我问道。"呃,好吧,我这就解释给你听。在地球上,这些落叶是树木赖以生存的根本。"他说,"我是说,土壤中的那些落叶和枯树为一颗种子提供了能让它长成参天大树的养分。可是在这儿……呃,好吧……这儿有些地方的确有落叶,不过到现在为止我连一棵枯树都没有看见。但毫无疑问,这儿的树都长得繁茂无比……呃,我想这儿的生态环境应该达到了某种……呃……某种平衡。这儿的一切好像都是被预先设

这儿的树都长得繁茂无比

计安排好的……呃,我不知道到底该怎么解释这种情况,这儿的一切真是匪夷所思。"其实,在当时我并不理解医生的质疑,在我看来,这些大树没有疾病和虫害健康地生长着是件大好事,并没有值得奇怪的地方。

走着走着,我们已经穿过了身后的这片树林,面前突然出现了一条延伸至地平线的丘陵和山脉。这些山丘并不像我们刚到月球时所看见的那些光秃秃的小土坡,而是被一些低矮的灌木和石楠花丛所覆盖。这些植被生长得很密集,看样子穿过它们得费不少力气。一如既往,在这些山上也鲜有落叶的存在,现在医生对此现象有了一个新的解释,他认为这和月球上的季节因素有关——确切地说是和月球上四季的缺乏有关。他告诉我们,月球上可能没有冬夏之分。看来,许多我们在地球上认为理所当然的事情,在月球上可能都不太一样,这点让我很是郁闷。

## 第八章

# 会唱歌的树

我们在这片丘陵地带行走了好几英里,终于来到了一处盆地。在这里,我们不仅发现了更多的巨人脚印,还发现了火焰留下的痕迹——在一个巨大的洞穴中,我们找到了一大片和沙子混在一起的灰烬。医生对这些灰烬很感兴趣,把它们和化学试剂混合在一起,做了不少试验,可还是没搞明白这些灰烬的成分。不过,他说他很确定我们发现了一处能够向地球发射信号的所在。就在我们从地球出发之前,猫头鹰吐吐就说他看到了一些烟雾从月亮后面冒出来(也就在那时,巨蛾降落在了医生的花园里),看样子这个盆地就是烟雾的源头了。

"那股烟绝对是从这儿升起来的。斯塔宾斯,"医生说,"我能肯定,你看,这个盆地有好几英里宽,明显是一场大爆炸造成的。不过,我还不清楚是什么引发了如此规模的大爆炸。"

"可是,我们看到的是烟雾,而不是一般的爆炸所带

## 第八章 会唱歌的树 049

我们终于来到了一处盆地

来的火焰啊。"我说。

"没错,"他答道,"肯定是某种未被发现的材料导致了爆炸。虽然刚才的试验没有结果,不过谁知道呢,也许我们过会儿就会有出乎意料的新发现。"

基于两个原因,医生一直不想让大家离开丛林太远:首先是我们得靠从丛林中采集来的野果果腹,其次是医生对丛林里的植物产生了浓厚的兴趣。约翰·杜立德医生相信这些植物中还有不少让地球上的自然学家们欣喜若狂的秘密。

根据医生的建议,我们在丛林边设立了营地。大家认认真真地搭建了帐篷,然后便分头沿着不同的路线穿过丛林去探险。不一会,我的笔记本上又写满了各种试验结果和研究资料。

我们的第一个重大发现是月球上的植物和动物(严格说来应该是昆虫)之间的关系并非像地球上那样是吃和被吃的关系。这两种生物之间和平相处的和谐景观给我们留下了很深的印象。

我们还花了三天时间调查那些无处不在的乐声。医生作为一名熟练的长笛演奏者,对于这个问题有着很强的好奇心。经过仔细的观察,我们发现这些声音是那些树木所发出的。它们在风中摆动枝条发出不同的音符,就好像一把竖琴在特定的角度被风吹过会产生不同的乐音一样,医生把它们称为"会唱歌的树"。他还特意让我把这天的日期用红色标在了笔记本上,用他的话来说就是"这真是难忘的一天"。我们像着了魔似的盯着那些树的树梢聆听歌声,就像是一场大自然的交响乐。有时一棵树会先慢慢迎着微风抬起一段树枝,发出一个轻柔的音符,接着另外三四棵树会一起挥舞枝条,演奏出一段美妙的和弦,在林间回荡。

医生发现这些树只能在有风的时候发出声响,此外

**会唱歌的树**

他还想知道它们所能发出声音的音阶范围。我对这些音乐概念不太了解,但这些乐声总是令人愉悦的。而且,奇怪的是,即便是我这样的门外汉也能听出这些树木之间的默契以及它们所采用的有着清晰的高音和低音部分的管弦乐演奏方法。

我很享受这场美妙的音乐会,而医生显然比我更兴奋。"嘿!斯塔宾斯,"他大声说道,"你知道这种现象代表了什么吗?——这真是有点吓人。如果这些树能演奏音乐——而且还是需要互相配合的齐奏,那它们一定有自己的语言——它们能互相交流!你能想象吗?植物的语言!说不定哪天我自己也能学会这种语言呢。斯塔宾斯,今天真是伟大的一天!"

和往常一样,医生一旦工作起来就废寝忘食。他会捧着笔记本连续看上好几个钟头,或者花上很长时间捣鼓他自己安装的用来研究植物语言的新仪器。

你应该还记得在我们开始月球之旅之前,医生就对巨蛾带来的几株月铃花进行了细致的研究,并且怀疑它们之间可能有某种交流方式。为了证明这个猜想,这几天医生一直盯着几株灌木和小树看个不停,想要找出它们之间交谈的方法。

## 第九章
# 植物语言的研究

这几天,医生和我聊天时总是会谈到朗·阿罗。我们真希望这个蛛猴岛上的印第安博物学家现在能和我们待在一起。虽然他从未说过自己在植物语言方面进行过研究,但他那些关于植物学和植物历史方面百科全书式的知识肯定能帮上大忙。尽管朗·阿罗——哥顿·阿罗之子,一生中从未动笔写下过任何植物学方面的记录——这一点也不奇怪,因为他不会拼写——但他却能随时随地告诉你,为什么这种颜色的蜜蜂喜欢在那种颜色的花儿上采蜜,为什么这种蛾子喜欢在那棵灌木上产卵以及为什么这只昆虫幼虫会附着在那株水草上之类的知识。

我们一般会在傍晚时分坐下,想象他现在会在哪儿、在做什么。虽然他没有和我们几个一同离开蛛猴岛,但我们谁都不敢说他现在一定还待在那座小岛上。他一向居无定所,自由自在,现在也许会在南、北美洲的任何一个角落。

医生也会经常提到我的父母。他显然对于带我不辞而别而对他们深感愧疚——虽然这并不是他的错,是我自己偷偷地吊在巨蛾肚子上离开了地球。诸如此类的无数想法一直骚扰着医生,不过他似乎总能在最后关头打住思绪,回到他所热爱的科学研究上来。

"斯塔宾斯,"他常常这么说,"你不该跟来的……是的,是的,我知道,你这么做是为了帮我。但是,你父亲雅各布,还有你母亲,他们肯定被你的突然消失搞得焦头烂额,而我则要为此负责。好吧,反正我们对此也做不了什么,还是继续手头的工作吧。"

随后,医生又会一头扎进某个新的研究课题中,直到某件往事再次打断他的思绪。

当我们对这儿的植物的了解逐渐加深时,对月球上的动物们仍然知之甚少。不过,每晚睡觉时,我们经常会有种奇怪的感觉,就好像附近有不少巨型的蛾子、蝴蝶和甲虫在飞来爬去。

有几次当我们在半夜醒来走出帐篷时,还会看见空中有巨大的黑影一飞而过。我们很难在它飞出我们的视线范围之前辨认出那是什么,不过看起来十有八九它是来窥探我们的动向的。除此以外,我们又再次发现了那些巨人留下的印迹,它们总是突兀地出现在奇怪的地方,然后又突然消失。我相信如果医生同意让波莉尼西娅和吱吱自由地去追踪这些足迹的话,我们可能很快就能发现巨人的秘密。但是约翰·杜立德医生还是希望大家能待在一起。虽然鹦鹉和猴子都算不上是一流的战士,但是他们出众的侦察和导航能力,让他们成为探险队伍里的宝贝。医生常常对我说,如果他要去蛮荒之地探险,带上他们两个比带上一个团的散兵游勇更让人放心。

空中有巨大的黑影一飞而过

我们在这几天里还花了不少时间研究生长在荒地上的开花灌木以及河里的巨型睡莲。

医生为了继续深入研究植物语言,决定回到巨蛾着陆的地方再去拿一些行李。一天天刚蒙蒙亮,我们就踏上了来时的路。这又是一段漫长难熬的路程。我们花了一天半的时间才走到那里,然后又足足花了两天,带着各种各样的大包小包回到了丛林。奇怪的是,在我们着陆点的四周也出现了不少巨人的脚印和其他的不明生物的印迹。很明显,我们现在已经时刻处在那些神秘动物们的视线范围内了。

约翰·杜立德医生在仔细检查了巨人脚印后告诉我们,巨人的右脚跨的步子比左脚步子大了一些,这说明巨人走起路来有些一瘸一拐,但是这丝毫不妨碍他成为一个力大无穷的可怕家伙。

我们回到了营地,开始把行李中的物件一件件拿出来。看起来,医生准备好了所有我们可能用得上的东西:斧头、绳子、钉子、锉刀、锯子,还有其他一些我们在月球上绝对没法手工制作出来的东西。稍微吃了一些东西后,医生就投入到了劳动中。不到一个小时,医生就用斧头和锯子在营地周围搭起了几幢小木屋。

医生用斧头和锯子在营地周围搭起了小木屋

第十章
# 月球上的麦哲伦

医生现在已经完全把一些烦恼都抛在了脑后,不再去想为什么月球上的动物召唤他来却一直不肯露面以及巨人究竟长什么样之类的问题,而是一门心思扑在了植物语言的研究上。这种耗费精力的工作让医生感到很充实。可是对我们几个来说,想要跟上医生的研究步伐实在很不容易。好在医生终于取得了一点成果,在一个午后,他激动地宣布自己确认了树木的交流方式:它们的确是用枝条做出不同的姿势来表达不同的意思。在了解到这一点后,医生现在正试着让自己站得像一棵树那样笔直,然后模仿它们的样子摆动手臂和这些丛林的原住民们对话。通过这些方式,医生还了解到这些树木还可以通过它们散发的气味来交谈。它们会用特定的方式散发出不同的气味,持续时间有长有短,就好像摩斯密码一样。

吱吱的任务是为大家准备食物。每过三个时辰,这

*医生一门心思扑在了植物语言的研究上*

只勤劳忠诚的猴子就会给我们带来他搜集到的各种野菜、野果,还有装在坚果壳里的清洁的水。

而我,作为这次探险的记录者(对此我感到非常自豪),我需要记录下医生所作的所有数学计算和博物学方面的笔记,我已经记录下了气温、气压和昼夜交替的规律,而医生开始着手计算我们从踏上月球之后行走的里程。这项工作的困难在于月球上的引力实在太小,以至

**吱吱的任务是为大家准备食物**

于我们跨出的步子要比在地球上大很多。所以，尽管医生随身带着一个计步器，但是却派不上什么用处。根据我的估计，我们在下坡时一步能毫不费力地跨出足足七英尺呢。

也正是在那段时间里，医生提出了在月球上旅行的想法。你应该记得，麦哲伦是第一个环游地球的人——他完成了一项前无古人的壮举。要知道，地球上的水域比陆地要广大得多，而月球上则正好相反，这里没有大

第十章 月球上的麦哲伦　061

下坡时一步能毫不费力地跨出足足七英尺

海,有的只是一串串的小溪。所以,如果我们要效仿麦哲伦探险的话,就只好依靠步行了,这也使得这项计划困难了不少。医生要求我严格详细地记录下行进的路程,就是为了给绕月旅行作准备。不过,我们并没有始终沿着直线前进,原因有二:一是缺乏可靠的参照物;二是因为新奇的事物(比如树木发出的音乐和巨人的脚印等等)总是会把我们带离预定的路线。同时,医生带来的指南针完全起不到作用,也给我们的旅行带来了困难。

为了解决这个难题,约翰·杜立德医生一如既往地投入了极大的精力。你知道,他可是一个非常棒的数学家。一天下午,他拿着一本笔记本和一本天文年历,开始测算天空中星星的方位。这些散发着微弱光芒的亮点虽然遥不可及,但是它们却是我们曾经在地球上也能看到的唯一东西,所以,这些星星给了我们一种很奇特的亲切感。

火引起的烟雾可以告诉我们风的方向

同时,为了制造出一个新的仪器来代替指南针,医生进行了无数次的尝试。一天,他好像突然想到了什么,对我大声说道:"斯塔宾斯!我想到了!风!这儿的风吹得很平稳,方向也不会常常变化,我想我们可以用它来判断我们所处的方位!"于是,我们开始着手制作一些装置,包括一个用树枝支撑起来的风向标。紧接着,医生又忽然想到可以利用烟雾来进行定位。

"如果我们在合适的地方生火,"他解释说,"那么火引起的烟雾也可以告诉我们风的方向,一旦我们闻不到烟味了,那么就说明风向改变了。"见医生说的有道理,我们就开始准备生火了。

# 第十一章
# 点火

我们首先决定要在四周都是光秃秃的小山坡上燃放火堆,这样火势就不会蔓延开来点燃四周的灌木丛。我们选好了一个合适的位置,但是问题来了,我们该用什么材料作为燃料呢?

这里根本就没有枯树,所以我们只得去砍伐一些树枝,等它们风干以后再用来引燃火堆。我刚刚砍了没几根树枝,忽然被医生制止了。他说他突然想到了一件事:既然这儿的树都会说话,那么几乎就能肯定它们也有感觉——它们能感觉到疼痛!这个想法把我们都吓坏了,我们甚至都不敢去看那些被砍伐下来的树枝。于是,我们只能采用那些最原始的办法了,就是四处捡拾那些断枝。这毫无疑问大大降低了我们的效率。但是,无论怎样困难,我们都一致认定用烟雾来指示风向是决定我们环游月球探险成败的关键,所以我们一定要十分的耐心。首先,我们得去丛林里搜集不同种类树木的断枝样本。

由于只有我和医生两人才能有能力和空闲搬运那些树枝，所以这项工作花了挺长的时间。虽然吱吱也想帮忙，但他还得花时间去帮我们搜集食物，所以到头来还是只有我和医生两个人。

在我们收集的几种树枝里面，有的压根就不能被点燃，还有的虽然能够燃烧，但却没有烟雾。

当我们试验到第五种树枝时，差点儿引发了一场事故。当时医生小心翼翼地用火柴点燃了好几根像竹子一样的树枝后，这些树枝突然劈劈啪啪地爆炸了，医生差点儿被炸伤。我和吱吱吓坏了，赶紧给医生做了一下检查，还好除了胡子被烧掉外，只有手上被烧了几个泡。我们从医生随身带的小黑包里找到了药水给医生涂上。我们都注意到了这些树枝燃烧时所冒出的滚滚白烟，经几个时辰还是久久不肯散去。医生非常肯定地告诉我们说，我们在帕德尔比小镇上看到的月亮上的白烟就是这种树枝经燃烧而产生的。

"老天！"我大喊道，"连我们在地球上都能看得到，这浓烟该有多厉害啊！要我说至少得有几千吨的树枝才够吧！"吱吱也插话道："是啊，可是有谁有这种本事呢？"有一会儿我们谁也没有说话，直到波莉尼西娅说出了我和医生心里想着的同一个答案。

"我敢保证，"她轻声说，"那个人肯定能在一天内搬走这么多的树枝。"

"你是说那个巨人发出了信号?"吱吱问道,他滑稽的小眼睛因为震惊而睁得大大的。

"为什么不能是他呢?"波莉尼西娅说。之后她便陷入了沉思,不管吱吱再怎么问也不再开口了。

"那好吧,"吱吱最后说,"看样子,正是那个巨人去找医生的,也许他需要医生的帮助。"

"你说是那个巨人发出的信号?"吱吱问道。

第十一章 点 火

他又朝医生看去,好像是要听听他的意见,不过医生也和波莉尼西娅一样不发一言。

好吧,除了这次小小的意外,烟雾试验非常成功,我们发现这种烟雾可以保持三到四天的时间,为我们显示方向十分有用。"当然啦,斯塔宾斯,"医生说,"在我们正式环游月球前还需要再做一次试验,毕竟过了一个星期后风向可能会改变。我们还得确保那些山脉不会挡住风或者让风改变方向——如果是这样,那我们就会走偏了。不过现在看来,这种方法应该能够代替指南针了。"

有那么一两次,当吱吱和波莉尼西娅都不在身旁的时候,我问约翰·杜立德他是否真的相信是巨人而不是其他动物召唤他到月球上来的。我原以为只有我们两人在的时候他谈这事会轻松一点,想不到他还是没说太多。"我不知道,斯塔宾斯。"他皱着眉头说,"我真的不知道。说实话,现在我压根就没在想这件事儿——我也没空想这事儿。光是月球上的植物研究就够我忙的了。我猜就是一两百位植物学家也要花上一两年才能基本了解它们,而我们才刚刚学到一点皮毛呢,我真希望能够学到更多——不过,谁知道呢?天啊,我多希望现在有一大群科学家和我在一起——绘图学家、地质学家,还有勘探员。想想吧,我们身处在一个崭新的世界中,但是我们甚至连自己的确切位置都不知道!我大概了解我们的路线,也尝试着把它们记了下来。但我更应该画几张地图——斯塔宾斯,真正的地图!那种标有每座山峰、每条河流、每片高原的地图!老天!我得尽量去完成这件事。"

## 第十二章
# 爱漂亮的百合花

现在回想起来,如果不是因为和地球相比,月球没有那么幅员辽阔的话,我们几乎是不可能完成这样一个壮举。想想看,一个医生、一个男孩、一只猴子和一只鹦鹉,就是一支探险队的全部成员。但是我们还是凭借自己的力量完成了探险。想当初在我们刚刚来到这个星球时,我们压根就没有想到能够环游月球,但是我们竟然就这么做到了。回想一下,我们先是一路疾行,希望能找到动物的踪迹,之后,医生开始了对植物语言的研究,然后为了探索和了解更多的知识而继续探险。我们每到一处都会留下一些标记,有时是一处营帐,有时是一个物资存放点,这样就算我们在探险途中遇到危险,也能找到退路和补给品。

探险途中波莉尼西娅总能派上大用场,医生总是让她先飞到前头去察看地形,再折回来告诉我们要做好哪些准备。另外医生还带上了一些微型的测量仪,他用这些小玩意儿在图表上标出我们的大致探索路线以及为了探查一些奇怪的地形所走过的弯路。

刚开始探险时,我们总是觉得不该走得离那片丛林太远,以免丧失了食物来源。不过,波莉尼西娅在一次侦察后告诉我们,在远处还有另一片丛林。为了慎重起见,我们还是先请丛林专家吱吱先去探索了一番。吱吱返回时兴高采烈地带来了比之前那片丛林中找到的更美味的野菜和浆果,于是我们便毫不犹豫地朝着月球深处走去。

随着时间的推移,我们身边的植物世界变得更加多姿多彩,医生对植物语言的了解也越来越深入。我们常常在途中扎营休息几天,那时医生总是会摆弄他的那些仪器来研究和植物的对话,在我看来,医生和植物的交流似乎是越来越顺利了。

我还记得第一次见到这种"爱漂亮的百合花"(这是医生后来给它们起的名字,真是令人难忘)时的情景。这些花朵有着巨大而艳丽的花瓣,花瓣的最外层是柔和的奶油色,内层以紫色和橙色为主,点缀着中心处黑色的花蕊,叶子则是橄榄绿的。花的直径差不多有十八英寸,形成喇叭状,细长的花径随风摆动,远看就像一群在舞会上热舞的舞者。特别是当我们靠近时,它们的摆动更加剧烈了,甚至连花苞都开始颤动起来,似乎对我们的到来很

爱漂亮的百合花

感兴趣。这真是我们所见过的最艳丽、最热情的花儿了,为了一探究竟,医生决定在附近休息,研究一番。

我们把食物和睡袋从包裹里拿了出来,一边吃晚餐,一边察看四周。远远望去,在这些美丽的花儿组成的花海后面,就是一片由灌木和攀援植物构成的丛林。吃过晚饭后,大家都有些劳累,便都早早睡下了。我把毯子裹紧,听见远处丛林中植物发出的音乐声,似乎在叽叽喳喳地议论我们这些不速之客。我们还听到了天上有什么东西在飞,是那些巨型昆虫在附近盘旋并且不知疲倦地注视着我们。

医生在这几天中对"爱漂亮的百合花"的研究,让我获得了对月球上植物的不少奇妙的知识。医生把这次进展归功于这种植物出众的智力。到了第三天,我、吱吱和波莉尼西娅惊讶地发现,医生已经几乎可以不借助任何仪器与那些花儿自由交谈了。他也发现这些百合花是通

医生几乎可以不借助任何仪器与那些花儿自由交谈了

过晃动花苞彼此进行交谈。我们日后还发现它们甚至可以通过这种方式与昆虫和鸟类进行交流。这些美丽的花儿的智慧比它们的外表更加出众。不管你对植物学有多么无知,你也可以分辨出它们和其他植物有多么不同,你甚至会幻想它们也许有着和人类同样的性格。

医生把他和百合花之间的对话足足写满了两大本笔记本,而且每当医生有了新的问题,便会立刻前去询问一番。他激动地告诉我们,这些花是整个植物王国里——包括地球和月球——拥有最高智商的种类。

# 第十三章
# 有多种气味的花

我们在长满了华丽百合花的那片沼泽地里还发现了这些植物的另一个古怪特点,那就是它们散发出的各种气味,使得这片花海周围方圆一英里之内丝毫没有其他植物的踪影,这些百合花看起来占据了整片沼泽地。当时,我们一靠近这片沼泽地,就分辨出了至少六种不同的气味。刚开始我们以为其中有些气味是被风吹来的其他花儿的味道,但后来我们发现这股风是从沙漠的方向吹来的,所以这些香味和风应该没什么关系。

医生第一个想到这些百合花可能就是这些香味的源泉——也就是说它们能散发出不止一种气味。他的试验也证明了这一点。不过他也觉得这次探险没能把小狗叽喳带来是个大大的遗憾。叽喳那专家级别的灵敏嗅觉在这儿肯定能派上大用场。不过即便我们的鼻子没有叽喳那么好使,我们也渐渐地能闻出这些花儿散发出的气味变得更多更复杂了,粗略算来大约有一打左右不同的种类。这些气味大多数都令人心旷神怡,但也有一两种气味几乎能把人弄晕。吱吱闻了其中一种后就直接晕了过去——这都是拜医生所赐。当时,他热切地询问那些花儿到底能释放出多少种不同的气味,那些花儿在解释的同时释放了一种气味,估计是毒气之类,弄不好还会跑到眼睛里去。我和医生只好扛着神志不清的吱吱飞也似的逃开了。

眼看自己造成了巨大的"损害",百合花们立刻释放出一种我这辈子闻到过的最香甜的味道。很明显它们不希望我和医生离开。这点在医生后来与它们的对话中(我把这段对话一字一句地记了下来)也得到了证实。这些花儿说尽管它们是植物,但也已经听说了伟大的博物学家约翰·杜立德的种种事迹,并且一直期盼着他的到来。通过和它们的对话,我们终于觉得在月球上遇到了可以聊天的朋友。

现在想来,如果我想给读者提供最直观的医生和植物间的交流场景,没有什么比摘录日记中的片段更合适的了。其实直到现在还有很多人不相信人类可以和植物进行对话。不过,我本人可是一路跟随着医生去过世界各地探险的,也见证了他一步步从鱼类到昆虫语言的学习,所以我毫不怀疑这个伟大的人对于植物语言的掌握。

*我一路跟随医生去过世界各地探险*

那是一天傍晚,我们几个正要离开营地去做研究,医生突然转身让我回营地去多拿一本笔记本来——他打算在那天要记录下一个重大的发现,于是我立刻拿来了三本笔记本跟了上去。我们在离百合花海还有大约二十步距离的地方停了下来(自从吱吱不小心中毒之后,我们把营地向后移了几百米),医生一屁股坐在地上,开始对着那些花儿摇头晃脑,那些花儿也立即摇头晃脑地予以回应。"准备好了吗,斯塔宾斯?"医生问道。

"好了,医生。"我答道,又看了看手头的铅笔,确认已经削好。"很好,"他说,"把我们的对话记录下来。"于是,我写道:

医生——"你们喜欢这种一成不变的生活吗?——我是说,你们喜欢一直待在同一个地方吗?不能移动难道不会令你们沮丧吗?"

百合花——(几株花儿一齐答道)"噢,当然不会,虽然我们一直待在同一个地方,但是我们一直都能听到外界的消息。"

医生——"那么你们是从哪里听说外界的消息的呢?"

百合花——"其他的植物啊,蜜蜂啊,或者各种各样的鸟儿。"

医生——"喔,你们还能和蜜蜂、鸟儿交流?"

百合花——"那是当然。怎么了?"

医生——"可是,你们完全是不同种类的生物啊!"

百合花——"这没错,但是那些蜜蜂成天飞过来采蜜,那些鸟儿尤其是夜莺,也常常飞来坐在我们的叶子上,对着我们唱歌,还叽叽喳喳地讲外面世界的见闻,久而久之,我们就都互相学会了对方的语言。"

医生——"哦,原来如此,原来如此。不过难道你们从来没幻想过要出门看看吗?"

百合花——"老天！当然没有！整天到处窜来窜去有什么意思！再怎么说，哪里也没有自己家好，不是吗？这儿又漂亮又安全——我们过得可是很开心呢。不像那些跑来跑去的伙计们——我是说，它们指不定什么时候就会摔个四脚朝天——我们可不用担心这个。再者说呢，我们在此休养，静观世界，还有蜜蜂和鸟儿们作伴——还有什么比这样的生活更值得向往呢？"

医生——"好吧，最后说一句，一想到你们能和蜜蜂还有鸟儿交谈，就让我感到难以置信。"

百合花——"哈，这对我们来说可是简单得很呐——对了，还得加上甲虫和飞蛾。"

也正是在这段谈话期间，我们还发现了另一个令人震惊的事实——这些百合花居然拥有视觉！我之前已经提到过了，月球上的光线十分暗淡。医生与百合花交谈到一半时，突然想抽烟了。于是他问那些花儿是否讨厌烟草味，花儿们说它们压根就不知道"烟草味"是什么。于是医生便掏出了他的烟斗，说如果它们不喜欢烟草味可以告诉他。说着，医生便燃起了一根火柴，就在这么一瞬间，我清楚地看到那些花儿们往后缩了缩，确保花苞没有正对着亮光。这时我们才注意到小小的一根火柴对这些早已习惯昏暗光线的生物造成了多大的影响。

第十三章 有多种气味的花　079

医生掏出烟斗说，如果它们不喜欢烟草味可以告诉他。

# 第十四章
# 送给百合花儿面镜子

医生注意到当他划亮火柴时百合花们都往回缩了缩,这让他觉得光线的变化能对百合花造成影响。医生对此感到兴奋不已。

"这是为什么呢,斯塔宾斯?"他小声说道,"我们和手里燃烧的火柴离它们那么远,它们肯定感受不到火焰的温度,所以肯定是火柴发出的亮光被它们觉察到了。这说明它们肯定有着某种对光线十分敏感的器官,就像人类的眼睛一样——它们很可能有着视力!看来这回我又有的忙了。"

于是他又开始询问百合花们各种有关它们视觉的问题。他还不停地伸出手臂,问那些花儿们他做了什么动作。虽然这些花儿完全搞不懂医生的目的,但它们每次都能准确地做出回应。甚至有一次,当医生伸出手臂时,一株硕大的百合花抬起了花苞一直"看"着他。

现在看来,毫无疑问这些百合花的确可以看得见东西,但是令人费解的是,它们并没有任何可以被称为"眼睛"的器官。

这个问题让医生既好奇又疑惑。在研究了好几个小时后,医生还是一头雾水。最后,他只好得出这样一个奇怪的结论:这些花朵所具有的并非视觉,而是另一种感觉,只不过成功地代替了视力罢了。"总之,斯塔宾斯,"他说,"不能因为我们人类只有五种感官,就认为其他物种也是这样。很久以前就有人怀疑鸟类有第六感,现在看来这些花儿也能用第六感来看见东西——尽管它们没有眼睛。"

那天晚上,医生在整理行李时,无意间发现了一份花卉的品种目录,应该是在出发前随手带上的,上面绘着精美的图画。医生是一位勤劳的园丁,整个英格兰的花卉与种子商人都会给他寄来这种目录。"嘿,斯塔宾斯!"他喊道,把手里的小册子高高举起,"这是个机会,我们可以观察一下这些百合花看到那些不同花儿的彩色插图时的反应。"

第二天一大早,医生就把这本精美的画册带到了场地上。他一页页地翻着,把一张张牵牛花、菊花还有葵花的图片展示给那些百合花儿看。连我和吱吱都看得出来,这些图片在百合花丛中引起了轰动。它们那些喇叭形的花苞不停地对着那本画册左看右看,然后又互相"看了看",好像在谈论着什么。

后来医生告诉了我它们在说些什么,我也将这些内容记在了笔记本上。看起来这些百合花们对画册里面的花的身份感到非常好奇,同时也感到非常亲切。医生后来把月球上的植物界称为"植物社会",主要原因就是这些百合花们的神态看上去就像地球上的贵妇人在对着异域风情的美景评头论足一般。

百合花们对于仪表的看重让医生感到十分惊奇,事实上,这就是医生称它们为"爱漂亮的百合花"的原因。好吧,当医生告诉它们这些画册里面花儿的尺寸比起月球上的植物来说要小得多时,它们显得有些失望,不过也隐约带有一点自豪。医生还告诉它们,在地球上没有任何一株植物能和动物交流,这也让那些花儿感到难以置信。

在经过一段时间的观察后,就连医生也被这些花儿花在打理自己身上的时间震惊了。它们每天都会花很多时间伸长茎秆想看看水里自己的倒影。如果有昆虫或小鸟飞过时一不小心把它们的花粉沾到了花瓣上,或者折弯了它们的花蕊,这些花儿便会伤心不已。就连那些长在水边的花儿也不好过。一旦水池干涸,它们就只能看着水底的黏土叹息不已了。于是医生打算出手帮助这些可怜的小家伙们——既然天然的镜子没了,何不自己动手做几面呢?

当然,我们手头也没有平面镜——除了医生挚爱的剃须时用的小镜子。不过,我们有装水果和沙丁鱼的锡罐子,于是,我们把这些锡罐压平了之后磨光,再用树枝固定在了地面上。啊哈!一面面镜子诞生了。

"事实上,斯塔宾斯,"医生说,"自然界的趋势就是让每种生物都长成它们心中最好的模样——因为这种模样一般都对那种生物本身有好处。而这些花儿有着自己的

我们用锡罐压平后磨光,送给百合花当镜子。

审美观,只是它们不太清楚自己真正的外表罢了。我们送给它们的镜子虽然简陋,但对于它们的进化也许会有决定性的帮助。"

在以后的月球探险中,我脑海中时常会想起这样一个场景:那些迷人的百合花们在柔和的天光中转动着它们的花瓣,柔软的茎秆随着微风的吹拂而摇摆。它们一边愉快地照着镜子,一边低声交谈。这真是一幅让人心动的画面。

## 第十五章
## 穿上新衣

一天,医生又开始琢磨起了月球生物的奇特行为,"我真是搞不懂巨蛾为什么把我们带到这里之后就不再出现了呢?"

"他可能也是身不由己,才这样做的。"波莉尼西娅压低了声音说道。

"此话怎讲?"医生有些疑惑。

"好吧,"波莉尼西娅慢吞吞地继续说道,"也许有什么东西在阻止他——也许也阻止了其他动物——靠近我们。"

"你是指那个巨人?"约翰·杜立德追问道。

但是,波莉尼西娅闭口不谈,大家也把话题转移开了。

过了一会儿,吱吱轻轻地说:"其实我担心的不是这个。"

大家都沉默了,我想大家都猜到了吱吱要说什么。

"我担心的是我们该怎么回去。"吱吱终于小心翼翼地说出了他的心思,"月亮上的伙计把我们带来了这个地方——虽然不知道他们的用意,但是如果他们一直躲着我们不肯露面的话,光靠咱几个可没法回到地球上去。"

没有谁能回答这个问题,大家心里都沉甸甸的。

"呃,好吧,"医生突然大声说道,"振作起来,振作起来!别整天想着这些还没发生的事了。再说了,谁能保证那个巨人就一定是个坏蛋呢?说不定他的性情就是这样慢吞吞的。你们必须记住一点:我们在他们眼中就和他们在我们眼中一样奇异。让我瞧瞧,我们才来了两个多星期,事情肯定会慢慢好起来的。你们也都看到了,这儿的植物对我们都挺友善的,这可是个好兆头。"

医生的话给大家带来了信心,大家开始七嘴八舌地聊起天来。大家都意识到了月亮上的食物对我们身体带来的影响,波莉尼西娅是第一个发现这一点的。

"汤米,"一天她对我说,"你看起来长高了不少,好像也胖多了,不是吗?"

"呃,有吗?"我说,"我的皮带最近确实是紧了一点,不过我想这应该是正常现象吧。"

"还有医生,"这只老鹦鹉又说道,"我敢发誓说他比以前壮多了——除非是我的眼睛出了什么毛病。"

"这很容易证明,"约翰·杜立德说,"我对自己的身高可是记得清清楚楚——五尺二寸半。我正好带了把两英尺长的直尺,我这就去找棵树量一下我有多高。"

测量的结果连医生自己也被震惊了,他发现自己竟然长高了三英寸。我不太记得自己来月球之前的身高了,但是测量结果远远超出了预期,我们俩的腰围也变粗了不少。就连吱吱看起来也长大了不少,体重也明显地增加了。至于波莉尼西娅,由于她的体型实在太小,所以

测量的结果连医生自己也被震惊了,他发现自己竟然长高了三英寸。

也看不出有什么明显的变化。

"好吧,"医生解释道,"依我看来这也算得上正常。毕竟这儿的一切——不管是植物还是昆虫——都比地球上同样的物种要大上不少。导致这种现象的种种因素——无论是气候、食物、空气成分,还是气压——都肯定对我们有同样的作用。这对生物学家和生理学家来说肯定是个有意思的话题。另外,既然这儿的环境能使动植物们轻轻松松地活上那么久,我相信只要一直住在这儿,我们个个都能长命百岁。我还记得那天和百合花聊天时它们告诉我说,一株植物哪怕被完全折断也能在缺水的情况下存活几周甚至几个月。哈!这下我们也知道为什么巨蛾带到帕德尔比的月铃花能保存得那么好了。看来月球给我们带来的惊喜真是太多了。不过,我还是希望回到地球之后体形能恢复正常,我可不想长得太过庞大——我的大衣已经有点紧了,我竟然一直没有注意到——看来,让我们操心的事情已经足够多了。"

此话不假,过去一段时间里我们一直被月球上的奇观和新颖的科学发现所吸引,以至于身高体重的变化被完全忽视了。但是,接下来一段时间的变化令我和医生都有点狼狈不堪,因为我们俩的衣服都开始开裂了。现在,我们开始打算在月球上寻找可靠的原料来做衣服了。

一天下午,在我们确认所有从地球带来的衣服都已经完全穿不下时,医生开口说话了:"让我想想这儿有什么理想的材料……棉花就别提了,就算这儿真的有这种植物,我们也不会纺线。至于亚麻,不,想都别想,我也没找到这种植物。剩下的好像只能用植物根部的纤维了,可是上帝保佑,我可不想让皮肤接触到那种粗糙的面料。看来我们只能再花时间找找了。"

于是,吱吱便带着我们在树林中搜巡。过了几天终于有了突破。我们找到了一种外形古怪、有着宽大柔软树叶的沼泽树,我们把它们的叶片晒干后就得到了结实可靠的"布料"。

吱吱和波莉尼西娅还给我们找来了一种特殊的细线——这是他俩从一些藤蔓的卷须上取得的,非常牢固。当一切准备就绪,我们就开始着手裁剪新衣了。"最好把衣服做得稍大一些,"医生嘱咐道,一边在一块大石头做成的工作台上挥动着剪子,"天知道我们的体型以后还会长到多大。"当这些衣服全部成型时,我们可乐坏了,迫不及待要穿上一试。

"我们看着就像鲁宾逊·克鲁索似的。"约翰·杜立德开玩笑说,"不过没关系,这身衣服穿着还不错。"我们还用剩下的"布料"简单地做了几件内衣内裤。毕竟月球上的气候温和,衣服不需要做得太厚。

我们开始着手裁剪新衣

"那么我们的鞋子该怎么办呢?"我一边穿上裤子一边问道,"我的鞋子都从顶上裂开了。"

"这还不简单,"吱吱说,"我在找野果时发现了一种树,它的树皮剥下来做鞋子再合适不过了,不过要编出像样的鞋带可要花点工夫。"于是,很快我们的脚上就多了一双别致的鞋子,看样子穿上一个星期不成问题。

"太好了!"医生说,"看来短时间内我们不必为穿衣服的事发愁了,现在终于可以继续我们的研究了!"

## 第十六章
# 月亮的传说

有一天,在寻找新奇植物的路上,大家聊起了月球的早期历史。那时候医生刚刚听说了一种名叫"轻语藤蔓"的攀援植物,可以依靠叶片发出的沙沙声相互交流。

"吱吱,"医生问道,"你还记得你祖母以前讲的那些有关月亮的传说里面的细节吗?我是说,她有没有提到过任何奇怪的树木或者其他的植物?"

"应该没有,"吱吱答道,"我祖母在讲故事时一般只会提到动物和人类,至于植物,她很少会提到。不过,她有时候也会描述一片区域是否被树木覆盖或是一片荒芜。怎么了?"

"好吧,"医生解释道,"在我看来,月球以前是地球的一部分,这是毫无疑问的,但是奇怪的是,月球上的植物和地球上的植物大不相同啊。"

"这可不一定,医生,"波莉尼西娅说,"这儿有大片的芦笋林啊。"

"这倒是,"医生点头道,"这儿的确有些物种让我想起了地球上的生物——当然,这儿的尺寸是大多了。而且,这儿的植物互相之间能够交谈,有着发达的社会性,因此我很好奇,地球上的植物为什么没有这种本事——正因如此,我们的自然学家们才会认为植物互相是不能交流的,也正因如此,了解一下远古时期的植物知识非常重要。"

"好吧,让我想想。"吱吱坐了下来,两手托着腮。

"好吧,让我想想。"吱吱坐下来,两手托着腮。

"不行,"过了一会儿,他开口说道,"我还是想不起来任何有关植物的故事,不过,我的祖母讲到史前艺术家奥托·布劳奇时曾经提到过一些木材,他用这些木材做成工具的手柄、家具或者装水的碗之类的玩意儿,但她从未说过有会说话的树或者类似的什么东西。"

到了正午时分,我们几个便坐在地上准备吃午餐了。我们虽然只走了两三个小时,但比起在地球上能走出的距离远得多。我们在过去的一个星期里每天都会出发去寻找"爱漂亮的百合花"说起过的各种植物,然后在夜幕降临前回到营地,接着用医生的仪器继续研究。那天傍晚,医生靠在一块大石头上,嚼着一块黄色的植物块根,这种食物是我们在丛林边发现的,十分有营养,已经成了我们每天的主食。

"吱吱,"医生说,"你能告诉我奥托·布劳奇的故事结尾吗?这真是我听过的最吸引人的故事。"

"我记得我说给你听过啊。"吱吱说,"我干脆从头开始再讲一遍好了。在月亮存在以前,奥托·布劳奇是个离群索居的人。他最大的爱好就是每天用石头做的工具在鹿角或骨头上作画。他一直有个愿望,就是想画一幅人类的画像,可是他从没见过了他自己以外的其他人。一天,当他又一次祷告希望有人能当他的模特时,他突然看见一个漂亮的女孩出现在了一块大石头上,单膝跪地。

医生靠在一块大石头上,嚼着一块黄色的植物块根,这种食物已经成了我们每天的主食。

奥托大喜过望,赶紧把她画在一块鹿角上——这也是他最棒的作品。可惜,当他刚刚画完,女孩的身影就慢慢消失在了山间的迷雾中。奥托大声地呼唤她,迷雾中传来女孩的声音,告诉他自己叫皮皮蒂帕,是一名仙女,不能在人间待太久。可怜的艺术家跑到那块大石头边,发现了皮皮蒂帕留下来的一串蓝色珠子。奥托难过地把珠子戴在了手腕上,不论白天黑夜都不肯取下来,希望仙女有一天能够回来。故事就这样结束了,像我这样的小猴子,总是缠着祖母让她继续说下去,毕竟这样的结局太悲伤了。可是祖母坚持说这就是结局,她还说不久之后奥托·布劳奇,这个鹿角画家突然消失了,连一丁点儿痕迹都没有留下,就好像大地把他一口吃掉了似的。"

"嗯嗯,"医生咕哝道,"你知道这个故事发生在什么时候吗?"

"不知道,"小猴子说,"我祖母从来没有说起过确切的时间或地点。这个故事也是她从她的父母和祖父母那儿听来的,但我想应该十有八九发生在大洪水那段时间左右吧,因为我祖母讲的故事中从来都只出现过两个时间段,月亮存在之前和之后,而艺术家奥托·布劳奇的名字只在月亮存在之前的故事中出现过。"

"我知道了,"医生一副若有所思的神情,"那么你祖母有没有说起过这两个时间的交替是什么时候发生的呢?"

"好像也没有,"吱吱答道,"我以前问过这个问题,还有大洪水发生的时间,但祖母都不清楚。这些事件无疑是曾经发生过的,这是肯定的,但是流传下来的传说少了很多细节。我们不知道是什么导致了月亮的出现,甚至也不知道月亮出现之后的一段时间内发生了什么。不过我猜这应该是一场大灾难——当时动物们肯定都只顾着逃命了,灾难过去以后,他们则分散开了,所以也很难保持统一的说法。不过我倒是记得祖母提到过,在月亮出现后的一个晚上,一群人类在山顶上对着月亮跪拜。这些虔诚的太阳崇拜者认为月亮是太阳的妻子。"

"呃,好吧,"医生说,"但是人们难道不知道月亮曾经是地球的一部分吗?"

"是啊,我也不太清楚,"吱吱说,"看来,我祖母的故事里缺了不少重要信息。不过,她倒是提起过那段时期中的一些细节:黑暗笼罩了大地,紧接而来的是一场剧烈的大爆炸,无数的动物失去了生命,然后海水倒灌进了炸出的大坑,造成了更加严重的破坏。人类和其他动物有的躲进了洞穴,有的爬到了山顶,还有的只能闭上眼睛听天由命了……我们猴子一族的历史学家认为,亲身经历过那场灾难的动物如今没有在世的了,但我一直对此表示怀疑。不过,在那场浩劫之后,人类成功地又聚集到了一起,恢复了大灾变前的秩序,可惜,好景不长,一场战争很快就爆发了。"

"那场战争的原因是什么?"医生好奇地问道。

"那时人类的数量已经翻了好几番,还建立了不少大城市。"吱吱回忆道,"至于战争的起因嘛,其实很简单:那些老派的太阳崇拜者们认为月亮是太阳的妻子或者女儿,所以把她视为女神;而另一些人认为既然月亮曾经是地球的一部分,那么只有地球才有资格和太阳一起被视为神,而不是月亮。还有一小群人认为太阳、地球和月亮组成了一个全能的大三角。这场战争真是残酷得很,成千上万的人类互相厮杀,我们猴子的祖先都被震惊到了。"

"天哪,天哪,"吱吱说完,医生喃喃自语道,"这可是史上第一场宗教战争啊!老天!真是让人费解,只要活得开心,做一个真诚友善的人,那么邻居家的信仰又有什么要紧呢?"

# 第十七章
# 我们听说了"理事会"


现在回想起来,那次寻找"轻语藤蔓"的旅程真是令人愉悦又收获颇丰。这些藤蔓生长在一座风景优美的峡谷之中,形态各异的爬藤从石壁上垂下来,一汪泉水镶嵌在峡谷底部,好似仙女们生活的世外桃源,也好似那些奇珍异兽的藏身之处。

波莉尼西娅灵巧地飞到了那片藤蔓上,突然,那些藤蔓就像波浪一样抖动起来,还发出一阵阵充耳可闻的"说话声"。显然,这些植物不喜欢被一只陌生的鸟儿打扰。波莉尼西娅见势不妙,赶紧拍打着翅膀飞了回来。

"真是糟糕,"她不满地摇了摇头说,"这个地方真叫我看不上眼。瞧那些蠕动的爬藤,看起来简直和蛇一模一样。"

"我说,波莉尼西娅,"医生发出一阵大笑,"他们只是不太习惯这种状况罢了,你可能已经吓坏他们了——让我去试试看能不能和他们聊上几句。"

波莉尼西娅灵巧地飞到了那片藤蔓上

鉴于医生有过与"会唱歌的树"和"爱漂亮的百合花"的交流经验,我猜想医生能够更加娴熟地运用肢体动作和语言来与藤蔓们交流。果然,医生很快就和他们开始聊天了,就好像他们以前就认识似的。

突然,有个可怕的念头萦绕在我的脑海,医生就像看穿了我的想法一样说道,"斯塔宾斯,这些植物和我对话如此轻松,只能有一个解释:他们之前肯定和其他人类有过交流,看,我甚至可以用声音和唇语来与他们谈话。"

医生放下了手中的仪器,开始轻轻地哼出一段旋律,听起来就像一首歌谣和一段对话的结合体。以前,约翰·杜立德一般都要等上好几个小时甚至好几天,才能没有障碍地和月球上的有些植物聊天,但是这次情况不一样,医生语音刚落,这些藤蔓就抬起了枝条,让风儿从一个特定的角度吹过,从而能够发出一种和医生哼唱的旋律极为相似的音色来作为回应。

"斯塔宾斯,他们说很高兴认识我们!"医生说,他的肩膀因为激动而抖个不停。

"真是太棒了,医生!"我说,"他们立刻作出了反应,我从没见过这样的事。"

"他们以前也和人类交流过,"医生重复道,"这是毫无疑问的,要确认这一点只需要——老天!你怎么了?"

他一回头就看到吱吱一脸紧张地扯着他的袖子,这只小猴子嚅动着嘴唇,另一只手在比画着什么,但是却一句话也说不出来。

"怎么了,吱吱?"医生问,"到底发生了什么?"

"看!"吱吱用尽全力从牙缝里挤出了一个字。他伸手指向泉水的一边。我们被他的神情吓坏了,赶紧爬上一块大石头想要看得更清楚些。只见那儿的沙滩上赫然有着两个和我们之前在湖边看到的一模一样的脚印。

"月亮巨人!"医生失声叫道,"好吧,看样子这些藤蔓

第十七章 我们听说了"理事会" 101

以前确实和人类对话过。我一直在想——"

"嘘!"波莉尼西娅突然打断了医生的自言自语,"等会儿你们抽空偷偷往左边的峭壁上瞥一眼,那里似乎有些东西在偷看我们,小心别被他们发现。"

于是,我和医生都装作若无其事地继续与爬藤们聊天,然后我漫不经心地挠了挠耳朵,顺势朝波莉尼西娅所指的方向看去,只见有几只鸟儿正躲在密密的藤蔓后面,显然在窥视着我们。就在这时,一个巨大的黑影遮住了

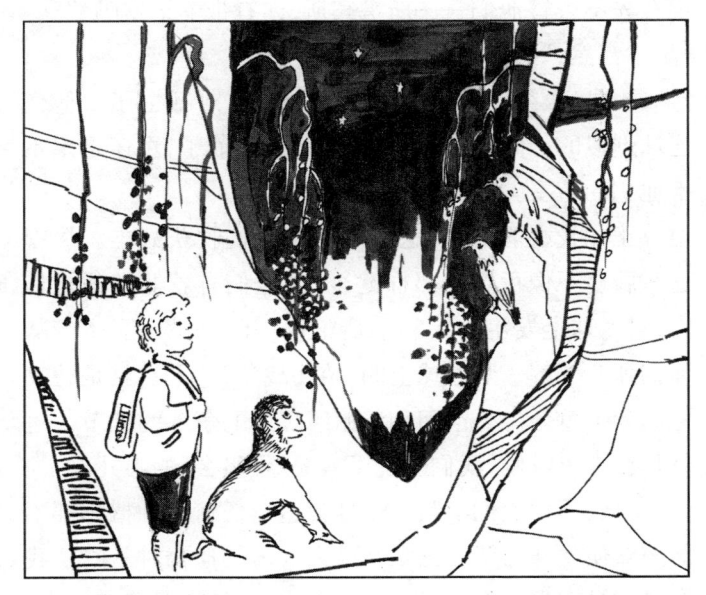

有几只鸟儿正躲在密密的藤蔓后面,显然在窥视我们。

山谷里的阳光,我们赶忙抬头,担心会不会遭到来自空中的袭击。不过,看起来是我们多虑了,一只和巨蛾同一种类的昆虫从我们头顶上徐徐飞过,转眼消失在了地平线上。

我们愕然无语。

"好吧,"医生拉长了声音说道,"我猜他们是故意现身的,也许他们已经决定要与我们进行接触了。看那些鸟儿啊,他们竟然还没有这儿的昆虫大。不管怎样,我们现在先不去管他们——斯塔宾斯,你有带笔记本吗?"

"当然,"我说,"时刻准备着。"

于是,医生便转头继续和那些藤蔓对话去了。他们连珠炮似的一问一答,我记得手都快抽筋了,可还是跟不上他们的节奏。

正如我之前所说,这次对话令我们收获颇丰。尽管这些藤蔓不像百合花那样健谈,但他们有着非凡的记忆力,对月球上发生的大小事情记得一清二楚。医生想从他们那儿了解一些月球上的"植物战争"——也就是植物之间为了争夺生长空间和资源所爆发的争斗的细节。也就是在那个时候,我们听说了有关"理事会"的事儿。

"哦,不,"他们不紧不慢地说道,"任何一种植物都不能随随便便地为了一己私利就去攻击其他物种。哈!我们早就没有那么低级了。很久以前,这种情况确实存在,虫子和虫子、植物和植物、鸟儿和鸟儿互相开战。不过如今,再也不会了。"

"你们是怎样办到的?"医生对此特别感兴趣,"如果两种物种想要同一样东西的话,你们是怎么处理的?"

"这种情况理事会会出面进行调停。"那些藤蔓答道。

"呃——不好意思,"医生说,"我还没有搞清楚,什么理事会?"

"好吧,好吧,"藤蔓慢悠悠地说,"在几百年前——那时的场景还历历在目——我们——"

"等等,"医生打断说,"你是说这儿的昆虫、植物和鸟儿都已经存在了几个世纪之久?"

"当然。有什么问题吗?"那些藤蔓抬了抬枝条,又慢条斯理地继续说下去,"还有年纪更大的呢。在这儿,如果你不满两百岁的话只能算是个年轻人。有几棵老树,还有几只动物,据说已经有一千岁了呢!"

"你是在开玩笑吧!"医生喊道,"我知道你们寿命很长,但是几百岁——或者一千岁——真是太匪夷所思,难以置信——噢,不好意思,请继续。"

"好的,"藤蔓们又说开了,"在我们设立理事会之前,这片土地上到处都有战争和毁灭。有一种体型巨大像蜥蜴一样的生物,在月球上横行霸道,他们身型庞大,食量惊人,几乎把植物给吃了个精光,不少植物根本活不到出芽繁殖的年龄。眼看植物界就要面临灭顶之灾,我们这些幸存者不得已聚到一起,商量该怎么办。"

"呃……你说什么?"医生问,"你说'聚到一起'是什么意思? 你们植物可是无法移动的,不是吗?"

"的确不能,"藤蔓答道,"但是我们可以让鸟儿们或者虫子们当作信使互相传话,我们把这种方式称作开会。"

"好吧,"医生又抛出了另一个问题,"大约是在多久之前动植物之间开始互相交流的呢?"

"嗯……我们实在没法告诉你一个确切的日期——你知道,有些交流方式已经有上千年的历史了,不过那些方式可没现在的那么好使。如今我们月球上各个物种之间的关系好多了。无论在哪个角落发生了什么事,用不了多久这儿的每只鸟儿、每只昆虫和每株植物都会知道。"

"嚯!"医生惊讶极了,"还有这样的事!"

# 第十八章
# 管事的

接下来,在"轻语藤蔓"的介绍中,我们了解了更多有关"理事会"的信息。这是一个类似委员会的组织,它的成员中包括动物和植物。成立这个组织的宗旨在于保障月球的和平,防止争斗和战乱。比如,当某种灌木想要获得更多的栖息地,而它的目标地区已经被其他植物——比如芦笋所占据,它可不能就这样直接入侵,而是需要把申请事先呈给理事会。又比如说,某种蝴蝶采蜜时,遭到了蜜蜂或甲虫的干扰,它们也可以向理事会求助,由它们来最终裁决。这些信息使得许多之前困扰我们的谜团终于得到了解释。

"你瞧,斯塔宾斯,"医生对我说道,"果然这儿奇特的一切都是有原因的。有了这样一个组织,怪不得动植物们都能安居乐业。看来我们亲爱的地球也可以从她的孩子身上学到不少东西呢——我们的故乡可是一个——呃,弱肉强食的世界。"

理事会成员包括动物和植物

医生摇了摇头，抬头看向天空，这时，地球正在一片暗淡的光晕中缓缓落下地平线，正如同我在帕德尔比日出时看到的月亮那样。

医生用一种更严肃的口气继续说道，"我们人类向来自命不凡却缺乏智慧和远见。斯塔宾斯，在地球上我们到处都能见到暴力——战争！战争！还是战争！还有什么'适者生存'的法则！我大半辈子都尝试着去帮助动物——那些所谓的'低等生物'！我不是在抱怨什么，我

地球在一片暗淡的光晕中缓缓落下地平线

很享受和动物们待在一起,并赢得它们的友谊。但是,我一直觉得依我一己之力改变不了什么。不过这个理事会又给了我信心。终有一天,地球上的生物们也能和平共处。"

"虽说是这样,"我对医生说,"但是这儿没有什么狮子老虎之类的猛兽啊!所以自然不会有'大鱼吃小鱼,小鱼吃虾米'的情况发生。"

"这倒没错,斯塔宾斯,"医生回答,"但是别忘了,大飞虫和小飞虫之间也会有掠食关系,更别提比他们更大的动物了——比方说地球上的人类与家蝇——之间的竞争了。再说,说不定这儿的某种动物将来也会进化成像狮子老虎之类的掠食动物呢。"

医生说完便转身又询问了几个问题,什么理事会有多少成员啊,会议多久举行一次啊,等等,而得到的回答和我们的预期也是八九不离十。

那时我打心底里希望自己是个高明的诗人或作家,因为以我贫瘠的语言几乎无法描绘出月球上最伟大的一幅图景:树木摇曳歌唱,花儿梳妆打扮,鸟儿与昆虫和植物们谈笑风生,好不热闹,而这美妙的一切都由一个博爱的"理事会"所守护。这儿的生物,不论体型大小、力量强弱,都共同拥有一片和平的天地,没有悲伤,也鲜有病痛。而要描绘这样一幅画卷,人类的华丽词藻显得多么渺小而又贫乏无力。

正当我独自沉思之时,医生又开口了:"很抱歉我还有最后一个问题,能告诉我你们是如何控制后代数量的吗?我是说,有时候你们播撒的种子会比理想数量多,不是吗?"

"这种情况一般是由鸟儿们处理的,"藤蔓回答,"他们的职责就是帮助我们吃掉所有多余的种子。"

"有意思。"医生突然像想起什么似的说,"对了,我希望有件事理事会能够帮我解答——但愿不会给他们添麻烦——有关我的园艺试验的事。我从地球上带来了几种不同植物的种子，但种下去后一点反应也没有，我想知道原因。"

那些细长的藤条轻轻晃动着，答道，"哦，医生，你忘了，我们的消息可是灵通得很哪。你一把它们种下去，这件事情就被报告给了理事会。你们一离开，长嘴鸟就被派去把每一粒种子都挖出来并销毁掉了。理事会的成员们对于外来物种很是担心，毕竟我们赖以生存的生态平

长嘴鸟被派去把每粒种子都挖出来并销毁掉

衡一旦被打破,天知道会发生什么。正因如此,管事的才会——"

突然,那三根正在说话的大藤条陷入了沉默,就好像一个发现自己说错了话的人类一样。瞬间,藤蔓丛中爆发出一阵骚动,它们在峭壁上晃动、扭转,有的还蜷缩成了一团。随着几声尖锐的叫声,三五只色彩鲜艳的鸟儿拍打着翅膀从藤蔓丛中飞了出来,越过两侧的山崖不见了。

色彩鲜艳的鸟儿拍打着翅膀从藤蔓丛中飞了出来,越过两侧的山崖不见了。

"什么情况——医生,发生了什么?"我一边问,一边看着更多的鸟儿从藏身之处向远方飞去。

"我不知道,斯塔宾斯,"医生说道,"我猜是谁说漏嘴了。"他又转向了那些藤蔓:"告诉我,谁是管事的?"

"他是理事会的领导。"他们迟疑了一会儿说道。

"我猜得到,"医生说,"但是他到底是什么?"

这时,攀附在山崖上的藤条又扭动起来,看起来像是某种警告。

终于,那三根大藤条说:"我们很抱歉,但是我们有规定要遵守,有些事是不能说的。"

"为什么? 有谁在阻止你们提起吗?"医生追问道。

但这次他们没有回答,无论医生怎么询问,他们始终一言不发。最后,我们只得放弃尝试,悻悻地回去了。

"依我之见,"在我们准备晚餐时,波莉尼西娅说道,"我们刚才似乎和月球社会闹了点儿不愉快。真奇怪,我这辈子还没见过这样一个地方呢——话说我见过的地方可不少。我猜我们几个和刚才说漏嘴的藤蔓已经成了月球上的新闻人物了。还有那个什么'管事的'搞得神神秘秘的,派头那么大,不知道的还以为他是圣徒彼得本人呢。"

"也许我们很快就能知道他的真实身份了,"医生一边切着野果一边说,"再怎么说,他们应该意识到没必要这么遮遮掩掩的。"

"但愿如此,"吱吱说道,"这个秘密让我有点害怕。我很想早点回到帕德尔比。冒险,我想我已经受够了冒险了。"

"哦,别担心,"医生说,"我敢保证,只要我搞清楚他们来找我的目的,然后履行我的职责就行了。至于回到地球的事,我相信他们自有安排。"

"但愿如此,"波莉尼西娅一边啄着坚果一边咕哝道,"但愿如此。"

# 第十九章
# 月亮巨人

那一晚我睡得很不安心。首先,我们的身体还在不停地生长,睡觉时手臂和腿总会伸到睡袋外面,硌在沙地上,更别提周围阵阵窸窸窣窣的声音和若隐若现的阴影了。我记得有一次半夜醒来,竟然听见医生、吱吱和波莉尼西娅一起说着梦话,看来白天发生的事情的确给了他们不小的压力。

终于熬到了天亮,我们睡意惺忪地爬了起来,开始准备早餐。波莉尼西娅很快就又变得精神饱满了,她开始仔细地检查营地周边的地面环境,饱经风霜的脸上显出严肃的神色:"看样子有不少家伙对我们感兴趣啊!""何出此言?"医生问道,"有什么异常的情况吗?""你自己瞧瞧就知道了。"鹦鹉一边说着一边把我们带到营地周围。

好吧,我们早就习惯在营地四周探查各种各样的痕迹了,但这次的痕迹远远超过了以往的任何一次,这些痕迹密密麻麻地出现在营地周围,几乎要把我们包围了,其中有着一些奇怪的昆虫印迹、巨大的鸟类足迹和十分明显的巨人脚印。

医生不以为然地耸耸肩说:"反正他们和我们保持了一定的距离,而且也并无恶意,那么让他们看着我们睡觉又有什么问题呢?还是先去吃早餐吧。"

不过医生的预言——就是那个说月球上的动物很快就会露面的预言——很快就成为了现实。当我正咀嚼着一块蘸了蜂蜜的番薯时,注意到一大片阴影笼罩住了我们。我抬头想看看是什么,但我简直不敢相信自己的眼睛:那只去帕德尔比接我们的巨蛾正缓缓从空中落下。和他相比,我们简直小得出奇,就像是站在大象边上的老鼠。

就在这时,又有两三只同样大小的飞蛾轻轻地开始降落。我们甚至还没搞清楚他们是从哪儿冒出来的,他们就已经停在了同伴身旁。

无数的鸟儿飞来了,既有那些曾经被我们发现躲在藤蔓后面的鸟儿,也有不少没有见过面的,有鹳鸟、天鹅和不少叫不上名字的。有的鸟儿比地球上的同种生物要稍大一些,更多的鸟儿体型硕大无朋,颜色和外形与地球上的同类也不尽相同。

无数的蜜蜂也飞来了。他们排着整齐的队列向我们

第十九章 月亮巨人 115

有的鸟儿比地球上的同种生物要稍大些,更多的鸟儿体型硕大无朋。

飞来。我认出了通体漆黑的大黄蜂、稍小一些的普通黄蜂、亮绿色飞得极快的小蜜蜂和其他不知名的蜜蜂。他们庞大的体型使得这些在地球上普通的小昆虫变成了恐怖的怪兽。

看得出来,可怜的吱吱已经吓得话都说不出来了。这并不奇怪,再强壮的动物看到这么一大群巨大的虫子也会觉得胆怯的。不过鉴于医生在场,我并不怎么慌乱。

再看医生本人,与其说是害怕,不如说是兴趣盎然。那些生物看起来也并无恶意,他们队形齐整,动作划一,看起来像是事先排练好的。

过了一会儿,当我们的营地四周已然成为一片昆虫与鸟类的海洋时,我们感到脚下的大地颤动起来,远处也传来了沉重的脚步声。虽然在月球上声音能传得很远,但这如同地震一般颤动的地面却让我们感到有个大东西正在接近。

吱吱害怕地钻进了医生的外套里面,大气也不敢出,波莉尼西娅站在旁边的一棵树桠上,看起来心烦意乱又充满好奇。我看见她圆溜溜的小眼睛正盯着我们右手边树林里一道剪子形的空地。她朝一侧伸长了脖子——这是她的标志性动作——想看清楚那边的状况。她一边瞧着,一边低声喃喃自语着什么(有可能是瑞典语,她心情不好时就喜欢说瑞典语),不过我一句也听不懂。这时,远处的树木开始摇动,一个巨大的生物出现在了地平线上。

天色慢慢暗了下来,那个生物离我们也越来越近了。因为体型过于庞大,他前进时显得有点一摇一摆,不小心被他踩到的大树就像细树枝一样被轻易折断。看着看着,我承认自己有点胆怯了。

慢慢地,慢慢地,那个生物完全从林子里走了出来,那些昆虫和鸟儿纷纷为他让路,我们也终于看清了他的外形:他身高体壮,两只手臂垂在身体两侧——这是一个人!

我们终于见到了月亮巨人!

"哎呀,老天!"波莉尼西娅尖声叫道,"你在这儿肯定是个厉害角色吧!怪不得我们要过了那么久才能见到你本尊呢!"虽然当时的气氛有点瘆人,这只伶牙俐齿的鸟儿还是把我给逗乐了。夜幕已经完全降临,星光倒映在

"我们终于见到月亮巨人了"

巨蛾和鸟儿们的眼睛里,闪耀着奇特的光芒,就好像一盏台灯的微光反射在猫眼里一样。我用余光瞥见约翰·杜立德站了起来,向着面前的巨人致意。"我很荣幸终于见到了阁下!"他用字正腔圆的英语一字一句地说道,但巨人只是发出了一阵含糊不清的咕哝声。

医生意识到巨人也许不懂英语,就开始尝试用其他语言和巨人进行交流。这个我所认识的最伟大的语言学家开始用地球上不同的人类语言逐一向巨人问好,可是这些无论是如今正在使用的,还是几乎已经失传的语言,都没能让巨人作出任何反应。于是医生改用了动物的语言,巨人似乎能听懂一两个词,等到医生用植物和昆虫的语言向他问好时,巨人显示出了浓厚的兴趣。我、吱吱和波莉尼西娅目不转睛地盯着医生和巨人之间的交谈。一个小时过去了,两个小时过去了,终于医生转身冲我做了一个手势,于是我心领神会抓起一本笔记本和一支铅笔,准备做记录。当我刚准备下笔时,在我旁边的吱吱突然高声喊道:"看!快看!快看巨人的右手手腕!"我们几个睁大了眼睛,果然看见巨人的右手腕上绑着什么东西。这时,吱吱又大叫起来:"看哪!是一串蓝色的珠子!你们看到了吗?虽然明显已经老旧不堪了——但他肯定就是奥托·布劳奇!那串珠子就是仙女皮皮蒂帕送给他的礼物!看哪!医生——这就是那位古代艺术家——他竟

第十九章 月亮巨人 119

然来到了月球!"

"快看哪!巨人右手戴着一串蓝色的珠子!"吱吱嚷道。

## 第二十章
# 医生和巨人


"没事,吱吱,没事。"医生说道,"你先等会儿,不要那么激动。"

虽然医生看上去十分冷静,但我看得出来他其实内心兴奋不已。在这个奇特的世界里待了那么久后,我们终于见到了令我们印象深刻的脚印的主人,相信没有人能按捺住激动之情。

我抬头看着面前高耸入云的巨人,意识到只要他愿意的话,就可以轻轻松松地碾碎我们。但是,和其他月球上的生物一样,我们在他身上看不到什么恶意,只不过看样子他对我们的小巧体型感到十分好奇。至于约翰·杜立德,我在他脸上根本看不到任何害怕的神情。很快他就开始尝试和巨人你一言我一语地对话了,而且好消息是,我们巨大的、穿着树皮衣服、头发乱糟糟垂在肩头的朋友似乎很乐意配合。医生一个劲地想着要让巨人听清自己的说话,不过两人巨大的身高差距使得这种尝试很

第二十章 医生和巨人

徒劳。最后,巨人伸出一只大手把医生托了起来,约翰·杜立德跳上了巨人的膝盖,开始一路向上爬,最后终于站到了他的肩膀上。现在医生只要踮起脚尖就能直接在巨人耳边说话了。过了一会儿,他从巨人身上又滑了下来,又站在了膝盖上。他向我大声喊道:"斯塔宾斯,我说斯塔宾斯!你手头有笔记本吗?"

医生站到了巨人的肩膀上,现在他只要踮起脚尖就能直接在巨人耳边说话了。

"有的,医生。我口袋里就有一本。你要我记些什么吗?"

"是的,"他又喊道,看起来就像是站在高楼上的工头,"我暂时还没能让他理解我准备要说的东西,不过我希望你能先记一些基础信息。你准备好了吗?"

事实证明,医生低估了与巨人交流的难度,眼看一个多小时过去了,医生仍没有取得任何进展。"哼!"波莉尼西娅不满地咕哝道,"真是搞不懂,医生为什么对这个傻大个这么痴迷。这家伙估计还没有一条毛毛虫聪明呢!而伟大的医生——约翰·杜立德,医学博士——还有我们,却为了这个野蛮人耽误了这么多时间!"

"就是说呀,"吱吱小声说道,眼睛不停地向上望,"但是——想想看,他年纪该有多大啊!打月球从地球上分离时起他就生活在这儿了——他少说也得有几万,不,几百万岁了吧? 老天爷! 真是个大寿星啊!"

"但是瞧他那副傻样,"鹦鹉仍不肯松口,"还有那种粗野的行为。难道仅仅因为体态臃肿、发育过剩就能对远道而来的客人如此怠慢吗?"

"噢,冷静,波莉尼西娅,"我说,"我们可不能忘了一点,他早就和人类文明彻底脱节了。哪怕他还保持着离开地球之时——我猜是石器时代的习惯,那也肯定不会是什么文明人的习惯。但令我惊奇的是,过了那么久的独居生活，他还能保持人性和思维，所以我说医生和他之间交流困难一点都不让人奇怪。"

"好吧，汤米·斯塔宾斯，"鹦鹉说，"这话可能听上去很有道理。但有一点不可否认，就是面前的这个大块头下令把我们接来月球，但是我们到了以后他又不闻不问的——搞得我们还要自己解决一日三餐。要我说，这可算不上热情好客。"

波莉尼西娅说，是面前这个大块头下令把我们接来月球。

"你可能忘了,波莉尼西娅,"我耐心地解释道,"医生他不是说起过吗?他可能也十分害怕我们——因为我们的体型小得出奇。对了,你有注意到他的跛脚吗?"

巨人可能也十分害怕我们——因为我们的体型小得出奇

"当然,"她说着转了转脑袋,"瞧他那条拖着的左腿,走起路来肯定一点都不稳。噗!我敢说他找医生过来就是为了治好他这条腿的——也许是风湿病或者脚趾扭了——我好奇的是他到底是从哪儿听说约翰·杜立德的大名的呢?毕竟这儿的世界和地球可不常联系。"

不过,我的注意力全都放在了医生和巨人身上。我实在想不出他们俩能用什么语言进行交流——这个巨人到底还记不记得远古时期他自己的母语呢?

事实上,要想获得这个问题的答案我还得再等上一会儿。医生直到很晚还在进行着他的语言研究。我看着昏昏欲睡的吱吱,自己也慢慢睡了过去。

当我醒来时已是日上三竿。医生还在锲而不舍地进行着研究,不过看上去似乎取得了显著的进展。我提醒他已经到了用早餐的时间了,他于是点了点头,又转头和巨人说了些什么——很明显是在邀请他和我们共进早餐。于是,巨人就在我们的桌边坐了下来,两眼直盯着上面摆放的食物,脸上的神情很好奇。我们给了巨人一些主食——黄番薯,但巨人摇了摇头,向医生说了些什么。医生告诉我巨人说这种植物是他巨大身材的罪魁祸首——其他植物的效果没有这么强大。

"那么给他几个瓜试试,医生。"吱吱提议。

这次,巨人愉快地接受了我们的馈赠,大口大口地嚼了起来。

这时,我开口问道,"医生,你究竟是怎么发现巨人使用的语言呢?"

"啊,"医生说,"这可不简单。刚开始的时候,我猜他还会记得某种人类的语言——也就是某种不同音节的组合,于是我就花了好几个小时顺着这种假设尝试,但他好像对此根本没有什么回应。当然啦,我想看看他是否仍有过去地球知识的记忆,于是我开始说起地球上的其他语言,结果发现他会说所有植物和昆虫语言的变体。这样看来,他没法告诉我一些史前人类的失传语言,不过他对植物和昆虫语言的深入了解一定会对我很有帮助。"

"噢,他有没有提起过他是怎样来到月球的?"波莉尼西娅问。

"没有,还没有,"医生说,"毕竟这才刚开始。一切都会好的。波莉尼西娅,一切都会好的。"

# 第二十一章
# 奥托·布劳奇来到月亮上的故事

事实证明,刚开始的时候,巨人的确为我们的小身板而惊惧不已,他也并不是一个想要碾碎我们的大坏蛋。事实上,一顿早餐过后,我就认定了他是我见过的脾气最好的人类——也许还是生物之一。他允许我们在他身上爬来爬去,而且看起来很高兴我们对他如此感兴趣。医生早就把他看成是一个值得信任的朋友,所以看到巨人这么和善并不惊讶,但我和吱吱却大大松了一口气。我在此无法一言不差地转述他们之间的对话,但大致的内容我会在接下来的段落中复述。

医生首先询问了巨人有关吱吱祖母流传下来的故事的真实性。虽然巨人对于这些陈年旧事明显记不大清了,但在医生向他完整讲述了猴子一族的传说后,他肯定了其中不少细节的准确性。对了,我忘了描述一下巨人的面部特征了。在白天时,他看起来就是一张聪明智慧的脸庞，而且看上去并没有他的实际年龄那么老。总之，这张脸并不带有任何野蛮人的特征，但总是有一种难以言表的怪异，我猜这是长时间不与其他人类接触的结果。不过，只要你在脑海中想象出一个尽其所能为其他生物谋福祉的人类面容，那肯定就和巨人长得十分相像。

医生接着又用奇怪的植物和昆虫语言向巨人发问。巨人说他依稀记得自己之前的确是叫奥托·布劳奇，也可能是个史前艺术家。至于那串手链，——没错，他说他戴着它是为了某个人——其他的他就不记得了——那个人是谁？好吧，他至少记得，在他之前，这串手链属于某个女人。那么他是怎么得到这串珠子的呢？——不记得了，毕竟那是很久很久以前的事了。好吧，既然如此，我们还有什么好问的呢？

其实我自己有个问题想问问他。就在前一晚上我和吱吱散步时，我发现巨人腰间挂着一个奇怪的圆形物体。那时，天色昏暗，我没有看清楚，今天早上我终于分辨出了上面的图像——是一名手持弓箭的女孩。我希望医生能询问有关这幅作品的来历。虽然我们从吱吱的故事里已经得知了女孩的身份，但我希望我们的询问能够唤起巨人的记忆，甚至能允许我们用其他东西来交换这幅作品。于是，医生便把话题转移到了这幅画上。巨人立刻举起了这块刻着图案的鹿角，并把它轻轻按在心口上，脸上露出了悲伤的神情,似乎突然想到了什么。我和医生面面相觑,决定还是不要谈起这个话题为妙。

医生接着迅速在巨人身上上下检查了一番,就好像是在仔细端详博物馆里的展品,不过,他一向做事谨慎温和,所以也没有什么冒犯之感。

"很好很好,"医生说,"我们已经确认了你就是那个史前艺术家奥托·布劳奇,也知道你在那次大爆炸中和月亮一起脱离了地球。不过,我们对你在理事会里的作

"知道你在那次大爆炸中和月亮一起脱离了地球"

为依然所知甚少——你应该是统领全局的吧?"

巨人晃着硕大的脑袋,看着站在自己手臂上的医生。

"理事会?"他有点儿心不在焉地答道,"哦,对,理事会——没错儿——我们当初意识到如果不能达到生态平衡的话,这儿会是一团糟——植物种子太多,草和树到处疯长,鸟蛋的数量多得要命,大片大片的蜂群成天飞来飞去,真是糟糕!——我猜你在地球上一定见过不少这样的状况吧?"

"是的,没错儿,"医生说,"请继续。"

"好吧,于是我们意识到只有一个方法可以抑制这种状况,就是减少物种间的竞争和战争,这就是理事会成立的原因。"

医生打断了巨人的话:"那么你知不知道你如此长寿的原因呢?没人知道月球是在多久以前从地球上分离出来的,所以说,和地球上的芸芸众生相比,你的寿命可是长的有点吓人啊!"

"呃,好吧,"月亮巨人说,"我始终不清楚我是怎么来到月球的。不过,这又怎么样呢?反正我已经在这儿待了那么久了。原先在地球上生活的记忆也已逐渐变得模糊不清——等等,我好像还记得些什么:月球飞离地球后,我感到难以呼吸——不过我决定要活下去,也许正是这种强烈的求生欲望让我支撑了下来。我还记得月亮停止旋转之时,土地一片荒芜,只有零星几株植物,所以我只能靠根茎之类的东西维生。过了一阵子,那些昆虫和鸟儿开始活跃了起来,一个新世界就这么诞生了。又过了很多很多年,我意识到我有责任帮助这个世界发展得更好,因为我拥有——呃,至少当时的确如此——比其他生物高得多的智力。我知道物种之间无端的争斗不会有好结果,于是我组织了理事会。从那时起——老天,那可是很久以前的事了——这儿的动植物就开始不断进化,直到他们变成现在的样子,就是这样。"

"哦,是的,是的,"医生说,"我能理解你的初衷——而且这是个很棒的法子。不过,我还有一个问题:你们是怎么听说关于我的事情的?月亮和地球之间可没有交流渠道啊。还有,我猜那只去帕德尔比找我的巨蛾也是你派去的吧?"

"是我和理事会派去的,"巨人纠正道,"至于我们是怎么听说你的,你说的没错,我们两个世界的交流极其有限,但并不是一点也没有。你们地球上发生自然灾害时,偶尔会把一些土壤、树木等碎片抛出地球的引力范围,而这些碎片一旦进入月球的引力范围,就会渐渐向我们靠近,最后变成月球的一部分。我记得,几个世纪前地球上发生的一场猛烈的飓风把一些灌木和石头抛出了地球,它们最终在月球上着陆了,结果这些植物种子就像疯了一样四处蔓延,最后我们费了好大力气才把它们控制住。"

"真有意思,"医生一边说一边还往我这儿看两眼,以确保我把这个故事记了下来,"你能否告诉我你是在哪次事件中听到了我的名字呢?"

"哦,那是一次火山爆发,"巨人说,"那次地球上的一座沉寂了数年的火山突然爆发,整个山头被炸掉了。这次剧烈的爆炸把好几吨各种各样的东西——泥土、木头之类的——抛进了太空。这些材料中的一部分向着月亮飞来,被我们的引力吸引住。你也知道,地球上的土石和树木中总会有些小动物存在,这回是一只火山爆发时正在附近湖边筑巢的翠鸟被带了上来。虽然有不少碎石砸在月球表面变成了粉末,但粘住翠鸟的那块碎石很幸运地落在了一座湖里。"

我相信这个令人震惊的故事的真实性,因为除此之外还能怎么解释医生在月球上的名气呢?说来也是运气,如果这个不速之客不擅长戏水,那么它十有八九会当场丧命,因为那个湖足足有五十英尺深。好在那只鸟儿立刻逃了出来,飞到了岸上。它能活着来到月球着实是个奇迹,我猜他穿过无空气带时的速度一定十分惊人,所以才能在没有辅助呼吸设备的情况下避免缺氧。

粘住翠鸟的那块碎石很幸运地落在了一座湖里

# 第二十二章
# 月球上的伙计听说了医生

那只翠鸟(看样子他已经被选为了理事会成员)于是被介绍给了医生。他告诉了我们不少有用的信息,其中不少是他来到月球之后的经历。他承认正是他告诉了月球生物们有关约翰·杜立德的种种事迹,他的医学技术还有他在飞禽走兽和鱼儿中的好名声。我们还从翠鸟那儿得知这次的大集会几乎召集来了所有的理事会成员,当然,除了那些不能移动的植物成员,但它们委托昆虫和鸟儿作为代表来参加集会,以确保它们的利益。

显然,今天对于月球上的生物来说是个大日子。我们和翠鸟聊天后发现有些动物正在相互争论什么,他们分成几个团体互相辩论,看起来就像是正在举行一场吵吵闹闹的政治磋商。不过,这些动物一听到医生大声询问巨人为何带他们来月球时都安静了下来。只听医生说道:"好吧,不管怎样,你们得明白我这个人真的很忙。我很荣幸能够受邀来到月球,但是我在地球上还有很多事

第二十二章 月球上的伙计听说了医生　135

那只翠鸟告诉了我们不少有用的信息

情要做。我相信你们找我来一定是有事情需要我帮忙，所以能不能现在就让我知道？"

暂时安静下来的动物们又开始窃窃私语，他们交头接耳谈论个不休，看起来医生刚才触及了某个敏感话题，就连巨人脸上也有些难堪的神情。

"好吧，"巨人终于开口了，"事实上，我们这儿太需要一位好医生了。我的脚板已经痛了很长很长时间了，还有那些大点儿的昆虫——尤其是蚱蜢——身体也很不好。和翠鸟谈话以后，我就觉得你正是我们要找的人。我想——呃，我想如果你知道我们的处境就不会怪我们把你带来月球了。千万告诉我你能帮助我们——我们自己的世界里实在是找不到这方面的人才。所以我们理事会在一次特别会议中决定邀你过来。"

医生没有作声。

"你得知道，"巨人继续说道，声音里充满了歉意，"我们派去的那只巨蛾也是历经千辛万苦才找到你的，而且他也成为了我们的英雄——因为不是任何动物都能担当此任——我们必须在大体型的鸟儿和昆虫中挑选，你知道，这趟行程会消耗很多体力——"

巨人无奈地摊开双手，这个动作倒是和地球上的人类颇为相像。医生赶紧开始安慰他。"哦，我当然会帮助你们，当然会。"医生说，"我——我们非常高兴能够来到这儿。虽然我在地球上的确事务缠身，但在这儿，我能够学到更多关于博物学的新知识。我得承认在地球上时我和巨蛾交流起来有不少困难，致使我的准备工作做得不够完善，但是我一点儿也不后悔来到这儿——毕竟探索一个新世界的机会可难得得很哪！当然，我是觉得你也许应该早些露面，不过现在想来你也许也有自己的难处，我猜你也是忙得很吧。"

"忙？"巨人说，"不不不，我一点儿都不忙。月亮上的生活可是悠闲得很。基本上我只要参加理事会的例行会议,然后每过一段时间就去巡视一下星球上的状况就可以了。我为什么没有早点露面的原因是……好吧,我得承认,是因为我有些害怕。在此之前地球上的人类从来没有来过月球,而且我本来以为你是一个人来,但是我的鸟儿们和昆虫、植物们给我通风报信说你们来了四个——我有点担心不知道你们会不会来对付我们,虽然翠鸟告诉我说你在地球上对动物们十分友好,但是我不确定你对我们会不会一视同仁——我很抱歉,没有尽到地主之谊,但希望你能理解。"

"噢,当然当然,"医生说,再次尝试让巨人平静下来。"你不用自责了,真的,我完全能够理解你的心情。不过,有几个问题还是令我们很困惑,希望你能给我们解答一下。首先,我们在帕德尔比的时候似乎看到月球上在冒烟——就是巨蛾刚找到我们那会——你知道是怎么回事吗?"

"知道,"巨人赶忙说道,"这就是我们干的。我刚才说过我们很担心孤身前去地球的巨蛾,也有点内疚把这么一个危险的任务交给了他——但是,很不幸,杰玛洛抽到了那张带记号的牌。"

"杰玛洛!"医生不知不觉中提高了音调,"带记号的牌?"

"是的,我们抽签决定执行任务的人选。"巨人解释道,"杰玛洛·巴伯利就是那只抽中签的蛾子。"

"我明白了,"医生说,"杰玛洛,不错不错。你们这儿的每只昆虫都有自己的名字——好吧,这也不难理解,毕竟他们也是这个社会的重要成员。我猜你能记得住这儿每只虫子的名字,哪怕是同一个种类的?"

"那是自然,"巨人答道,"我们这儿有差不多十万只蜜蜂,而我叫得出他们中每一个名字和他所属的家族及部落。好了,言归正传,杰玛洛被选中了,他体格健壮,沉默寡言,但是我总是有些担心,因为从未有过月球生物去往地球的先例。于是,我们和杰玛洛约定,他一落地就要和我们发个信号——无论是以什么方式,然后我们也要作出回应。不过看样子,他在你的花园里降落时可没少吃苦头。由于我们一直没能等到他发回来的信号,开始担心他的命运。不过我们想如果他看到了我们的信号,知道我们还在等他回来,就一定能振作起来。于是,我们便开始施放烟雾。"

"啊,是的,"医生说,"我看到你们的信号了。不过,你们是怎么燃烧出那么多的烟雾的?它看起来至少有一座小山那么大。"

"那是,"巨人说,"杰洛玛出发前二十天,我和一些大个的动物们就开始在森林里收集惊-惊树皮了。"

第二十二章 月球上的伙计听说了医生　139

"收集什么?"医生大惑不解。

"惊-惊树皮,"巨人又重复了一遍,"这是一种特别的树枝,能造成大爆炸。"

"那么你们是怎么燃烧它的呢?"

"摩擦,"巨人说,"我们用硬木棒在软木块上摩擦取火。我们把成吨的树皮堆在山谷里,这样它们燃烧时就不会波及其他植物——你知道,我们这儿可是一个小世界,所以特别怕森林大火。我用一块块石片把燃

巨人说,他们用硬木棒在软木块上摩擦取火。

烧着的灰倒在树皮上,在发生爆炸前转身离开。那场爆炸真是震耳欲聋,烟雾熏得我们直咳嗽,过了好几天才散去。"

# 第二十三章
# 一位王

在那段进行了足有一天半的对话期间,理事会成员们一直不停地抛出一个个问题,由巨人转告给医生,希望他能够回答。至于医生,尽管他很希望能够尽早回到地球,但是他也实在有太多问题要问了。

"你还记不记得,"他问巨人,"当月球在她自己的轨道上稳定下来后,你们是如何开始适应这儿的新环境的?我们几个刚来这儿时,可是受了不少罪,不同的空气、奇异的引力、神秘的乐音……你们是怎么挺过来的?"

巨人皱了皱眉头,硕大的手掌在前额上搓了几下。

"那真是很久以前的事了。"他说,"其实我差一点就没能撑下来。刚开始那几个月,我连填饱肚子都成问题。不过等到吃饭问题解决了之后,我就开始探索这个新世界了。我发现鸟儿和昆虫也在艰难求生,我还发现整个月球除了我没有别的人类。噢!这太让人懊丧了!那时我多想有个伴啊!'好吧,'我对自己说,'我还是花时间研究鸟儿和昆虫的学问吧。'慢慢地,我发现鸟儿们也已经适应了月球的生活,而且我还发现他们其实也很喜欢和我作伴并且相互帮助。当然啦,我时刻都小心翼翼地避免伤害到任何生物。这是因为,第一,我本来就不是一个粗暴的人;第二,我也意识到如果我在这儿树敌的话,不会有好日子过的。我在这儿孤单极了,连个说话的人也没有,于是我决心开始学习鸟儿的语言——我那时经常听鸟儿们歌唱,觉得他们之间绝对有着独特的交流方式。我花了好几年的时间进行研究,期间好几次都想放弃了,因为进度实在太慢了,但是想要交流的愿望终于让我坚持了下来,后来渐渐地我开始用吹口哨的方式和他们做短暂的交谈了。这让我受到了鼓舞,然后在鸟儿的帮助下,我又学会了昆虫的语言,接下来是植物的语言——蜜蜂帮了我的大忙,他们会说几乎所有植物的语言。然后嘛……呃……"

"请继续吧。"医生说,他的口吻听上去十分平静,但我看得出他早已被这个故事深深吸引。

"噢,请原谅,"巨人发出一声叹息,有些烦躁,"我的记忆,你知道的,对于那么久远的事情已经很模糊了。你可能觉得我的苍鹭语言和天竺葵方言说得很好,但我真的一点儿都记不起来是如何学会它们的。我只记得植物语言比起任何动物语言都要难得多。还有,一开始的时

第二十三章 一位王　143

巨人渐渐地开始用吹口哨的方式和鸟儿们做短暂的交谈了

候,我们一直都没能记录下这个世界的历史,直到最近——大约从一千年前开始,我们才尝试着留下一些重大事件的记录,而且这些记录做得还不错,只可惜你似乎只对一千年前的故事感兴趣。"

"好吧,请不要在意,"医生说,"在这种情况下能取得这样的成就已经很了不起了。我希望能亲眼看看你说的那些记录——当然,这是以后的事。"

接着他们便开始了又一长段的谈话,其中大部分和动植物的进化有关,医生一边说话一边紧盯着我,生怕我漏记了哪怕一个回答。老天!这次谈话简直没完没了。巨人是怎么意识到植物十分希望能与他合作并交谈的?他为什么相信蜜蜂和他所造访的花朵之间有着交流关系?他又是如何找到那些可食用的野果并且成功避免食物中毒的……这次谈话进行了足足有好几个小时。虽然最后我似乎已经有点神游天外了,但我发誓我还是记下了大部分的信息。

这次谈话进行了足足有好几个小时

第二十三章 一位王

巨人的回答仍然存在着时间混乱的问题。这是因为在一个人孤身生活了那么久之后，可能已经丧失了时间概念。哪怕讲起最引以为豪的过去一千年有历史记载的事件时，我们也能从中找到不少自相矛盾的地方，那些足有一个世纪偏差的时间错误比比皆是。

这一千年间发生的事件被用符号和图画的形式刻在一块宽大的岩石壁上，看上去奥托"史前艺术家"的天分

这一千年间发生的事件被用符号和图画的形式刻在一块宽大的岩石壁上

帮了他大忙。尽管这些图像远不及"跪地少女"那幅精美,却也足以令人赞叹不已。

虽然有着这样那样的时间错误,通过巨人的回忆和岩石壁上的记载,我们最终得到了一份有关月球社会的详尽资料。这份弥足珍贵的资料不仅仅是一部新世界的进化史,更是关于一个人如何仅仅凭借自己的双手和智慧,在一场大灾难之后成为一位新世界的仁慈帝王的故事——他所统治的王国比地球上的人类所能想象出来的最好的国度更美妙,而他自己的头衔不过就是"理事会主席",至于他在管理这个新世界时所遭遇到的困难,也只有我们这些身临其境的人才能想象。

当这段长谈终于结束的时候,我长舒了一口气,躺倒在地,开始伸展我写字写到抽筋的右手。波莉尼西娅等得有点不耐烦了,她咕哝了几句,抬了抬眉毛:"瞧瞧!汤米,我都跟你说了些什么?风湿!这就是医生大老远跑来要治的病——风湿病!当然啦,如果只是给巨人治病的话,我一点儿也不会介意的,毕竟他是个很老很老的老人了。但是那些蚱蜢!想想看他们大老远地把约翰·杜立德医学博士弄来这几十亿英里远的(波莉尼西娅偶尔会在计算上出点小错)地方,就是为了来看看这一大群蚱蜢!我——"

这之后,她又换成了瑞典语,这下我就不知道她到底

我长舒了一口气躺倒在地上,伸展我写字写到抽筋的右手。

在说些什么了。

这时,医生转向巨人开口说道:"请问我什么时候可以开始为你和那些生病的昆虫们检查身体?我很乐意为你们服务,不过你们也得了解我想尽快返回地球的愿望。"

在作出回应前,巨人和理事会成员们先讨论了一小会儿,然后转过身来对医生说:"真是多谢了,我们明天会过来,我们都很感激你愿意前来帮助我们,也希望不会给你添太多麻烦。另外我们衷心希望你能了解我们多么需要你。"

"噢,当然,当然,"医生赶忙说,"虽然我现在已经成了一名博物学家,但是我的本职工作还是治病救人的医生。对了,你们明天什么时候过来?"

"黎明时分,"巨人说道,他对于时间的概念简单得出奇,"我们会在日出时等着你。好了,晚安!祝好梦!"

## 第二十四章
# 杜立德医生在月亮上做手术

那天晚上,在长时间的交谈和找到不少令人兴奋的发现之后,我们都十分劳累,连晚饭也没吃,衣服也没换就进入了梦乡,就连一向唠叨的波莉尼西娅也一声不吭。第二天,当我们从沉沉睡梦中醒来时,天才刚蒙蒙亮。我不太确定谁是第一个醒来的(很可能是约翰·杜立德),但我无疑是第一个从睡袋中钻出来并看到这样罕见一幕的人:在晨光中,数以百计——也许是数以千计的庞大昆虫病人,把我们的营地围了个水泄不通,盯着不远万里前来为他们治病的小不点医生看个没完。其中有些昆虫是我们在环游月球时从未见过的:深受痛风病困扰的差不多有一整条小街那么长的毛毛虫、双眼疼痛的巨大甲虫、足有三层楼高的蚱蜢——关节上还缠着奇怪的枝条,我们甚至还看到了几只大鸟,他们的翅膀以一种奇怪的姿势歪在一边,看起来痛极了。我们的营地立刻成为了一间诊所,四周聚集着月球上所有生病的动物。

庞大的昆虫病人把营地围个水泄不通

医生,这个伟大的人,起床之后匆匆忙忙地吃了几口瓜果,又喝了几口掺了蜂蜜的水,随后便开始了工作。

我们带来的那个小小的黑色手提包——这个忠实的伙计跟了医生好几年,去过不少遥远又神秘的土地——显然装不下足够的手术器材。绷带是第一个被用光的,于是我和吱吱只好把带来的毯子和衬衣全都撕成一条条的布条来应急。然后那些涂搽的药剂也用完了,接着是

第二十四章 杜立德医生在月亮上做手术 151

医生匆匆忙忙吃了几口瓜果，喝了几口掺了蜂蜜的水，便开始了工作。

碘酒和其他的消炎药水。不过好在医生在以前的植物学研究中已经发现了月球上不少可以药用的植物，所以吱吱和波莉尼西娅立刻被派去寻找那些急需的草药。

我们连续工作了好几个小时不曾休息。虽然病人们排的长队一眼望不到头，不过黄昏时分我们终于治好了最后一个病人。这时，我们才意识到还没有看见巨人，看来他是把自己排在了最后一个。医生站起身来四处查看,看到远处的树林边上有一个巨大的的人影。"老天!"医生低声地自语道,"我怎么把他给忘了?瞧瞧,多么大公无私的人,我敢保证这就是他颇受爱戴的原因。我得赶紧去看看他怎么样了。"

约翰·杜立德一路小跑穿过那片开阔地带去询问巨人的状况。巨人伸出一条左腿给医生查看,医生上上下下地四处检查,又是捏又是掐。

"这是痛风,"他最后用不容置疑的口吻说道,"而且状况也不大妙。现在,奥托·布劳奇,听好了。"

然后,他便开始向巨人讲解种种关于缓解痛风的知识:注意饮食啦,多多锻炼啦什么的,还告诉了他一些有关生理学的基本知识。在医生的长篇大论结束之后,巨人向医生不停道谢——他看起来受益匪浅,然后转身走了,大地随着他的脚步而震动。

在结束了这一天的工作之后,我们都腰酸背痛昏昏欲睡了。

"好吧,"医生盖上他仅剩的一条毯子,说道,"我想我们在这儿的工作已经完成了,明天——也许是后天——我们就可以——当然,如果一切顺利的话——准备启程返回帕德尔比了。"

"嘘!"波莉尼西娅提醒道,"有人在偷听,我保证——就躲在那几棵树后头。"

## 第二十四章 杜立德医生在月亮上做手术 153

医生向巨人讲解缓解痛风的知识,巨人向医生道谢后转身走了,大地随着他的脚步而震动。

"噢,不管他,"医生说,"隔着那么远,谁都听不见的。"

"但是别忘了,声音在月球上传得比地球上更远。"鹦鹉又说。

"可是老天,"医生说,"他们也知道我们总有一天得回去啊,我们几个也不可能一辈子都待在这儿啊。再说,我不是已经和巨人说过了吗,如果他们真的十分迫切地需要我,我自然义不容辞,但对于斯塔宾斯来说就不一样了,他来这儿之前都没告诉他的父母亲。我不知道雅各布会怎么想,还有他的妻子,他们一定担心极了,我——"

"嘘!嘘!"波莉尼西娅又说,"我不是告诉过你了吗,我说了有人在偷听——除非是我的耳朵出了问题。看在上帝的分上,别说话,去睡觉!"

我们全都听从了老鹦鹉的建议,很快营地中传出了阵阵鼾声。

第二天早上,我们没有像往常一样早早醒来,因为今天没有什么任务要完成,所以可以一觉睡到自然醒。当我们终于开始新的一天时,已经是中午了。一向负责为我们打水的吱吱今天被临时派去采集一些草药,所以我自告奋勇去执行这个任务。由于之前有过"打水工"的经历,所以我成功地找到了取水源的路。我提着几个空葫芦向着森林方向走去,不过还没走几步,就被波莉尼西娅叫住了。

"汤米,小心!"她站在我的肩膀上,用一种奇特的音调小声说道。

"什么?怎么了?"我问她,"出了什么问题吗?"

"我也说不清楚,"她说,"但我有种不祥的预感。听着,我们昨天治好了这儿所有的病人,这之后他们就再也没有出现过了。"

"可是,"我说,"这没什么奇怪的吧,病人看完病后不

我提着空葫芦向着森林方向走去,不过没走几步就被波莉尼西娅叫住了

再当回头客,这难道不是一件好事吗?他们治好了病,拿好了药,自然不会再来打搅医生了。"

"没错,没错,"她说,"但我总觉得有些蹊跷。我总是觉得有什么落下了,好像并非所有月球上的病人都来了。再说,昨天之后我就没再见到过巨人,我到处找他,但正如我们刚来那会儿,他又躲了起来……好吧,你自己小心点,我得回去了,但是汤米,睁大眼睛注视四周情况,祝你好运!"

我完全没搞懂这只鸟儿想要警告我什么,只好带着满腹猜疑上路了。

就在那儿,我发现了巨人的踪迹。那时,我正蹲在湖边往葫芦瓢里盛水,抬头一看,只见巨人就站在我的面前。他脸上还是带着一如既往的和蔼笑容,但这次我看到他就觉得有点心慌。以他的体型,我肯定是逃不掉的,而且我们语言不通,我也没法向他问话,再者,我现在独自一人身处森林中央,我的呼救声肯定不会被医生听到。

我走投无路,巨人伸出右手一把将我拎了起来,就好像一个人类采了一朵花一样。他带着我大步流星地走出了森林,每走一步都能跨过我每半小时才能走完的路程。和以前相比,他今天的走路声音轻得出奇,似乎有意不想让别人听到或感觉到。他最终走到了一片空地上,那只载我们来月球的巨蛾——杰玛洛·巴伯利已经在那儿等着了。巨人把我放在了这只大昆虫的背上,这时,我意识到——自己被绑架了。

# 第二十五章
# 又见帕德尔比

我这辈子还从来没有过那么无助的时刻。正当巨人把我放到巨蛾背上时,我想如果现在大声呼救,也许还有一丝机会,于是我便用尽全身力气大声哭叫起来。但巨人立刻伸出一只大拇指按在了我的脸上,阻止了我的求救。随后我感到巨蛾动了一下,他好像就要起飞了。就算医生刚才听见了我的叫声他也来不及过来救我了。巨人松开了拇指,随后巨蛾立刻开始了滑行,巨大的翅膀在我耳边呼呼生风。我尝试着做最后一博,我冲向巨蛾的右翼奋力一跳,结果重重地摔在了巨人的腰上。我拼命挣扎着,大声呼喊着医生的名字。但巨人又一把把我拎了起来,丢到了巨蛾背上。这时,我的手无意中从巨人腰上抽走了什么——原来是那幅皮皮蒂帕的画儿。巨人那会儿正忙着对付我,又忙着给正在前进的巨蛾下命令,所以完全没有注意到他丢失了的宝贝。

不过当时我的心思完全不在这上面。我只想着我正在远离医生而去,显然,巨蛾是要把我一个人带回地球。正当巨蛾开始加速前进时,我听到耳边传来一阵拍打翅膀的声音。我转头一看,感谢上苍!是波莉尼西娅!她一见到我,就连珠炮似的开了腔,着急得连话都说不清楚。

"汤米!——他们知道了医生担心你长时间离家不归的事了。我昨晚就说了要小心隔墙有耳,他们果真听见了——他们害怕你如果留下的话,医生会想要尽快和你一起回去,所以——"

这时,巨蛾的足部已经离开了地表,他的脑袋直直地伸向前面,从空地边的树顶上掠过。我耳旁快速向后的气流又让我想起了来时的场景。波莉尼西娅只得使出浑身解数才能和这巨大的太空船保持一致。

"不用慌,汤米!"她大叫道,"虽然我之前一直找不着巨人,但我的直觉让我猜到会发生什么,于是我赶紧去警告了医生。他说一旦你真的被他们送走就让我给你带个口信。他希望你能照看好帕德尔比的老房子马厩里的瘸腿老马,再去给果树浇浇水,还有,他让你不用担心,他自己也能想到办法回来的——(之后,波莉尼西娅就逐渐被拉下了,她的声音也小了许多)再见!祝你好运——"

我试图回答她,但我一张嘴就会有空气倒灌进来,于是只得闭上了嘴,而"再见!祝你好运"也成了我在月球上听到的最后一句话。

为了抵御凛冽的寒风,我尽量压低身子,躲在巨蛾的绒毛之中。我的手碰到了什么东西,原来是几朵月铃花。巨人还算是周到地考虑到了我这个普通人类的需求。我赶紧把头埋进花蕊,我知道我们必须穿过那片糟糕的"死亡地带"。我对此无能为力,只好躺在巨蛾背上告诉自己尽量放轻松,直到我再次看到帕德尔比那座有着大花园的小房子。

这次返程和去时很不一样。虽然我已经知道这样的旅程对我并没有什么危险,但没了医生的陪伴,我总是觉得孤单。我伤心极了,还感到了深深的内疚。我把医生独自一人留在了月球上,而他却从不曾抛弃过我或任何一个朋友。我一遍遍地告诉自己这并不是我的过错,但我仍然希望自己能够做些什么。也许当时我只要小心一点、反应快一点,这一切就都不会发生。现在这样,我该如何面对拍拍和叽喽,告诉他们医生还留在月球上呢?

这段航程简直了无尽头,我发现巨人为我准备了一些果子,但我一接近死亡地带,我就开始发晕,一点也吃不下,在接下来的很长一段时间里也是无精打采的。

最后,巨蛾的飞行速度终于慢了下来,我也能够坐起身来抬头向前望了。我们离地球已经不远了,它在阳光照射下熠熠生辉,顿时,我感到了一丝轻松,我这才发现我在过去的几个月里思乡之情有多深。

巨蛾终于降落在了索尔兹伯里平原上。虽然我对这片土地不熟，但我以前在图画里看到过索尔兹伯里大教堂的外形，而我越过平坦的草地能看到这幢建筑的轮廓。我不知道现在这儿到底是几点钟，但看天色应该是清晨时分。在月球那样的独特环境下待了一段时间之后，地球上稍强的气压和引力也得花时间才能适应。我艰难地

巨蛾终于降落在了索尔兹伯里平原上。我越过平坦的草地能看到教堂的轮廓。

从巨蛾背上爬了下来,开始环顾四周。阵阵薄雾从地表慢慢升起,这就是我们亲爱的地球啊。在太空中看起来这地方迷人极了,但当我真正置身其间时,却觉得景色也是稀松平常。

当雾渐渐散去,我远远看到有个人正在一条小路上赶路。毫无疑问,这是一位赶去工作的农场工人。他看起来体型好小啊,难道是个侏儒不成?好久没有见过除了医生以外的其他地球人类了,我非常迫切地想上前和他交谈。我迈着沉重的步子向他走去(刚才经历的漫长旅程和地球上的重力让我走起路来像个醉鬼)。当我走到他跟前差不多二十步时,我和他打了个招呼。但他的反应着实出乎我的意料。他转过头来,一看到我时整张脸瞬间变得煞白,然后就像一只兔子似的跑掉了。

我站在路边,突然想到了我现在的形象。我打量了一下自己:九尺多的身高,腰围也有五十多寸,穿着自制的树皮和树叶编成的衣裳,还有植物根茎做成的鞋子,头发垂到肩膀。难怪那个突然在索尔兹伯里平原上遇见我的可怜人会受到这样的惊吓。我又想起了杰玛洛·巴伯利,我希望他能给医生带个话,当然前提是他能听得懂我的话——或者我写点什么让他带去就好了。于是我四处寻找他,但是丝毫不见他的踪影。也许是因为我在迷雾中迷失了方向,又或许是他已经踏上了返程。

我九尺多的身高,腰围也有五十多寸。

于是乎,我这么一个稻草人打扮的巨人,独自一人身处陌生的地区,身无分文,除了一块刻着史前图案的驯鹿角外一无所有,我知道那农夫的反应会是所有人看到我的反应,我也知道,从索尔兹伯里到帕德尔比可是有很长一段路,我还知道这一路上没有车马费和食物可是不行的。

我跌跌撞撞地走下小路,远远地一幢农舍映入眼帘,我还闻到了阵阵培根的香味。我饿极了,觉得应该冒险

## 第二十五章　又见帕德尔比

尝试一下。我走上台阶,轻轻敲了敲门。一个妇人开了门,吓得尖叫起来,猛地关上了大门。过了一会儿,一个男人打开窗子,手里端着一柄猎枪。"赶紧离开我的地盘,"他吼道,"快点!不然我就一枪打爆你的脑袋!"

我失魂落魄地继续走着。我究竟怎么了?我能把事情的真相告诉谁?有谁会相信我的离奇经历?但无论如何,我都必须回到帕德尔比。我得承认去把这个消息带给医生的动物们实在不是个好差事,但我必须这么做。哪怕医生没有让我照顾老马和那些果树,我也会做出同样的选择,因为我的职责就是在医生不在的时候代替他。还有我的父母——可怜的人!他们还认得出我来吗?

走啊走,忽然,我发现了一群吉卜赛人,他们正坐在路边的荆豆丛中休息,看样子还在准备早餐,诱人的香味让我空空如也的胃难以抗拒。奇怪的是,他们是所有见过我的人中仅有的不害怕我的人。他们纷纷从马车上下来,把我围在中间,目瞪口呆地看着我,不过我感到他们眼神中好奇多过恐惧。他们邀请我坐下来和他们一同进餐。他们的头领——一位长者,告诉我他们正要去一处乡村集市,并且很高兴与我同行。

我万分感激,如今任何一段友情都是值得去争取的。不过后来我发现,那位老者是想雇我在他们马戏团里扮演巨人。可是话说回来,我可不想拒绝这份工作。我需要钱,我可不想穿得破破烂烂地出现在帕德尔比。我还需要衣服、车马费,我更需要赖以生存的食物。

马戏团的老板其实是个相当不错的人。他原本希望我在他那儿演出一年,但我拒绝了。他又提议说六个月,但我还是摇头反对。我的心思是一赚到足够的能体面回家的钱就离开。马戏团老板似乎愿意付出一切代价让我留下来,哪怕只能工作一小段时间。最后老板同意我在马戏团工作一个月。

接下来就是讨论戏服的问题了。一开始他想让我留着长发,只穿着一条围裙,并且称呼我是"火星来的远古人类"或者类似的什么玩意儿。但我告诉他我不想被这么称呼(虽然他肯定没想到他的胡思乱想和事实有多么接近)。然后他又想称呼我是"南美大草原的巨人牛仔",这回我得戴着一顶巨大的太阳帽,穿着羊毛裤子,配上左轮枪套和马刺。这套服装显然也不怎么吸引我,正如同我绝对不会穿着一套周日礼服出现在帕德尔比一样。最后,我意识到这个生意人为了让我同意演出什么都愿意做,于是我想我也许可以自己挑选服装。

"先生,你瞧!"我对他说,"我可不想成为一个我自己都不认识的人。我是一名科学家,也是一名从化外之地归来的探险家。我独特的体型得归功于那儿奇特的气候和饮食习惯。我不会把自己包装成野人或牛仔来欺骗观众。给我弄一套黑西服——就是读书人穿的那样。我保证能给你的观众们讲一些他们做梦都想不到的探险经历,不过我只会在这儿工作一个月。成交吗?"

马戏团老板最终同意了我的要求。我的工钱是一天三先令,而我的衣服在合同到期后就会是我的个人财产。我能使用一辆单独的马车和一张自己的床。我的演出时间是严格规定好了的,而其他时间段则由我自由支配。

我的工作不算累。我的出场时间定在每天上午十点到十二点,下午三点到五点,晚上八点到十点。一位裁缝专门为我做了一件看着不错的西服,他们还请了一位理发师来给我剪发。在工作时间,我得在自己的照片上签名,再让马戏团以三便士一张的价格卖出去。一天中有两次我要为观众们讲述我的冒险故事。但我从来不会提到"月球"二字,只是管它叫做"化外之地"——其实也差不多。

终于,我的合同到期了。我可以带着赚来的三镑十五先令、穿着还不错的衣服回家了。我乘上了一辆开往帕德尔比方向的马车,一路上又换乘了好几次,最后在离我的家乡小镇不远的地方停了下来。一路上,有不少人盯着我的巨大体型看个不停,但我一点儿也不介意——至少现在我的模样实在算不上可怕。

到了帕德尔比,我想到的第一件事就是去看望我的父母。虽然这时候已经很晚了,但有什么能比让我父母放心更重要的事情要做呢。

当我见到父母时,他们高兴极了,迫切想要知道我去了什么地方,做了些什么。我惊讶地发现父母并没有对我的不辞而别感到太过担忧,但当我了解到原因后也就释怀了。原来他们发现医生和我一起失踪了,就猜想是医生把我带去了什么地方。既然有这么一个值得信赖的人和我在一起,那么还有什么好担心的呢?

我也很高兴他们还认得出我。事实上,他们甚至为我的体型感到骄傲,说我就像凯撒一样"成为巨人"。我们一起坐在壁炉前面,分享着我在月球上的种种奇闻轶事。说来也怪,他们俩对我所讲的在许多人眼里荒谬透顶的经历深信不疑。我想,世上除了他们两人以外——当然,还得算上马修·马格——就再也不会有人对我如此信任了。他们问我医生什么时候会回来,我告诉他们波莉尼西娅所说的——当医生准备好离开月球时就会施放一个烟雾信号。但我得承认我不太确定他是否真的能从那样一个如此需要他的地方逃脱。我又再次为自己的离去感到内疚,我的父母安慰我说我已经尽力了,他们还要求我先在家里住上一晚,明早再去向医生的动物们报告消息。母亲说我看上去累坏了,于是,我便说服自己不要再胡思乱想,快快上床睡觉。

## 第二十五章　又见帕德尔比

第二天,我去找了马修·马格,那个卖猫食的男人。我希望当我出现在那幢带着大花园的小房子里时,他能在一旁陪着。但我花了不下两个小时回答他连珠炮似的询问我们月球见闻的问题。

最后,我终于站在了医生的家门口。我的手还没有碰到门栓,就发现自己已经被动物们团团围住了。我猜,是猫头鹰吐吐,这个机警的哨兵,一直都在房顶上放哨,然后一声大叫如同火警警铃一般把大家都召唤到了花园里。大家有无数的问题要问我:怎么长得这么高?为什么模样也变了?不过没有谁怀疑我就是汤米·斯塔宾斯。不过,当他们看到我一个人失神地回到房中时都安静了下来。他们簇拥着我回到了厨房,在那个壁炉边坐下。就在那个伟大的人常常给我们讲故事的地方,我把月球上的经历从头到尾讲了一遍。故事讲完后他们个个眼泪汪汪,小猪咕咕开始嚎啕大哭。"我们再也见不到他了!"他喊道,"他们不会放他走的。噢,汤米,你怎么能把他一个人留在那儿啊?""安静!"小狗叽噗阻止了他,"他也是没办法。你没听他说吗?他被绑架了!不过,别担心,我们会密切注意月亮上的烟雾的。约翰·杜立德一定能回到我们身边的,不要怕。记住,波莉尼西娅可是和他在一起呢。"

"对咯!"白老鼠吱吱地叫道,"她肯定有办法的。"

我终于站在了医生的家门口，猫头鹰在放哨。

"我也不怎么担心，"鸭子拍拍抽泣着说，用一只翅膀擦去了眼泪，又用另一只翅膀把壁橱上的苍蝇赶跑，"但这儿没了他该有多冷清啊！"吐吐也发话了："要我说他肯定回得来。"这时，窗边传来一阵敲击声。"是奇普赛"，拍拍说，"汤米，放他进来。"于是，我抬起了窗框，这只说话带着伦敦腔的麻雀便飞了进来，停在了厨房的餐桌上——他最喜欢在那儿捡管家拍拍不小心落下的面包屑。吐吐用几句言简意赅的话告诉了他目前的情况。

"老天保佑!"这只麻雀说,"你们为什么都是一副苦瓜脸?约翰·杜立德被困月球?无稽之谈!无稽之谈!医生不会被任何地方困住。哦!拍拍!这回你大清扫的时候又没给我留面包屑,不是吗?要是有野鼠住在你这儿的话可不会有好日子过!"

好吧,就是这样。我很高兴能够回到这幢老房子里。我知道我迟早都能恢复原来的体型和食量。与此同时,住在这儿的我可以不用抛头露面。于是,我便安心住了下来,修剪果树,照料老马,不时注视着月亮上的动向,寻找可能的烟雾迹象。每天清晨,破晓时分,当我垂头丧气地回屋时,叽喋都会把他的脑袋在我的腿上蹭几下,说:"汤米,不用担心,医生一定会回来的。记住,这个人可是和波莉尼西娅在一起啊,他们俩肯定能有办法的——他们总是有办法的。"

(完)

# DOCTOR DOLITTLE ON THE MOON

Hugh Lofting

· 1 ·
# WE LAND UPON A NEW WORLD

In writing the story of our adventures in the Moon I, Thomas Stubbins, secretary to John Dolittle, M.D. (and son of Jacob Stubbins, the cobbler of PuddlebyontheMarsh), find myself greatly puzzled. It is not an easy task, remembering day by day and hour by hour those crowded and exciting weeks. It is true I made many notes for the Doctor, books full of them. But that information was nearly all of a highly scientific kind. And I feel that I should tell the story here not for the scientist so much as for the general reader. And it is in that I am perplexed.

For the story could be told in many ways. People are so different in what they want to know about a voyage. I had thought at one time that Jip could help me; and after reading him some chapters as I had first set them down I asked for his opinion. I discovered he was mostly interested in whether we had seen any rats in the Moon. I found I could not tell him. I didn't remember seeing any; and yet I am sure there must have been some—or some sort of creature like a rat.

Then I asked GubGub. And what he was chiefly concerned to hear was the kind of vegetables we had fed on. (DabDab snorted at me for my pains and said I should have known better than to ask him.) I tried my mother. She wanted to know how we had managed when our underwear wore out—and a whole lot of other matters about our living conditions, hardly any of which I could answer. Next I went to Matthew Mugg. And the things he wanted to learn were worse than either my mother's or Jip's: Were there any shops in the Moon? What were the dogs and cats like? The good Cats'meatMan seemed to have imagined it a place not very different from Puddleby or the East End of London.

No, trying to get at what most people wanted to read concerning the Moon did not bring me much profit. I couldn't seem to tell them any of the things they were most anxious to know. It reminded me of the first time I had come to the Doctor's house, hoping to be hired as his assistant, and dear old Polynesia the parrot had questioned me. "Are you a good noticer?" she had asked. I had always thought I was—pretty good, anyhow. But now I felt I had been a very poor noticer. For it seemed I hadn't noticed any of the things I should have done to make the story of our voyage interesting to the ordinary public.

The trouble was of course attention. Human attention is like butter: you can only spread it so thin and no thinner. If you try to spread it over too many things at once you just don't remember them. And certainly during all our waking hours upon the Moon there was so much for our ears and eyes and minds to take in it is a wonder, I often think, that any clear memories at all remain.

The one who could have been of most help to me in writing my impressions of the Moon was Jamaro Bumblelily, the giant moth who carried us there. But as he was nowhere near me when I set to work upon this book I decided I had better not consider the particular wishes of Jip, GubGub, my mother, Matthew or any one else, but set the story down in my own way. Clearly the tale must be in any case an imperfect, incomplete one. And the only thing to do is to go forward with it, step by step, to the best of my recollection, from where the great insect hovered, with our beating hearts pressed close against his broad back, over the near and glowing landscape of the Moon.

## 1. WE LAND UPON A NEW WORLD

Any one could tell that the moth knew every detail of the country we were landing in. Planing, circling and diving, he brought his widewinged body very deliberately down towards a little valley fenced in with hills. The bottom of this, I saw as we drew nearer, was level, sandy and dry.

The hills struck one at once as unusual. In fact all the mountains as well ( for much greater heights could presently be seen towering away in the dim greenish light behind the nearer, lower ranges) had one peculiarity. The tops seemed to be cut off and cuplike. The Doctor afterwards explained to me that they were extinct volcanoes. Nearly all these peaks had once belched fire and molten lava but were now cold and dead. Some had been fretted and worn by winds and weather and time into quite curious shapes; and yet others had been filled up or half buried by drifting sand so that they had nearly lost the appearance of volcanoes. I was reminded of "The Whispering Rocks" which we had seen in Spidermonkey Island. And though this scene was different in many things, no one who had ever looked upon a volcanic landscape before could have mistaken it for anything else.

The little valley, long and narrow, which we were apparently making for did not show many signs of life, vegetable or animal. But we were not disturbed by that. At least the Doctor wasn't. He had seen a tree and he was satisfied that before long he would find water, vegetation and creatures.

At last when the moth had dropped within twenty feet of the ground he spread his wings motionless and like a great kite gently touched the sand, in hops at first, then ran a little, braced himself and came to a standstill.

We had landed on the Moon!

By this time we had had a chance to get a little more used to the new air. But before we made any attempt to "go ashore" the Doctor thought it best to ask our gallant steed to stay where he was a while, so that we could still further accustom ourselves to the new atmosphere and conditions.

This request was willingly granted. Indeed, the poor insect himself, I imagine, was glad enough to rest a while. From somewhere in his packages John Dolittle produced an emergency ration of chocolate which he had been saving up. All four of us munched in silence, too hungry and too awed by our new surroundings to say a word.

The light changed unceasingly. It reminded me of the Northern Lights, the Aurora Borealis. You would gaze at the mountains above you, then turn away a moment, and on looking back find everything that had been pink was now green, the shadows that had been violet were rose.

Breathing was still kind of difficult. We were compelled for the moment to keep the "moonbells" handy. These were the great orange coloured flowers that the moth had brought down for us. It was their perfume (or gas) that had enabled us to cross the airless belt that lay between the Moon and the Earth. A fit of coughing was always liable to come on if one left them too long. But already we felt that we could in time get used to this new air and soon do without the bells altogether.

The gravity too was very confusing. It required hardly any effort to rise from a sitting position to a standing one. Walking was no effort at all—for the muscles—but for the lungs it was another question. The most extraordinary sensation was jumping. The least little spring from the ankles sent you flying into the air in the most fantastic fashion. If it had not been for this problem of breathing properly (which the Doctor seemed to feel we should approach with great caution on account of its possible effect on the heart) we would all have given ourselves up to this most lighthearted feeling which took possession of us. I remember, myself, singing songs—the melody was somewhat indistinct on account of a large mouthful of chocolate—and I was most anxious to get down off the moth's back and go bounding away across the hills and valleys to explore this new world.

But I realize now that John Dolittle was very wise in making us wait. He issued orders (in the low whispers which we found necessary in this new clear air) to each and all of us that for the present the flowers were not to be left behind for a single moment.

There were cumbersome things to carry but we obeyed orders. No ladder was needed now to descend by. The gentlest jump sent one flying off the insect's back to the ground where you landed from a twenty-five foot drop with ease and comfort. Zip! The spring was made. And we were wading in the sands of a new world.

· 2 ·

# THE LAND OF COLOURS
# AND PERFUMES

We were after all, when you come to think of it, a very odd party, this, which made the first landing on a new world. But in a great many ways it was a peculiarly good combination. First of all, Polynesia: she was the kind of bird which one always supposed would exist under any conditions, drought, floods, fire or frost. I've no doubt that at that time in my boyish way I exaggerated Polynesia's adaptability and endurance. But even to this day I can never quite imagine any circumstances in which that remarkable bird would perish. If she could get a pinch of seed (of almost any kind) and a sip of water two or three times a week she would not only carry on quite cheerfully but would scarcely even remark upon the strange nature or scantiness of the rations.

Then Chee-Chee: he was not so easily provided for in the matter of food. But he always seemed to be able to provide for himself anything that was lacking. I have never known a better forager than Chee-Chee. When every one was hungry he could go off into an entirely new forest and just by smelling the wild fruits and nuts he could tell if they were safe to eat. How he did this even John Dolittle could never find out. Indeed Chee-Chee himself didn't know.

Then myself: I had no scientific qualifications but I had learned how to be a good secretary on natural history expeditions and I knew a good deal about the Doctor's ways.

Finally there was the Doctor. No naturalist has ever gone afield to grasp at the secrets of a new land with the qualities John Dolittle possessed. He never claimed to know anything, beforehand, for certain. He came to new problems with a childlike innocence which made it easy for himself to learn and the others to teach.

Yes, it was a strange party we made up. Most scientists would have laughed at us no doubt. Yet we had many things to recommend us that no expedition ever carried before.

As usual the Doctor wasted no time in preliminaries. Most other explorers would have begun by planting a flag and singing national anthems. Not so with John Dolittle. As soon as he was sure that we were all ready he gave the order to march. And without a word Chee-Chee and I (with Polynesia who perched herself on my shoulder) fell in behind him and started off.

I have never known a time when it was harder to shake loose the feeling of living in a dream as those first few hours we spent on the Moon. The knowledge that we were treading a new world never before visited by Man, added to this extraordinary feeling caused by the gravity, of lightness, of walking on air, made you want every minute to have some one tell you that you were actually awake and in your right senses. For this reason I kept constantly speaking to the Doctor or Chee-Chee or Polynesia—even when I had nothing particular to say. But the uncanny booming of my own voice every time I opened my lips and spoke above the faintest whisper merely added to the dream-like effect of the whole experience.

However, little by little, we grew accustomed to it. And certainly there was no lack of new sights and impressions to occupy our minds. Those strange and ever changing colours in the landscape were most bewildering, throwing out your course and sense of direction entirely. The Doctor had brought a small pocket compass with him. But on consulting it, we saw that it was even more confused than we were. The needle did nothing but whirl around in the craziest fashion and no amount of steadying would persuade it to stay still.

Giving that up, the Doctor determined to rely on his moon maps and his own eyesight and bump of locality. He was heading towards where he had seen that tree—which was at the end of one of the ranges. But all the ranges in this section seemed very much alike. The maps did not help us in this respect in the least. To our rear we could see certain peaks which we thought we could identify on the charts. But ahead nothing fitted in at all. This made us feel surer than ever that we were moving toward the Moon's other side which earthly eyes had never seen.

"It is likely enough, Stubbins," said the Doctor as we strode lightly forward over loose sand which would ordinarily have been very heavy going, "that it is *only* on the other side that water exists. Which may partly be the reason why astronomers never believed there was any here at all."

For my part I was so on the look-out for extraordinary sights that it did not occur to me, till the Doctor spoke of it, that the temperature was extremely mild and agreeable. One of the things that John Dolittle had feared was that we should find a heat that was unbearable or a cold that was worse than Arctic. But except for the difficulty of the strange new quality of the air, no human could have asked for a nicer climate. A gentle steady wind was blowing and the temperature seemed to remain almost constantly the same.

We looked about everywhere for tracks. As yet we knew very little of what animal life to expect. But the loose sand told nothing, not even to Chee-Chee, who was a pretty experienced hand at picking up tracks of the most unusual kind.

Of odours and scents there were plenty—most of them very delightful flower perfumes which the wind brought to us from the other side of the mountain ranges ahead. Occasionally a very disagreeable one would come, mixed up with the pleasant scents. But none of them, except that of the moon bells the moth had brought with us, could we recognize.

On and on we went for miles, crossing ridge after ridge and still no glimpse did we get of the Doctor's tree. Of course crossing the ranges was not nearly as hard travelling as it would have been on Earth. Jumping and bounding both upward and downward was extraordinarily easy. Still, we had brought a good deal of baggage with us and all of us were pretty heavy-laden; and after two and a half hours of travel we began to feel a little discouraged. Polynesia then volunteered to fly ahead and reconnoitre, but this the Doctor was loath to have her do. For some reason he wanted us all to stick together for the present.

However, after another half-hour of going he consented to let her fly straight up so long as she remained in sight, to see if she could spy out the tree's position from a greater height.

· 3 ·
# THIRST!

So we rested on our bundles a spell while Polynesia gave an imitation of a soaring vulture and straight above our heads climbed and climbed. At about a thousand feet she paused and circled. Then slowly came down again. The Doctor, watching her, grew impatient at her speed. I could not quite make out why he was so unwilling to have her away from his side, but I asked no questions.

Yes, she had seen the tree, she told us, but it still seemed a long way off. The Doctor wanted to know why she had taken so long in coming down and she said she had been making sure of her bearings so that she would be able to act as guide. Indeed, with the usual accuracy of birds, she had a very clear idea of the direction we should take. And we set off again, feeling more at ease and confident.

The truth of it was of course that seen from a great height, as the tree had first appeared to us, the distance had seemed much less than it actually was. Two more things helped to mislead us. One, that the moon air, as we now discovered, made everything look nearer than it actually was in spite of the soft dim light. And the other was that we had supposed the tree to be one of ordinary earthly size and had made an unconscious guess at its distance in keeping with a fair-sized oak or elm. Whereas when we did actually reach it we found it to be unimaginably huge.

I shall never forget that tree. It was our first experience of moon life, *in* the Moon. Darkness was coming on when we finally halted beneath it. When I say *darkness* I mean that strange kind of twilight which was the nearest thing to night which we ever saw in the Moon. The tree's height, I should say, would be at least three hundred feet and the width of it across the trunk a good forty or fifty. Its appearance in general was most uncanny. The whole design of it was different from any tree I have ever seen. Yet there was no mistaking it for anything else. It seemed—how shall I describe it? — *alive*. Poor Chee-Chee was so scared of it his hair just stood up on the nape of his neck and it was a long time before the Doctor and I persuaded him to help us pitch camp beneath its boughs.

Indeed we were a very subdued party that prepared to spend its first night on the Moon. No one knew just what it was that oppressed us but we were all conscious of a definite feeling of disturbance. The wind still blew—in that gentle, steady way that the moon winds always blew. The light was clear enough to see outlines by, although most of the night the Earth was invisible, and there was no reflection whatever.

I remember how the Doctor, while we were unpacking and laying out the rest of our chocolate ration for supper, kept glancing uneasily up at those strange limbs of the tree overhead.

Of course it was the wind that was moving them—no doubt of that at all. Yet the wind was so deadly regular and even. And the movement of the boughs wasn't regular at all. That was the weird part of it. It almost seemed as though the tree were doing some moving on its own, like an animal chained by its feet in the ground. And still you could never be sure—because, after all, the wind *was* blowing all the time.

And besides, it moaned. Well, we knew trees moaned in the wind at home. But this one did it differently—it didn't seem in keeping with that regular even wind which we felt upon our faces.

I could see that even the worldly-wise practical Polynesia was perplexed and upset. And it took a great deal to disturb her. Yet a bird's senses towards trees and winds are much keener than a man's. I kept hoping she would venture into the branches of the tree; but she didn't. And as for Chee-Chee, also a natural denizen of the forest, no power on earth, I felt sure, would persuade him to investigate the mysteries of this strange specimen of a Vegetable Kingdom we were as yet only distantly acquainted with.

After supper was despatched, the Doctor kept me busy for some hours taking down notes. There was much to be recorded of this first day in a new world. The temperature; the direction and force of the wind; the time of our arrival—as near as it could be guessed; the air pressure (he had brought along a small barometer among his instruments) and many other things which, while they were dry stuff for the ordinary mortal, were highly important for the scientist.

Often and often I have wished that I had one of those memories that seem to be able to recall all impressions no matter how small and unimportant. For instance, I have often wanted to remember exactly that first awakening on the Moon. We had all been weary enough with excitement and exercise, when we went to bed, to sleep soundly. All I can remember of my waking up is spending at least ten minutes working out where I was. And I doubt if I could have done it even then if I had not finally realized that John Dolittle was awake ahead of me and already pottering around among his instruments, taking readings.

The immediate business now on hand was food. There was literally nothing for breakfast. The Doctor began to regret his hasty departure from the moth. Indeed it was only now, many, many hours after we had left him in our unceremonious haste to find the tree and explore the new world, that we realized that we had not as yet seen any signs of animal life. Still it seemed a long way to go back and consult him; and it was by no means certain that he would still be there.

Just the same, we needed food, and food we were going to find. Hastily we bundled together what things we had unpacked for the night's camping. Which way to go? Clearly if we had here reached one tree, there must be some direction in which others lay, where we could find that water which the Doctor was so sure must exist. But we could scan the horizon with staring eyes or telescope as much as we wished and not another leaf of a tree could we see.

This time without waiting to be ordered Polynesia soared into the air to do a little scouting.

"Well," she said on her return, "I don't see any actual trees at all. The beastly landscape is more like the Sahara Desert than any scenery I've ever run into. But over there behind that higher range-the one with the curious hat-shaped peak in the middle—you see the one I mean?"

"Yes," said the Doctor. "I see. Go on."

"Well, behind that there is a dark horizon different from any other quarter. I won't swear it is trees. But myself, I feel convinced that there is something else there besides sand. We had better get moving. It is no short walk."

Indeed it *was* no short walk. It came to be a forced march or race between us and starvation. On starting out we had not foreseen anything of the kind. Going off without breakfast was nothing after all. Each one of us had done that before many a time. But as hour after hour went by and still the landscape remained a desert of rolling sand-dunes, hills and dead dry volcanoes, our spirits fell lower and lower.

This was one of the times when I think I saw John

Dolittle really at his best. I know, although I had not questioned him, that he had already been beset with anxiety over several matters on the first steps of our march. Later he spoke of them to me: not at the time. And as conditions grew worse, as hunger gnawed at our vitals and the most terrible thirst parched our tongues—as strength and vitality began to give way and mere walking became the most terrible hardship, the Doctor grew cheerier and cheerier. He didn't crack dry jokes in an irritating way either. But by some strange means he managed to keep the whole party in good mood. If he told a funny story it was always at the right time and set us all laughing at our troubles. In talking to him afterwards about this I learned that he had, when a young man, been employed on more than one exploration trip to keep the expedition in good humour. It was, he said, the only way he could persuade the chief to take him, since at that time he had no scientific training to recommend him.

Anyway, I sincerely doubt whether our party would have held out if it had not been for his sympathetic and cheering company. The agonies of thirst were something new to me. Every step I thought must be my last.

Finally at what seemed to be the end of our second day, I vaguely heard Polynesia saying something about

"Forests ahead!" I imagine I must have been half delirious by then. I still staggered along, blindly following the others. I know we *did* reach water because before I fell and dozed away into a sort of half faint I remember Chee-Chee trickling something marvellously cool between my lips out of a cup made from a folded leaf.

· 4 ·
# CHEE-CHEE THE HERO

When I awoke I felt very much ashamed of myself. What an explorer! The Doctor was moving around already—and, of course, Chee-Chee and Polynesia. John Dolittle came to my side immediately he saw I was awake.

As though he knew the thoughts that were in my mind he at once started to reprimand me for feeling ashamed of my performance. He pointed out that after all Chee-Chee and Polynesia were accustomed to travelling in hot dry climates and that so, for that matter, was he himself.

"Taken all in all, Stubbins," said he, "your own performance has been extremely good. You made the trip, the whole way, and only collapsed when relief was in sight. No one could ask for more than that. I have known many experienced explorers who couldn't have done nearly as well. It was a hard lap—a devilish hard lap. You were magnificent. Sit up and have some breakfast. Thank goodness, we've reached food at last!"

Weak and frowsty, I sat up. Arranged immediately around me was a collection of what I later learned were fruits. The reliable Chee-Chee, scared though he might be of a moving tree or a whispering wind, had served the whole party with that wonderful sense of his for scenting out wild foodstuffs. Not one of the strange courses on the bill of fare had I or the Doctor seen before. But if Chee-Chee said they were safe we knew we need not fear.

Some of the fruits were as big as a large trunk; some as small as a walnut. But, starving as we were, we just dived in and ate and ate and ate. Water there was too, gathered in the shells of enormous nuts and odd vessels made from twisted leaves. Never has a breakfast tasted so marvellous as did that one of fruits which I could not name.

Chee-Chee! —Poor little timid Chee-Chee, who conquered your own fears and volunteered to go ahead of us alone, into the jungle to find food when our strength was giving out. To the world you were just an organ-grinder's monkey. But to us whom you saved from starvation, when terror beset you at every step, you will for ever be ranked high in the list of the great heroes of all time. Thank goodness we had you with us! Our bones might to-day be mouldering in the sands of the Moon if it had not been for your untaught science, your jungle skill—and, above all, your courage that overcame your fear!

Well, to return: as I ate these strange fruits and sipped the water that brought life back I gazed upward and saw before me a sort of ridge. On its level top a vegetation, a kind of tangled forest, flourished; and trailing down from this ridge were little outposts of the Vegetable Kingdom, groups of bushes and single trees, that scattered and dribbled away in several directions from the main mass. Why and how that lone tree survived so far away we could never satisfactorily explain. The nearest John Dolittle could come to it was that some underground spring supplied it with enough water or moisture to carry on. Yet there can be no doubt that to have reached such enormous proportions it must have been there hundreds—perhaps thousands—of years. Anyway, it is a good thing for us it *was* there. If it had not been, as a pointer towards this habitable quarter of the Moon—it is most likely our whole expedition would have perished.

When the Doctor and I had finished our mysterious breakfast we started to question Chee-Chee about the forest from which he had produced the food we had eaten.

"I don't know how I did it," said Chee-Chee when we asked him. "I just shut my eyes most of the time—terribly afraid. I passed trees, plants, creepers, roots. I smelt—Goodness! I too was hungry, remember. I smelt hard as I could. And soon of course I spotted food, fruits. I climbed a tree—half the time with my eyes shut. Then I see some monster, golly! What a jungle—different from any monkey ever see before—Woolly, woolly! —Ooh, ooh! All the same, nuts smell good. Catch a few. Chase down the tree. Run some more. Smell again. Good! — Up another tree. Different fruit, good just the same. Catch a few. Down again. Run home. On the way smell good root. Same as ginger—only better. Dig a little. Keep eyes shut—don't want to see monster. Catch a piece of root. Run all the way home. Here I am. Finish!"

Well, dear old Chee-Chee's story was descriptive of his own heroic adventures but it did not give us much idea of the moon forest which we were to explore. Nevertheless, rested and fit, we now felt much more inclined to look into things ourselves.

Leaving what luggage we had brought with us from our original landing point, we proceeded towards the line of trees at the summit of the bluff, about four miles ahead of us. We now felt that we could find our way back without much difficulty to the two last camps we had established.

The going was about the same, loose sand—only that as we approached the bluff we found the sand firmer to the tread.

On the way up the last lap towards the vegetation line we were out of view of the top itself. Often the going was steep. All the way I had the feeling that we were about to make new and great discoveries—that for the first time we were to learn something important about the true nature of the mysterious Moon.

## · 5 ·
# ON THE PLATEAU

Indeed our first close acquaintance with the forests of the Moon was made in quite a dramatic manner. If it had been on a stage it could not have been arranged better for effect. Suddenly as our heads topped the bluff we saw a wall of jungle some mile or so ahead of us. It would take a very long time to describe those trees in detail. It wasn't that there were so many kinds but each one was so utterly different from any tree we had seen on the Earth. And yet, curiously enough, they did remind you of vegetable forms you had seen, but not of trees.

For instance, there was one whole section, several square miles in extent apparently, that looked exactly like ferns. Another reminded me of a certain flowering plant (I can't recall the name of it) which grows a vast number of small blossoms on a flat surface at the top. The stems are a curious whitish green. This moon tree was *exactly* the same, only nearly a thousand times as big.

The denseness of the foliage (or flowering) at the top was so compact and solid that we later found no rain could penetrate it. And for this reason the Doctor and I gave it the name of the *Umbrella Tree*. But not one single tree was there which was the same as any tree we had seen before. And there were many, many more curious growths that dimly reminded you of something, though you could not always say exactly what.

One odd thing that disturbed us quite a little was a strange sound. Noises of any kind, no matter how faint, we already knew could travel long distances on the Moon. As soon as we had gained the plateau on top of the bluff we heard it. It was a musical sound. And yet not the sound of a single instrument. It seemed almost as though there was a small orchestra somewhere playing very, very softly. We were by this time becoming accustomed to strange things. But I must confess that this distant hidden music upset me quite a little, and so, I know, it did the Doctor.

At the top of the bluff we rested to get our wind before we covered the last mile up to the jungle itself. It was curious how clearly marked and separated were those sections of the Moon's landscape. And yet doubtless the smaller scale of all the geographical features of this world, so much less in bulk than our own, could partly account for that. In front of us a plateau stretched out, composed of hard sand, level and smooth as a lake, bounded in front by the jungle and to the rear of us by the cliff we had just scaled. I wondered as I looked across at the forest what scenery began on the other side of the woods and if it broke off in as sharp a change as it did here.

As the most important thing to attend to first was the establishment of a water supply, Chee-Chee was asked to act as guide. The monkey set out ahead of us to follow his own tracks which he had made last night. This he had little difficulty in doing across the open plateau. But when we reached the edge of the forest it was not so easy. Much of his travelling here had been done by swinging through the trees. He always felt safer so, he said, while explaining to us how he had been guided to the water by the sense of smell. Again I realized how lucky we had been to have him with us. No one but a monkey could have found his way through that dense, dimly lit forest to water. He asked us to stay behind a moment on the edge of the woods while he went forward to make sure that he could retrace his steps. We sat down again and waited.

"Did you wake up at all during the night, Stubbins?" the Doctor asked after a little.

"No," I said. "I was far too tired. Why?"

"Did you, Polynesia?" he asked, ignoring my question.

"Yes," said she, "I was awake several times."

"Did you hear or see anything—er—unusual?"

"Yes," said she. "I can't be absolutely certain. But I sort of felt there was something moving around the camp keeping a watch on us.

"Humph!" muttered the Doctor. "So did I."

Then he relapsed into silence.

Another rather strange thing that struck me as I gazed over the landscape while we waited for Chee-Chee to return was the appearance of the horizon. The Moon's width being so much smaller than the Earth's, the distance one could see was a great deal shorter. This did not apply so much where the land was hilly or mountainous; but on the level, or the nearly level it made a very striking difference. The *roundness* of this world was much more easily felt and understood than was that of the world we had left. On this plateau, for example, you could only see seven or eight miles, it seemed, over the level before the curve cut off your vision. And it gave quite a new character even to the hills, where peaks showed behind other ranges, dropping downward in a way that misled you entirely as to their actual height.

Finally Chee-Chee came back to us and said he had successfully retraced his steps to the water he had found the night before. He was now prepared to lead us to it. He looked kind of scared and ill at ease. The Doctor asked him the reason for this, but he didn't seem able to give any.

"Everything's all right, Doctor," said he—"at least I suppose it is. It was partly that—oh, I don't know—I can't quite make out what it is they have asked you here for. I haven't actually laid eyes on any animal life since we left the moth who brought us. Yet I feel certain that there's lots of it here. It doesn't appear to want to be seen. That's what puzzles me. On the Earth the animals were never slow in coming forward when they were in need of your services."

"You bet they were not!" grunted Polynesia. "No one who ever saw them clamouring around the surgery door could doubt that."

"Humph!" the Doctor muttered, "I've noticed it myself already. I don't understand it quite—either. It almost looks as though there were something about our arrival which they didn't like.... I wonder.... Well, anyway, I wish the animal life here would get in touch with us and let us know what it is all about. This state of things is, to say the least—er—upsetting."

· 6 ·

# THE MOON LAKE

And so we went forward with Chee-Chee as guide to find the water. Our actual entrance into that jungle was quite an experience and very different from merely a distant view of it. The light outside was not bright; inside the woods it was dimmer still. My only other experience of jungle life had been in Spidermonkey Island. This was something like the Spidermonkey forest and yet it was strikingly different.

From the appearance and size of that first tree we had reached, the Doctor had guessed its age to be very, very great. Here the vegetable life in general seemed to bear out that idea beyond all question. The enormous trees with their gigantic trunks looked as though they had been there since the beginning of time. And there was surprisingly little decay—a few shed limbs and leaves. That was all. In unkept earthly forests one saw dead trees everywhere, fallen to the ground or caught half-way in

## 6. THE MOON LAKE

the crotches of other trees, withered and dry. Not so here. Every tree looked as though it had stood so and grown in peace for centuries.

At length, after a good deal of arduous travel—the going for the most part was made slow by the heaviest kind of undergrowth, with vines and creepers as thick as your leg—we came to a sort of open place in which lay a broad calm lake with a pleasant waterfall at one end. The woods that surrounded it were most peculiar. They looked like enormous asparagus. For many, many square miles their tremendous masts rose, close together, in ranks. No creepers or vines had here been given a chance to flourish. The enormous stalks had taken up all the room and the nourishment of the crowded earth. The tapering tops, hundreds of feet above our heads, looked good enough to eat. Yet I've no doubt that if we had ever got up to them they would have been found as hard as oaks.

The Doctor walked down to the clean sandy shore of the lake and tried the water. Chee-Chee and I did the same. It was pure and clear and quenching to the thirst. The lake must have been at least five miles wide in the centre.

"I would like," said John Dolittle, "to explore this

by boat. Do you suppose, Chee-Chee, that we could find the makings of a canoe or a raft anywhere?"

"I should think so," said the monkey. "Wait a minute and I will take a look around and see."

So, with Chee-Chee in the lead, we proceeded along the shore in search of materials for a boat. On account of that scarcity of dead or dried wood which we had already noticed, our search did not at first appear a very promising one. Nearly all the standing trees were pretty heavy and full of sap. For our work of boat-building a light hatchet on the Doctor's belt was the best tool we had. It looked sadly small compared with the great timber that reared up from the shores of the lake.

But after we had gone along about a mile I noticed Chee-Chee up ahead stop and peer into the jungle. Then, after he had motioned to us with his hand to hurry, he disappeared into the edge of the forest. On coming up with him we found him stripping the creepers and moss off some contrivance that lay just within the woods, not more than a hundred yards from the water's edge.

We all fell to, helping him, without any idea of what it might be we were uncovering. There seemed almost no end to it. It was a long object, immeasurably long. To me it looked like a dead tree—the first dead, lying tree we had seen.

"What do you think it is, Chee-Chee?" asked the Doctor.

"It's a boat," said the monkey in a firm and matter-of-fact voice. "No doubt of it at all in my mind. It's a dug-out canoe. They used to use them in Africa."

"But, Chee-Chee," cried John Dolittle, "look at the length! It's a full-sized Asparagus Tree. We've uncovered a hundred feet of it already and still there's more to come."

"I can't help that," said Chee-Chee. "It's a dug-out canoe just the same. Crawl down with me here underneath it, Doctor, and I'll show you the marks of tools and fire. It has been turned upside down."

With the monkey guiding him, the Doctor scrabbled down below the queer object; and when he came forth there was a puzzled look on his face.

"Well, they might be the marks of tools, Chee-Chee," he was saying. "But then again they might not. The traces of fire are more clear. But that could be accidental. If the tree burned down it could very easily—"

"The natives in my part of Africa," Chee-Chee interrupted, "always used fire to eat out the insides of their dug-out canoes. They built little fires all along the tree, to hollow out the trunk so that they could sit in it. The tools they used were very simple, just stone scoops to chop out the charred wood with. I am sure this is a canoe, Doctor. But it hasn't been used in a long time. See how the bow has been shaped up into a point."

"I know," said the Doctor. "But the Asparagus Tree has a natural point at one end anyhow."

"And, Chee-Chee," put in Polynesia, "who in the name of goodness could ever handle such a craft? Why, look, the thing is as long as a battleship!"

Then followed a half-hour's discussion, between the Doctor and Polynesia on the one side and Chee-Chee on the other, as to whether the find we had made was, or was not, a canoe. For me, I had no opinion. To my eyes the object looked like an immensely long log, hollowed somewhat on the one side, but whether by accident or design I could not tell.

In any case it was certainly too heavy and cumbersome for us to use. And presently I edged into the argument with the suggestion that we go on further and find materials for a raft or boat we could handle.

The Doctor seemed rather glad of this excuse to end a fruitless controversy, and soon we moved on in search of something which would enable us to explore the waters of the lake. A march of a mile further along the shore brought us to woods that were not so heavy. Here the immense asparagus forests gave way to a growth of smaller girth; and the Doctor's hatchet soon felled enough poles for us to make a raft from. We laced them together with thongs of bark and found them sufficiently buoyant when launched to carry us and our small supply of baggage with ease. Where the water was shallow we used a long pole to punt with; and when we wished to explore greater depths we employed sweeps, or oars, which we fashioned roughly with the hatchet.

From the first moment we were afloat the Doctor kept me busy taking notes for him. In the equipment he had brought with him there was a fine-meshed landing net; and with it he searched along the shores for signs of life in this moon lake, the first of its kind we had met with.

"It is very important, Stubbins," said he, "to find out what fish we have here. In evolution the fish life is a very important matter."

"What is evolution?" asked Chee-Chee.

I started out to explain it to him but was soon called upon by the Doctor to make more notes—for which I was not sorry, as the task turned out to be a long and heavy one. Polynesia, however, took it up where I left off and made short work of it.

"Evolution, Chee-Chee," said she, "is the story of how Tommy got rid of the tail you are carrying—because he didn't need it any more—and the story of how you grew it and kept it because you did need it…. Evolution! Proof! —Professors' talk. A long word for a simple matter."

It turned out that our examination of the lake was neither exciting nor profitable. We brought up all sorts of water-flies, many larvæ of perfectly tremendous size, but we found as yet no fishes. The plant life—water plant I mean—was abundant.

"I think," said the Doctor, after we had poled ourselves around the lake for several hours, "that there can be no doubt now that the Vegetable Kingdom here is much more important than the Animal Kingdom. And what there is of the Animal Kingdom seems to be mostly insect. However, we will camp on the shore of this pleasant lake and perhaps we shall see more later."

So we brought our raft to anchor at about the place from which we had started out and pitched camp on a stretch of clean yellow sand.

I shall never forget that night. It was uncanny. None of us slept well. All through the hours of darkness we heard things moving around us. Enormous things. Yet never did we see them or find out what they were. The four of us were nevertheless certain that all night we were being watched. Even Polynesia was disturbed. There seemed no doubt that there was plenty of animal life in the Moon, but that it did not as yet want to show itself to us. The newness of our surroundings alone was disturbing enough, without this very uncomfortable feeling that something had made the moon folks distrustful of us.

· 7 ·
# TRACKS OF A GIANT

Another thing which added to our sleeplessness that night was the continuance of the mysterious music. But then so many strange things contributed to our general mystification and vague feeling of anxiety that it is hard to remember and distinguish them all.

The next morning after breakfasting on what remained of our fruits we packed up and started off for further exploration. While the last of the packing had been in progress Chee-Chee and Polynesia had gone ahead to do a little advanced scouting for us. They formed an admirable team for such work. Polynesia would fly above the forest and get long-distance impressions from the air of what lay ahead while Chee-Chee would examine the more lowly levels of the route to be followed, from the trees and the ground.

The Doctor and I were just helping one another on with our packs when Chee-Chee came rushing back to us in great excitement. His teeth were chattering so he could hardly speak.

"What do you think, Doctor!" he stammered. "We've found tracks back there. Tracks of a man! But so enormous! You've no idea. Come quick and I'll show you."

The Doctor looked up sharply at the scared and excited monkey, pausing a moment as though about to question him. Then he seemed to change his mind and turned once more to the business of taking up the baggage. With loads hoisted we gave a last glance around the camping ground to see if anything had been forgotten or left.

Our route did not lie directly across the lake, which mostly sprawled away to the right of our line of march. But we had to make our way partly around the lower end of it. Wondering what new chapter lay ahead of us, we fell in behind Chee-Chee and in silence started off along the shore.

After about half an hour's march we came to the mouth of a river which ran into the upper end of the lake. Along the margin of this we followed Chee-Chee for what seemed like another mile or so. Soon the shores of the stream widened out and the woods fell back quite a distance from the water's edge. The nature of the ground was still clean firm sand. Presently we saw Polynesia's tiny figure ahead, waiting for us.

When we drew up with her we saw that she was standing by an enormous footprint. There was no doubt about its being a man's, clear in every detail. It was the most gigantic thing I have ever seen, a barefoot track fully four yards in length. There wasn't only one, either. Down the shore the trail went on for a considerable distance; and the span that the prints lay apart gave one some idea of the enormous stride of the giant who had left this trail behind him.

Questioning and alarmed, Chee-Chee and Polynesia gazed silently up at the Doctor for an explanation.

"Humph!" he muttered after a while. "So Man is here, too. My goodness, what a monster! Let us follow the trail."

Chee-Chee was undoubtedly scared of such a plan. It was clearly both his and Polynesia's idea that the further we got away from the maker of those tracks the better. I could see terror and fright in the eyes of both of them. But neither made any objection; and in silence we plodded along, following in the path of this strange human who must, it would seem, be something out of a fairy tale.

But alas! It was not more than a mile further on that the footprints turned into the woods where, on the mosses and leaves beneath the trees, no traces had been left at all. Then we turned about and followed the river quite a distance to see if the creature had come back out on the sands again. But never a sign could we see. Chee-Chee spent a good deal of time too at the Doctor's request trying to find his path through the forest by any signs, such as broken limbs or marks in the earth which he might have left behind. But not another trace could we find. Deciding that he had merely come down to the stream to get a drink, we gave up the pursuit and turned back to the line of our original march.

Again I was thankful that I had company on that expedition. It was certainly a most curious and extraordinary experience. None of us spoke very much, but when we did it seemed that all of us had been thinking the same things.

The woods grew more and more mysterious, and more and more *alive*, as we went onward towards the other side of the Moon, the side that earthly Man had never seen before. For one thing, the strange music seemed to increase; and for another, there was more movement in the limbs of the trees. Great branches that looked like arms, bunches of small twigs that could have been hands, swung and moved and clawed the air in the most uncanny fashion. And always that steady wind went on blowing, even, regular and smooth.

All of the forest was not gloomy, however. Much of it was unbelievably beautiful. Acres of woods there were which presented nothing but a gigantic sea of many-coloured blossoms, colours that seemed like something out of a dream, indescribable, yet clear in one's memory as a definite picture of something seen.

The Doctor as we went forward spoke very little; when he did it was almost always on the same subject: "the absence of decay," as he put it.

"I am utterly puzzled, Stubbins," said he, in one of his longer outbursts when we were resting. "Why, there is hardly any leaf-mould at all!"

"What difference would that make, Doctor?" I asked.

"Well, that's what the trees live on, mostly, in our world," said he. "The forest growth, I mean—the soil that is formed by dying trees and rotting leaves—that is the nourishment that brings forth the seedlings which finally grow into new trees. But here! Well, of course there is *some* soil—and some shedding of leaves. But I've hardly seen a dead tree since I've been in these woods. One would almost think that there were some—er—balance. Some *arrangement* of—er—well—I can't explain it.... It beats me entirely."

I did not, at the time, completely understand what he meant. And yet it did seem as though every one of these giant plants that rose about us led a life of peaceful growth, undisturbed by rot, by blight or by disease.

Suddenly in our march we found ourselves at the end of the wooded section. Hills and mountains again spread before us. They were not the same as those we had first seen, however. These had vegetation, of a kind, on them. Low shrubs and heath plants clothed this rolling land with a dense growth—often very difficult to get through.

But still no sign of decay—little or no leaf-mould. The Doctor now decided that perhaps part of the reason for this was the seasons—or rather the lack of seasons. He said that we would probably find that here there was no regular winter or summer. It was an entirely new problem, so far as the struggle for existence was concerned, such as we knew in our world.

· 8 ·

# THE SINGING TREES

Into this new heath and hill country we travelled for miles. And presently we arrived upon a rather curious thing. It was a sort of basin high up and enclosed by hills or knolls. The strange part of it was that here there were not only more tracks of the Giant Man, just as we had seen lower down, but there were also unmistakable signs of *fire*. In an enormous hollow ashes lay among the sands. The Doctor was very interested in those ashes. He took some and added chemicals to them and tested them in many ways. He confessed himself at last entirely puzzled by their nature. But he said he nevertheless felt quite sure we had stumbled on the scene of the smoke signalling we had seen from Puddleby. Curiously long ago, it seemed, that time when Too-Too, the owl, had insisted he saw smoke burst from the side of the Moon. That was when the giant moth lay helpless in our garden. And yet—how long was it? Only a few days!

"It was from here, Stubbins," said the Doctor, "that the signals we saw from the Earth were given out, I feel certain. This place, as you see, is miles and miles across. But what was used to make an explosion as large as the one we saw from my house I have no idea."

"But it was smoke we saw," said I, "not a flash."

"That's just it," he said. "Some curious material must have been used that we have as yet no knowledge of. I thought that by testing the ashes I could discover what it was. But I can't. However, we may yet find out."

For two reasons the Doctor was anxious for the present not to get too far from the forest section. (We did not know then, you see, that there were other wooded areas beside this through which we had just come.) One reason was that we had to keep in touch with our food supply which consisted of the fruits and vegetables of the jungle. The other was that John Dolittle was absorbed now in the study of this Vegetable Kingdom which he felt sure had many surprises in store for the student naturalist.

After a while we began to get over the feeling of uncanny creepiness, which at the beginning had made us so uncomfortable. We decided that our fears were mostly caused by the fact that these woods and plants were so different from our own. There was no unfriendliness in these forests after all, we assured ourselves—except that we *were* being watched. That we knew—and that we were beginning to get used to.

As soon as the Doctor had decided that we would set up our new headquarters on the edge of the forest, and we had our camp properly established, we began making excursions in all directions through the jungle. And from then on I was again kept very busy taking notes of the Doctor's experiments and studies.

One of the first discoveries we made in our study of the Moon's Vegetable Kingdom was that there was practically no warfare going on between it and the Animal Kingdom. In the world we had left we had been accustomed to see the horses and other creatures eating up the grass in great quantities and many further examples of the struggle that continually goes on between the two. Here, on the other hand, the animals (or, more strictly speaking, the insects, for there seemed as yet hardly any traces of other animal species) and the vegetable life seemed for the most part to help one another rather than to fight and destroy. Indeed we found the whole system of Life on the Moon a singularly peaceful business. I will speak of this again later on.

## 8. THE SINGING TREES

We spent three whole days in the investigation of the strange music we had heard. You will remember that the Doctor, with his skill on the flute, was naturally fond of music; and this curious thing we had met with interested him a great deal. After several expeditions we found patches of the jungle where we were able to see and hear the tree music working at its best.

There was no doubt about it at all: The trees were making the sounds and they were doing it *deliberately*. In the way that an Æolian harp works when set in the wind at the right angle, the trees moved their branches to meet the wind so that certain notes would be given out. The evening that the Doctor made this discovery of what he called the *Singing Trees* he told me to mark down in the diary of the expedition as a Red Letter Date. I shall never forget it. We had been following the sound for hours, the Doctor carrying a tuning-fork in his hand, ringing it every once in a while to make sure of the notes we heard around us. Suddenly we came upon a little clearing about which great giants of the forest stood in a circle. It was for all the world like an orchestra. Spellbound, we stood and gazed up at them, as first one and then another would turn a branch to the steady blowing wind and a note would boom out upon the night, clear and sweet.

Then a group, three or four trees around the glade, would swing a limb and a chord would strike the air, and go murmuring through the jungle. Fantastic and crazy as it sounds, no one could have any doubt who heard and watched that these trees were actually making sounds, which they *wanted to make*, with the aid of the wind.

Of course, as the Doctor remarked, unless the wind had always blown steadily and evenly such a thing would have been impossible. John Dolittle himself was most anxious to find out on what scale of music they were working. To me, I must confess, it sounded just mildly pleasant. There *was* a time: I could hear that. And some whole phrases repeated once in a while, but not often. For the most part the melody was wild, sad and strange. But even to my uneducated ear it was beyond all question a quite clear effort at orchestration; there were certainly treble voices and bass voices and the combination was sweet and agreeable.

I was excited enough myself, but the Doctor was worked up to a pitch of interest such as I have seldom seen in him.

"Why, Stubbins," said he, "do you realize what this means? —It's terrific. If these trees can sing, a choir understands one another and all that, *they must have a* language.—They can talk! A language in the Vegetable Kingdom! We must get after it. Who knows? I may yet learn it myself. Stubbins, this is a great day!"

And so, as usual on such occasions, the good man's enthusiasm just carried him away bodily. For days, often without food, often without sleep, he pursued this new study. And at his heels I trotted with my note book always ready—though, to be sure, he put in far more work than I did because frequently when we got home he would go on wrestling for hours over the notes or new apparatus he was building, by which he hoped to learn the language of the trees.

You will remember that even before we left the Earth John Dolittle had mentioned the possibility of the moon bells having some means of communicating with one another. That they could move, within the limits of their fixed position, had been fully established. To that we had grown so used and accustomed that we no longer thought anything of it. The Doctor had in fact wondered if this might possibly be a means of conversation in itself—the movement of limbs and twigs and leaves, something like a flag signal code. And for quite a long while he sat watching certain trees and shrubs to see if they used this method for talking between themselves.

## · 9 ·
# THE STUDY OF PLANT LANGUAGES

About this time there was one person whom both the Doctor and I were continually reminded of, and continually wishing for, and that was Long Arrow, the Indian naturalist whom we had met in Spidermonkey Island. To be sure, he had never admitted to the Doctor that he had had speech with plant life. But his knowledge of botany and the natural history of the Vegetable Kingdom was of such a curious kind we felt that here he would have been of great help to us. Long Arrow, the son of Golden Arrow, never booked a scientific note in his life. How would he—when he was unable to write? Just the same he could tell you why a certain coloured bee visited a certain coloured flower; why *that* moth chose *that* shrub to lay its eggs in; why this particular grub attacked the roots of this kind of water plant.

Often of an evening the Doctor and I would speak of him, wondering where he was and what he was doing. When we sailed away from Spidermonkey Island he was left behind. But that would not mean he stayed there. A natural-born tramp who rejoiced in defying the elements and the so-called laws of Nature, he could be looked for anywhere in the two American continents.

And again, the Doctor would often refer to my parents. He evidently had a very guilty feeling about them—despite the fact that it was no fault of his that I had stowed away aboard the moth that brought us here. A million and one things filled his mind these days, of course; but whenever there was a let-down, a gap, in the stream of his scientific inquiry, he would come back to the subject.

"Stubbins," he'd say, "you shouldn't have come.... Yes, yes, I know, you did it for me. But Jacob, your father—and your mother too—they must be fretting themselves sick about your disappearance. And I am responsible.... Well, we can't do anything about that now, I suppose. Let's get on with the work."

And then he'd plunge ahead into some new subject and the matter would be dropped—till it bothered him again.

Throughout all our investigations of the Moon's Vegetable Kingdom we could not get away from the idea that the animal life was still, for some unknown reason, steering clear of us. By night, when we were settling down to sleep, we'd often get the impression that huge moths, butterflies or beetles were flying or crawling near us.

We made quite sure of this once or twice by jumping out of our beds and seeing a giant shadow disappear into the gloom. Yet never could we get near enough to distinguish what the creatures were before they escaped beyond the range of sight. But that they had come—whatever they were—to keep an eye on us seemed quite certain. Also that all of them were winged. The Doctor had a theory that the lighter gravity of the Moon had encouraged the development of wings to a much greater extent than it had on the Earth.

And again those tracks of the strange Giant Man. They were always turning up in the most unexpected places; I believe that if the Doctor had allowed Polynesia and Chee-Chee complete liberty to follow them that the enormous Human would have been run down in a very short time. But John Dolittle seemed still anxious to keep his family together. I imagine that with his curiously good instinctive judgment he feared an attempt to separate us. And in any case of course both Chee-Chee and

Polynesia were quite invaluable in a tight place. They were neither of them heavy-weight fighters, it is true; but their usefulness as scouts and guides was enormous. I have often heard John Dolittle say that he would sooner have that monkey or the parrot Polynesia with him in savage countries than he would the escort of a dozen regiments.

With some of our experimental work we wandered off long distances into the heath lands to see what we could do with the gorgeous flowering shrubs that thronged the rolling downs; and often we followed the streams many miles to study the gigantic lilies that swayed their stately heads over the sedgy banks.

And little by little our very arduous labours began to be repaid.

I was quite astonished when I came to realize how well the Doctor had prepared for this expedition. Shortly after he decided that he would set to work on the investigation of this supposed language of the plants he told me we would have to go back and fetch the remainder of our baggage which we had left at the point of our first arrival.

So the following morning, bright and early, he, Chee-Chee and I set out to retrace our steps. Polynesia was left behind. The Doctor told none of us why he did this, but we decided afterwards that, as usual, he knew what he was doing.

It was a long and hard trip. It took us a day and a half going there and two days coming back with the load of baggage. At our original landing-place we again found many tracks of the Giant Human, and other strange marks on the sands about our baggage-dump which told us that here too curious eyes had been trying to find out things without being seen.

A closer examination of the tracks made by the Giant Human in these parts where they were especially clear told the Doctor that his right leg stride was considerably longer than his left. The mysterious Moon Man evidently walked with a limp. But with such a stride he would clearly be a very formidable creature anyway.

When we got back and started unpacking the bundles and boxes which had been left behind, I saw, as I have already said, how well the Doctor had prepared for his voyage. He seemed to have brought everything that he could possibly need for the trip: hatchets, wire, nails, files, a hand-saw, all the things we couldn't get on the Moon. It was so different from his ordinary preparations for a voyage—which hardly ever consisted of more than

## 9. THE STUDY OF PLANT LANGUAGES

the little black bag and the clothes he stood in.

As usual he rested only long enough to get a few mouthfuls of food before he set to work. There seemed to be a dozen different apparatuses he wanted to set up at once, some for the testing of sound, others for vibrations, etc., etc. With the aid of a saw and an axe and a few other tools, half a dozen small huts had sprung up in an hour around our camp.

· 10 ·

# THE MAGELLAN OF THE MOON

Laying aside for the present all worry on the score of why he had been summoned to the Moon—of why the Animal Kingdom continued to treat us with suspicion, of why the Giant Human so carefully kept out of our way, the Doctor now plunged into the study of plant languages heart and soul.

He was always happy so, working like a demon, snatching his meals and his sleep here and there when he thought of such earthly matters. It was a most exhausting time for the rest of us, keeping pace with this firebrand of energy when he got on an interesting scent. And yet it was well worth while too. In one and a half days he had established the fact that the trees *did* converse with one another by means of branch gestures. But that was only the first step. Copying and practising, he rigged himself up like a tree and talked in the glade—after a fashion—with these centuries-old denizens of the jungle.

## 10. THE MAGELLAN OF THE MOON

From that he learned still more—that language, of a kind, was carried on by using other means—by scents given out, in a definite way—short or long perfumes, like a regular Morse Code; by the tones of wind-song when branches were set to the right angle to produce certain notes; and many other odd strange means.

Every night, by bed-time, I was nearly dead from the strain and effort of taking notes in those everlasting books, of which he seemed to have brought an utterly inexhaustible supply.

Chee-Chee looked after the feeding of us—Thank goodness! —or I fear we would easily have starved to death, if overwork itself hadn't killed us. Every three hours the faithful little monkey would come to us wherever we were at the moment with his messes of strange vegetables and fruits and a supply of good clean drinking water.

As official recorder of the Expedition (a job of which I was very proud even if it was hard work) I had to book all the Doctor's calculations as well as his natural history notes. I have already told you something of temperature, air pressure, time and what not. A further list of them would have included the calculation of distance travelled. This was quite difficult. The Doctor had brought with him a pedometer (that is a little instrument which when carried in the pocket tells you from the number of strides made the miles walked). But in the Moon, with the changed gravity, a pace was quite different from that usual on the Earth. And what is more, it never stayed the same. When the ground sloped downward it was natural to spring a step that quite possibly measured six or seven feet—this with no out-of-the-way effort at all. And even on the up grade one quite frequently used a stride that was far greater than in ordinary walking.

It was about this time that the Doctor first spoke of making a tour of the Moon. Magellan, you will remember, was the first to sail around our world. And it was a very great feat. The Earth contains more water area than land. The Moon, on the contrary, we soon saw, had more dry land than water. There were no big oceans. Lakes and chains of lakes were all the water area we saw. To complete a round trip of this world would therefore be harder, even though it was shorter, than the voyage that Magellan made.

It was on this account that the Doctor was so particular about my booking a strict record of the miles we travelled. As to direction, we had not as yet been so careful about maintaining a perfectly straight line. Because it was by no means easy for one thing; and for another, the subjects we wished to study, such as tree-music, tracks, water supply, rock formation, etc., often led us off towards every quarter of the compass. When I say the *compass* I mean something a little different from the use of that word in earthly geography. As I have told you, the magnetic compass which John Dolittle had brought with him from Puddleby did not behave in a helpful manner at all. Something else must be found to take its place.

John Dolittle, as usual, went after that problem too with much energy. He was a very excellent mathematician, was the Doctor. And one afternoon he sat down with a note book and the Nautical Almanac and worked out tables which should tell him from the stars where he was and in what direction he was going. It was curious, that strange sense of comfort we drew from the stars. They, the heavenly bodies which from the Earth seemed the remotest, most distant, unattainable and strangest of objects, here suddenly became friendly; because, I suppose, they were the only things that really stayed the same. The stars, as we saw them from the Moon, were precisely as the stars we had seen from the

Earth. The fact that they were nearly all countless billions of miles away made no difference. For us they were something that we had seen before and knew.

It was while we were at work on devising some contrivance to take the place of the compass that we made the discovery of the explosive wood. The Doctor after trying many things by which he hoped to keep a definite direction had suddenly said one day:

"Why, Stubbins, I have it.—The wind! It always blows steady—and probably from precisely the same quarter—or at all events with a regular calculable change most likely. Let us test it and see."

So right away we set to work to make various wind-testing devices. We rigged up weather-vanes from long streamers of light bark. And then John Dolittle hit upon the idea of smoke.

"That is something," said he, "if we only place it properly, which will warn us by smell if the wind changes. And in the meantime we can carry on our studies of the Animal Kingdom and its languages." So without further ado we set to work to build fires—or rather large smoke smudges—which should tell us how reliable our wind would be if depended on for a source of direction.

· 11 ·
# WE PREPARE TO CIRCLE THE MOON

We went to a lot of trouble working out how we could best place these fires so that they should give us the most satisfactory results. First of all we decided with much care on the exact position where we would build them. Mostly they were on bare knolls or shoulders, where they couldn't spread to the underbrush and start a bush-fire. Then came the question of fuel: —What would be the best wood to build them of?

There were practically no dead trees, as I have said. The only thing to do then was to cut some timber down and let it dry.

This we proceeded to do but did not get very far with it before the Doctor suddenly had qualms of conscience. Trees that could talk could, one would suppose, also *feel*. The thought was dreadful. We hadn't even the courage to ask the trees about it—yet. So we fell back upon gathering fallen twigs and small branches.

This made the work heavier still because, of course, we needed a great deal of fuel to have fires big enough to see and smell for any distance.

After a good deal of discussion we decided that this was a thing which couldn't be hurried. A great deal depended on its success. It was a nuisance, truly, but we had just got to be patient. So we went back into the jungle-lands and set to work on getting out various samples of woods to try.

It took a longish time, for the Doctor and myself were the only ones who could do this work. Chee-Chee tried to help by gathering twigs; but the material we most needed was wood large enough to last a fair time.

Well, we harvested several different kinds. Some wouldn't burn at all when we tried them. Others, we found, were pretty fair burners, but not smoky enough.

With about the fifth kind of wood, I think it was that we tested out, we nearly had a serious accident. Fire seemed to be (outside of the traces we had found of the smoke signal apparatus) a thing quite unusual in the Moon. There were no traces of forest burnings anywhere, so far as we had explored. It was therefore with a good deal of fear and caution that we struck matches to test out our fuel.

## 11. WE PREPARE TO CIRCLE THE MOON

About dusk one evening the Doctor set a match to a sort of fern wood (something like a bamboo) and he narrowly escaped a bad burning. The stuff flared up like gunpowder.

We took him off, Chee-Chee and I, and examined him. We found he had suffered no serious injuries, though he had had a very close shave. His hands were somewhat blistered and he told us what to get out of the little black bag to relieve the inflammation.

We had all noticed that as the wood flared up it sent off dense masses of white smoke. And for hours after the explosion clouds of heavy fumes were still rolling round the hills near us.

When we had the Doctor patched up he told us he was sure that we had stumbled by accident on the fuel that had been used for making the smoke signals we had seen from Puddleby.

"But my goodness, Doctor," said I, "what an immense bonfire it must be visible all that distance! —Thousands of tons of the stuff, surely, must have been piled together to make a smudge which could be seen that far."

"And who could have made it?" put in Chee-Chee.

For a moment there was silence. Then Polynesia

spoke the thought that was in my mind—and I imagine in the Doctor's too.

"The man who made those torches," said she quietly, "could move an awful lot of timber in one day, I'll warrant."

"You mean you think it was *he* who sent the signals?" asked Chee-Chee, his funny little eyes staring wide open with astonishment.

"Why not?" said Polynesia. Then she lapsed into silent contemplation and no further questioning from Chee-Chee could get a word out of her.

"Well," said the monkey at last, "if he *did* send it that would look as though he were responsible for the whole thing. It must have been he who sent the moth down to us—who needed the Doctor's assistance and presence here."

He looked towards John Dolittle for an answer to this suggestion. But the Doctor, like Polynesia, didn't seem to have anything to say.

Well, in spite of our little mishap, our wood tests with smoke were extremely successful. We found that the wind as a direction-pointer could certainly be relied on for three or four days at a time.

"Of course, Stubbins," said the Doctor, "we will

have to test again before we set off on our round trip. It may be that the breeze, while blowing in one prevailing direction now, may change after a week or so. Also we will have to watch it that the mountain ranges don't deflect the wind's course and so lead us astray. But from what we have seen so far, I feel pretty sure that we have here something to take the place of the compass."

I made one or two attempts later, when Polynesia and Chee-Chee were out of earshot, to discover what John Dolittle thought about this idea that it had really been the Moon Man who had brought us here and not the Animal Kingdom. I felt that possibly he might talk more freely to me alone on the subject than he had been willing to with all of us listening. But he was strangely untalkative.

"I don't know, Stubbins," said he, frowning, "I really don't know. To tell the truth, my mind is not occupied with that problem now—at all events, not as a matter for immediate decision. This field of the lunar Vegetable Kingdom is something that could take up the attention of a hundred naturalists for a year or two. I feel we have only scratched the surface. As we go forward into the unknown areas of the Moon's further side we are liable to make discoveries of—well, er—who can tell?

When the Moon Man and the Animal Kingdom make up their minds that they want to get in touch with us, I suppose we shall hear from them. In the meantime we have our work to do—more than we can do.... Gracious, I wish I had a whole staff with me! —Surveyors, cartographers, geologists and the rest. Think of it! Here we are, messing our way along across a new world—and we don't even know where we are! I think I have a vague idea of the line we have followed. And I've tried to keep a sort of chart of our march. But I should be making maps, Stubbins, real maps, showing all the peaks, valleys, streams, lakes, plateaux and everything.—Dear, dear! Well, we must do the best we can."

## · 12 ·
# THE VANITY LILIES

Of course on a globe larger than that of the Moon we could never have done as well as we did. When you come to think of it, one man, a boy, a monkey and a parrot, as a staff for the exploration of a whole world, makes the expedition sound, to say the least, absurd.

We did not realize, any of us, when we started out from our first landing that we were going to make a circular trip of the Moon's globe. It just worked out that way. To begin with, we were expecting every hour that some part of the Animal Kingdom would come forward into the open. But it didn't. And still we went on. Then this language of the trees and flowers came up and got the Doctor going on one of his fever-heat investigations. That carried us still further. We always took great care when departing from one district for an excursion of any length to leave landmarks behind us, camps or dumps, so that we could find our way back to food and shelter if we should get caught in a tight place.

In this sort of feeling our way forward Polynesia was most helpful. The Doctor used to let her off regularly now to fly ahead of us and bring back reports. That gave us some sort of idea of what we should prepare for. Then in addition to that, the Doctor had brought with him several small pocket surveying instruments with which he marked on his chart roughly the points at which we changed course to any considerable extent.

In the earlier stages of our trip we had felt we must keep in touch with the first fruit section we had met with, in order to have a supply of vegetables and fruits to rely on for food. But we soon discovered from Polynesia's scouting reports, that other wooded sections lay ahead of us. To these we sent Chee-Chee, the expert, to investigate. And when he returned and told us that they contained even a better diet than those further back, we had no hesitation in leaving her old haunts and venturing still further into the mysteries of the Moon's Further Side.

The Doctor's progress with the language of the trees and plants seemed to improve with our penetration into the interior. Many times we stopped and pitched camp for four or five days, while he set up some new apparatus and struggled with fresh problems in plant language. It seemed to grow easier and easier for him all the time. Certainly the plant life became more elaborate and lively. By this we were all grown more accustomed to strange things in the Vegetable Kingdom. And even to my unscientific eyes it was quite evident that here the flowers and bushes were communicating with one another with great freedom and in many different ways.

I shall never forget our first meeting with the Vanity Lilies, as the Doctor later came to call them. Great gaudy blooms they were, on long slender stems that swayed and moved in groups like people whispering and gossiping at a party. When we came in sight of them for the first time, they were more or less motionless. But as we approached, the movement among them increased as though they were disturbed by, or interested in, our coming.

I think they were beyond all question the most beautiful flowers I have ever seen. The wind, regular as ever, had not changed. But the heads of these great masses of plants got so agitated as we drew near, that the Doctor decided he would halt the expedition and investigate.

We pitched camp as we called it—a very simple

business in the Moon, because we did not have to raise tents or build a fire. It was really only a matter of unpacking, getting out the food to eat and the bedding to sleep in.

We were pretty weary after a full day's march. Beyond the lily beds (which lay in a sort of marsh) we could see a new jungle district with more strange trees and flowering creepers.

After a short and silent supper, we lay down and pulled the covers over us. The music of the forest grew louder as darkness increased. It seemed almost as though the whole vegetable world was remarking on these visitors who had invaded their home.

And then above the music of the woods we'd hear the drone of flying, while we dropped off to sleep. Some of the giant insects were hovering near, as usual, to keep an eye on these creatures from another world.

I think that of all our experiences with the plant life of the Moon that with the Vanity Lilies was perhaps the most peculiar and the most thrilling. In about two days the Doctor had made extraordinary strides in his study of this language. That, he explained to me, was due more to the unusual intelligence of this species and its willingness to help than to his own efforts. But of course if he had not already done considerable work with the trees and bushes it is doubtful if the lilies could have got in touch with him as quickly as they did.

By the end of the third day Chee-Chee, Polynesia and I were all astonished to find that John Dolittle was actually able to carry on conversation with these flowers. And this with the aid of very little apparatus. He had now discovered that the Vanity Lilies spoke among themselves largely by the movement of their blossoms. They used different means of communication with species of plants and trees other than their own—and also (we heard later) in talking with birds and insects; but among themselves the swaying of the flower-heads was the common method of speech.

The lilies, when seen in great banks, presented a very gorgeous and wonderful appearance. The flowers would be, I should judge, about eighteen inches across, trumpet-shaped and brilliantly coloured. The background was a soft cream tone and on this great blotches of violet and orange were grouped around a jet-black tongue in the centre. The leaves were a deep olive green.

But it was that extraordinary look of alive intelligence that was the most uncanny thing about them. No one, no matter how little he knew of natural history in general or of the Moon's Vegetable Kingdom, could see those wonderful flowers without immediately being arrested by this peculiar character. You felt at once that you were in the presence of people rather than plants; and to talk with them, or to try to, seemed the most natural thing in the world.

I filled up two of those numerous note books of the Doctor's on his conversations with the Vanity Lilies. Often he came back to these flowers later, when he wanted further information about the Moon's Vegetable Kingdom. For as he explained to us, it was in this species that Plant Life—so far at all events as it was known on either the Moon or the Earth—had reached its highest point of development.

## · 13 ·
# THE FLOWER OF MANY SCENTS

Another peculiar thing that baffled us completely, when we first came into the marshy regions of the Vanity Lily's home, was the variety of scents which assailed our noses. For a mile or so around the locality there was no other flower visible; the whole of the marsh seemed to have been taken up by the lilies and nothing else intruded on their domain. Yet at least half a dozen perfumes were distinct and clear. At first we thought that perhaps the wind might be bringing us scents from other plants either in the jungle or the flowering heath lands. But the direction of the breeze was such that it could only come over the sandy desert areas and was not likely to bring perfumes as strong as this.

It was the Doctor who first hit upon the idea that possibly the lily could give off more than one scent at will. He set to work to find out right away. And it took no more than a couple of minutes to convince him that it could. He said he was sorry he had not got Jip with him. Jip's expert sense of smell would have been very useful here. But for ordinary purposes it required nothing more delicate than an average human's nose to tell that this flower, when John Dolittle had communicated the idea to it, was clearly able to give out at least half a dozen different smells as it wished.

The majority of these perfumes were extremely agreeable. But there were one or two that nearly knocked you down. It was only after the Doctor had asked the lilies about this gift of theirs that they sent forth obnoxious ones in demonstrating all the scents that they could give out. Chee-Chee just fainted away at the first sample. It was like some deadly gas. It got into your eyes and made them run. The Doctor and I only escaped suffocation by flight—carrying the body of the unconscious monkey along with us.

The Vanity Lilies, seeing what distress they had caused, immediately threw out the most soothing lovely scent I have ever smelled. Clearly they were anxious to please us and cultivate our acquaintance. Indeed it turned out later from their conversation with the Doctor (which I took down word for word) that in spite of being a stationary part of the Moon's landscape, they had heard of John Dolittle, the great naturalist, and had been watching for his arrival many days. They were in fact the first creatures in our experience of the Moon that made us feel we were among friends.

I think I could not do better, in trying to give you an idea of the Doctor's communication with the Vegetable Kingdom of the Moon, than to set down from my diary, word for word, some parts of the conversation between him and the Vanity Lilies as he translated them to me for dictation at the time. Even so, there are many I am sure who will doubt the truth of the whole idea: that a man could talk with the flowers. But with them I am not so concerned. Any one who had followed John Dolittle through the various stages of animal, fish, and insect languages would not, I feel certain, find it very strange, when the great man did at last come in touch with plant life of unusual intelligence, that he should be able to converse with it.

On looking over my diary of those eventful days the scene of that occasion comes up visibly before my eyes. It was about an hour before dusk—that is the slight dimming of the pale daylight which proceeded a half darkness, the nearest thing to real night we ever saw on the Moon. The Doctor, as we left the camp, called back over his shoulder to me to bring an extra note book along as he expected to make a good deal of progress to-night. I armed myself therefore with three extra books and followed him out.

Halting about twenty paces in front of the lily beds (we had camped back several hundred yards from them after they had nearly suffocated Chee-Chee) the Doctor squatted on the ground and began swaying his head from side to side. Immediately the lilies began moving their heads in answer, swinging, nodding, waving, and dipping.

"Are you ready, Stubbins?" asked John Dolittle.

"Yes, Doctor," said I, making sure my pencil point would last a while.

"Good," said he.—"Put it down":

*The Doctor*—"Do you like this stationary life—I mean, living in the same place all the time, unable to move?"

*The Lilies*—(Several of them seemed to answer in chorus)—"Why, yes—of course. Being stationary doesn't bother us. We hear about all that is going on."

*The Doctor*—"From whom, what, do you hear it?"

*The Lilies*—"Well, the other plants, the bees, the

birds, bring us news of what is happening."

*The Doctor*-"Oh, do you communicate with the bees and the birds?"

*The Lilies*-"Why, certainly, of course!"

*The Doctor*—"Yet the bees and the birds are races different from your own."

*The Lilies*—"Quite true, but the bees come to us for honey. And the birds come to sit among our leaves—especially the warblers—and they sing and talk and tell us of what is happening in the world. What more would you want?"

*The Doctor*-"Oh, quite so, quite so. I didn't mean you should be discontented. But don't you ever want to move, to travel?"

*The Lilies*—"Good gracious, no! What's the use of all this running about? After all, there's no place like home—provided it's a good one. It's a pleasant life we lead—and very safe. The folks who rush around are always having accidents, breaking legs and so forth. Those troubles can't happen to us. We sit still and watch the world go by. We chat sometimes among ourselves and then there is always the gossip of the birds and the bees to entertain us."

*The Doctor*—" And you really understand the

language of the birds and bees! —You astonish me."

*The Lilies*—"Oh, perfectly—and of the beetles and moths too."

It was at about this point in our first recorded conversation that we made the astonishing discovery that the Vanity Lilies could *see*. The light, as I have told you, was always somewhat dim on the Moon. The Doctor, while he was talking, suddenly decided he would like a smoke. He asked the lilies if they objected to the fumes of tobacco. They said they did not know because they had never had any experience of it. So the Doctor said he would light his pipe and if they did not like it he would stop.

So taking a box of matches from his pocket he struck a light. We had not fully realized before how soft and gentle was the light of the Moon until that match flared up. It is true that in testing our woods for smoke fuel we had made much larger blazes. But then, I suppose we had been more intent on the results of our experiments than on anything else. Now, as we noticed the lilies suddenly draw back their heads and turn aside from the flare, we saw that the extra illumination of a mere match had made a big difference to the ordinary daylight they were accustomed to.

## · 14 ·
# MIRRORS FOR FLOWERS

When the Doctor noticed how the lilies shrank away from the glow of the matches he became greatly interested in this curious unexpected effect that the extra light had had on them.

"Why, Stubbins," he whispered, "they could not have felt the heat. We were too far away. If it is the glare that made them draw back it must be that they have some organs so sensitive to light that quite possibly *they can see*! I must find out about this."

Thereupon he began questioning the lilies again to discover how much they could tell him of their sense of vision. He shot his hand out and asked them if they knew what movement he had made. Every time (though they had no idea of what he was trying to find out) they told him precisely what he had done. Then going close to one large flower he passed his hand all round it; and the blossom turned its head and faced the moving hand all the way round the circle.

There was no doubt in our minds whatever, when we had finished our experiments, that the Vanity Lilies could in their own way see—though where the machinery called eyes was placed in their anatomy we could not as yet discover.

The Doctor spent hours and days trying to solve this problem. But, he told me, he met with very little success. For a while he was forced to the conclusion (since he could not find in the flowers any eyes such as we knew) that what he had taken for a sense of vision was only some other sense, highly developed, which produced the same results as seeing.

"After all, Stubbins," said he, "just because we ourselves only have five senses, it doesn't follow that other creatures can't have more. It has long been supposed that certain birds had a sixth sense. Still, the way those flowers feel light, can tell colours, movement, and form, makes it look very much as though they had found a way of seeing—even if they haven't got eyes.... Humph! Yes, one might quite possibly see with other things besides eyes."

Going through his baggage that night after our day's work was done, the Doctor discovered among his papers

## 14. MIRRORS FOR FLOWERS   255

an illustrated catalogue which had somehow got packed by accident. John Dolittle, always a devoted gardener, had catalogues sent to him from nearly every seed merchant and nurseryman in England.

"Why, Stubbins!" he cried, turning over the pages of gorgeous annuals in high glee—"Here's a chance; if those lilies can see we can test them with this.—Pictures of flowers in colour!"

The next day he interviewed the Vanity Lilies with the catalogue and his work was rewarded with very good results. Taking the brightly coloured pictures of petunias, chrysanthemums and hollyhocks, he held them in a good light before the faces of the lilies. Even Chee-Chee and I could see at once that this caused quite a sensation. The great trumpet-shaped blossoms swayed downwards and forwards on their slender stems to get a closer view of the pages. Then they turned to one another as though in critical conversation.

Later the Doctor interpreted to me the comments they had made and I booked them among the notes. They seemed most curious to know *who* these flowers were. They spoke of them (or rather of their species) in a peculiarly personal way. This was one of the first occasions when we got some idea or glimpses of lunar

*Vegetable Society*, as the Doctor later came to call it. It almost seemed as though these beautiful creatures were surprised, like human ladies, at the portraits displayed and wanted to know all about these foreign beauties and the lives they led.

This interest in personal appearance on the part of the lilies was, as a matter of fact, what originally led the Doctor to call their species the Vanity Lily. In their own strange tongue they questioned him for hours and hours about these outlandish flowers whose pictures he had shown them. They seemed very disappointed when he told them the actual size of most earthly flowers. But they seemed a little pleased that their sisters of the other world could not at least compete with them in that. They were also much mystified when John Dolittle explained to them that with us no flowers or plants (so far as was known) had communicated with Man, birds, or any other members of the Animal Kingdom.

Questioning them further on this point of personal appearance, the Doctor was quite astonished to find to what an extent it occupied their attention. He found that they always tried to get nearer water so that they could see their own reflections in the surface. They got terribly upset if some bee or bird came along and disturbed the pollen powder on their gorgeous petals or set awry the angle of their pistils.

The Doctor talked to various groups and individuals; and in the course of his investigations he came across several plants who, while they had begun their peaceful lives close to a nice pool or stream which they could use as a mirror, had sadly watched while the water had dried up and left nothing but sun-baked clay for them to look into.

So then and there John Dolittle halted his questioning of the Vanity Lilies for a spell while he set to work to provide these unfortunates, whose natural mirrors had dried up, with something in which they could see themselves.

We had no regular looking-glasses of course, beyond the Doctor's own shaving mirror, which he could not very well part with. But from the provisions we dug out various caps and bottoms of preserved fruits and sardine tins. These we polished with clay and rigged up on sticks so that the lilies could see themselves in them.

"It is a fact, Stubbins," said the Doctor, "that the natural tendency is always to grow the way you want to grow. These flowers have a definite conscious idea of what they consider beautiful and what they consider ugly. These contrivances we have given them, poor though they are, will therefore have a decided effect on their evolution."

That is one of the pictures from our adventures in the Moon which always stands out in my memory: the Vanity Lilies, happy in the possession of their new mirrors, turning their heads this way and that to see how their pollen-covered petals glowed in the soft light, swaying with the wind, comparing, whispering and gossiping.

I truly believe that if other events had not interfered, the Doctor would have been occupied quite contentedly with his study of these very advanced plants for months. And there was certainly a great deal to be learned from them. They told him for instance of another species of lily that he later came to call the *Poison Lily* or *Vampire Lily*. This flower liked to have plenty of room and it obtained it by sending out deadly scents (much more serious in their effects than those unpleasant ones which the Vanities used) and nothing round about it could exist for long.

Following the directions given by the Vanity Lilies we finally ran some of these plants down and actually conversed with them—though we were in continual fear that they would be displeased with us and might any moment send out their poisonous gases to destroy us.

From still other plants which the Vanities directed us to the Doctor learned a great deal about what he called "methods of propagating." Certain bushes, for example, could crowd out weeds and other shrubs by increasing the speed of their growth at will and by spreading their seed abroad several times a year.

In our wanderings, looking for these latter plants, we came across great fields of the "moon bells" flourishing and growing under natural conditions. And very gorgeous indeed they looked, acres and acres of brilliant orange. The air was full of their invigorating perfume. The Doctor wondered if we would see anything of our giant moth near these parts. But though we hung about for several hours we saw very few signs of insect life.

## · 15 ·
# MAKING NEW CLOTHES

"I don't understand it at all," John Dolittle muttered. "What reason at least can the moth who brought us here have for keeping out of our way?"

"His reasons may not be his own," murmured Polynesia.

"What do you mean?" asked the Doctor.

"Well," said she, "others may be keeping him—and the rest, away from us."

"You mean the Moon Man?" said John Dolittle.

But to this Polynesia made no reply and the subject was dropped.

"That isn't the thing that's bothering me so much," said CheeChee.

There was a pause. And before he went on I know that all of us were quite sure what was in his mind.

"It's our getting back home," he said at last. "Getting here was done for us by these moon folks—for

## 15. MAKING NEW CLOTHES    261

whatever reason they had. But we'd stand a mighty poor chance of ever reaching the Earth again if they're going to stand off and leave us to ourselves to get back."

Another short spell of silence—during which we all did a little serious and gloomy thinking.

"Oh, well," said the Doctor, "come, come! Don't let's bother about the stiles till we reach them. After all we don't know for certain that these—er—whoever it is—are definitely unfriendly to us. They may have reasons of their own for working slowly. You must remember that we are just as strange and outlandish to them as they and their whole world are to us. We mustn't let any idea of that kind become a nightmare. We have only been here, let's see, not much over two weeks. It is a pleasant land and there is lots to be learned. The Vegetable Kingdom is clearly well disposed towards us. And if we give them time I'm sure that the—er—others will be too, in the end."

Another matter which came up about this time was the effect of moon food on ourselves. Polynesia was the first to remark upon it.

"Tommy," said she one day, "you seem to be getting enormously tall—and fat, aren't you?"

"Er—am I?" said I. "Well, I had noticed my belt

seemed a bit tight. But I thought it was just ordinary growing."

"And the Doctor too," the parrot went on. "I'll swear he's bigger—unless my eyesight is getting queer."

"Well, we can soon prove that," said John Dolittle. "I know my height exactly—five feet two and a half. I have a twofoot rule in the baggage. I'll measure myself against a tree right away."

When the Doctor had accomplished this he was astonished to find that his height had increased some three inches since he had been on the Moon. Of what my own had been before I landed, I was not so sure; but measurement made it too a good deal more than I had thought it. And as to my waist line, there was no doubt that it had grown enormously. Even CheeChee, when we came to look at him, seemed larger and heavier. Polynesia was of course so small that it would need an enormous increase in her figure to make difference enough to see.

But there was no question at all that the rest of us had grown considerably since we had been here.

"Well," said the Doctor, "I suppose it is reasonable enough. All the vegetable and insect world here is tremendously much larger than corresponding species in our own world. Whatever helped them to grow—climate, food, atmosphere, airpressure, etc.—should make us do the same. There is a great deal in this for the investigation of biologists and physiologists. I suppose the long seasons—or almost no seasons at all, you might say—and the other things which contribute to the long life of the animal and vegetable species would lengthen our lives to hundreds of years, if we lived here continually. You know when I was talking to the Vampire Lilies the other day they told me that even cut flowers—which with them would mean of course only blossoms that were broken off by the wind or accident—live perfectly fresh for weeks and even months—provided they get a little moisture. That accounts for the moon bells which the moth brought down with him lasting so well in Puddleby. No, we've got to regard this climate as something entirely different from the Earth's. There is no end to the surprises it may spring on us yet. Oh, well, I suppose we will shrink back to our ordinary size when we return home. Still I hope we don't grow too gigantic. My waistcoat feels most uncomfortably tight already. It's funny we didn't notice it earlier. But, goodness knows, we have had enough to keep our attention occupied."

It had been indeed this absorbing interest in all the new things that the Moon presented to our eyes that had prevented us from noticing our own changed condition. The following few days, however, our growth went forward at such an amazing pace that I began seriously to worry about it. My clothes were literally splitting and the Doctor's also. Finally, taking counsel on the matter, we proceeded to look into what means this world offered of making new ones.

Luckily the Doctor, while he knew nothing about tailoring, did know something about the natural history of those plants and materials that supply clothes and textile fabrics for Man.

"Let me see," said he one afternoon when we had decided that almost everything we wore had become too small to be kept any longer: "Cotton is out of the question. The spinning would take too long, even if we had any, to say nothing of the weaving. Linen? No, likewise.—I haven't seen anything that looked like a flax plant. About all that remains is root fibre, though heaven help us if we have to wear that kind of material next our skins! Well, we must investigate and see what we can find."

With the aid of CheeChee we searched the woods. It

took us several days to discover anything suitable, but finally we did. It was an oddlooking swamp tree whose leaves were wide and soft. We found that when these were dried in the proper way they kept a certain pliability without becoming stiff or brittle. And yet they were tough enough to be sewn without tearing.

Chee-Chee and Polynesia supplied us with the thread we needed. This they obtained from certain vine tendrils—very fine—which they shredded and twisted into yarn. Then one evening we set to work and cut out our new suits.

"Better make them large enough," said the Doctor, waving a pair of scissors over our rock worktable, "Goodness only knows how soon we'll outgrow them."

We had a lot of fun at one another's expense when at length the suits were completed and we tried them on.

"We look like a family of Robinson Crusoes," said John Dolittle. "No matter: they will serve our purpose. Any port in a storm."

For underwear we cut up all we had and made one garment out of two or three. We were afraid as yet to try our new tailoring next the skin. Luckily we only had to provide for a very mild climate.

"Now what about footwear?" said I when I had my

coat and trousers on. "My shoes are all split across the top."

"That part is easy," said Chee-Chee. "I know a tree in the jungle which I found when hunting for fruits. The bark strips off easily and you can cut it into sandals that will last quite a while. The only hard part will be plaiting thongs strong enough to keep them in place on your feet."

He guided us to the tree he had spoken of and we soon had outfitted ourselves with footgear which would last us at least a week.

"Good!" said the Doctor. "Now we need not worry about clothes for a while anyway, and can give our attention to more serious matters."

## · 16 ·
# MONKEY MEMORIES OF THE MOON

It was when we were on our way to visit still another new kind of plant that the subject of the Moon's early history came up again in conversation. The Doctor had heard of a "whispering vine" which used, as a method of conversation, the rattling or whispering of its leaves.

"Do you remember, Chee-Chee," the Doctor asked, "if your grandmother ever spoke, in her stories of very ancient times, of any peculiar or extraordinary plants or trees?"

"I don't think so, Doctor," he replied. "My grandmother in her talks of the Time Before There Was a Moon kept pretty much to animals and people. She hardly ever mentioned the trees or vegetable world, except to say of this country or that, that it was heavily wooded, or bare and desert. Why?"

"Well, of course in my mind there is no doubt that

the Moon was once a part of the Earth, as many scientists believe. And if so I am wondering why we do not see more plants and trees of our own home kinds here."

"Well, but we have, Doctor," said Polynesia. "How about the Asparagus Forests?"

"Quite so," said the Doctor. "There have been many that reminded one of earthly species in their shapes, even if they have grown into giants here. But this speech among plants and trees—and other evidences of social advance and development in the Vegetable Kingdom—is something so established and accepted here I am all the time wondering if something like it had not started on the Earth long ago—say in the Days Before There Was a Moon. And it was merely because our naturalists were not quick enough to—er—catch on to it, that we supposed there was no means of communication among flowers and trees."

"Let me think," said Chee-Chee, and he held his forehead tightly with both hands.

"No," he said after a while, "I don't recall my grandmother's speaking of things like that at all. I remember in her story of Otho Bludge, the prehistoric artist, that she told us about certain woods he used to make handles for his flint chisels and other tools and

## 16. MONKEY MEMORIES OF THE MOON

household implements. She described the wood, for instance, that he used to make bowls out of for carrying water in. But she never spoke of trees and plants that could talk."

It was about midday and we had halted for lunch on our excursion in search of the Whispering Vines we had been told of. We were not more than two or three hours' walk from our old base camp. But that, with the speed so easy in moon marching, means a much greater distance than it does on the Earth. From this camp where the Doctor had set up his apparatus for his special botanical studies, we had now for nearly a week been making daily expeditions in search of the various new species that the Vanity Lilies had described for us. But we always got back before nightfall. Well, this noon the Doctor was leaning back, munching a large piece of yellow yam—a vegetable we got from the edges of the jungle and which we had found so nourishing we had made it almost our chief article of diet.

"Tell me, Chee-Chee," said he, "what was the end of that story about Otho Bludge the prehistoric artist? It was a most fascinating tale."

"Well, I think I have told you," said Chee-Chee, "pretty nearly all there was to tell. In the Days Before

There Was a Moon, as Grandmother always began, Otho Bludge was a man alone, a man apart. Making pictures on horn and bone with a stone knife, that was his hobby. His great ambition was to make a picture of Man. But there was no one to draw from, for Otho Bludge was a man alone. One day, when he wished aloud for some one to make a picture from, he saw this beautiful girl—Pippiteepa was her name—kneeling on a rock waiting for him to make a portrait of her. He made it—the best work he ever did, carved into the flat of a reindeer's antler. About her right ankle she wore a string of blue stone beads. When the picture was finished she started to disappear again into the mountains' evening mist, as mysteriously as she had come. Otho called to her to stay. She was the only human being he had ever seen besides his own image in the pools. He wanted her company, poor Otho Bludge, the carver of horn, the man apart. But even as she passed into the twilight for ever she cried out to him that she could not stay—for she was of the Fairy Folk and not of his kin. He rushed to the rock where she had knelt; but all he found was the string of blue stone beads which she had worn about her ankle. Otho, broken-hearted, took them and bound them on his own wrist where he wore them night and day, hoping always that she would come back.

"There is nothing more. We youngsters used to pester my grandmother for a continuance of the tale. It seemed so sad, so unsatisfying, an ending. But the old lady insisted that that *was* the end. Not long after apparently Otho Bludge, the carver of horn and the man apart, just disappeared, completely, as though the Earth had swallowed him up."

"Humph!" muttered the Doctor. "Have you any idea when?"

"No," said the monkey. "You see, even my grandmother's ideas of time and place in these stories she told us were very hazy. She had only had them handed down to her by her parents and grandparents, just as she passed them on to us. But I am pretty sure it was around the time of the Great Flood. Grandmother used to divide her stories into two periods: those belonging to the Days Before There Was a Moon and those that happened after. The name of Otho Bludge the artist only came into those before."

"I see," said the Doctor thoughtfully. "But tell me: can you recall anything your grandmother said about the time of the change—I mean, when the one period left off and the other began?"

"Not a very great deal," said Chee-Chee. "It was the same when we questioned her about the Flood. That that event had taken place, there was no doubt; but, except for a few details, very little seemed to have been handed down as to how it came about, or of what was going on on the Earth at the time, or immediately after it. I imagine they were both great catastrophes—perhaps both came together—and such confusion fell upon all creatures that they were far too busy to take notes, and too scattered afterwards to keep a very clear picture in their minds. But I do remember that my grandmother said the first night when the Moon appeared in the sky some of our monkey ancestors saw a group of men kneeling on a mountain-top worshipping it. They had always been sun-worshippers and were now offering up prayers to the Moon also, saying it must be the Sun's Wife,"

"But," asked the Doctor, "did not Man know that the Moon must have flown off from the Earth?"

"That is not very clear," said Chee-Chee. "We often questioned my grandmother on this point. But there were certainly some awful big gaps in her information. It was like a history put together from odd bits that had been seen from different sides of the Earth and filled in by gossip and hearsay generations after. It seems that to begin with the confusion was terrible. Darkness covered the Earth, the noise of a terrible explosion followed and there was great loss of life. Then the sea rushed into the hole that had been made, causing more havoc and destruction still. Man and beast slunk into caves for shelter or ran wild across the mountains, or just lay down and covered their eyes to shut out the dreadful vision. From what Monkey History has to relate, none lived who had actually seen the thing take place. But that I have always doubted. And much later there was a regular war among mankind when human society had pulled itself together again sufficiently to get back to something like the old order."

"What was the war about?" asked the Doctor.

"Well, by that time," said Chee-Chee, "Man had multiplied considerably and there were big cities everywhere. The war was over the question: Was the Moon a goddess, or was she not? The old sun-worshippers said she was the wife or daughter of the Sun and was therefore entitled to adoration. Those who said the Moon had flown off from the flanks of the Earth had given up worshipping the Sun. They held that if the Earth had the power to shoot off another world like that, that *it* should be adored, as the Mother Earth from which we got everything, and not the Sun. They said it showed the Earth was the centre of all things, since the Sun had never shot off children. Then there were others who said that the Sun and the new Earth should be adored as gods—and yet others that wanted all three, Sun and Earth and Moon, to form a great triangle of Almighty Power. The war was a terrible one, men killing one another in thousands—greatly to the astonishment of the Monkey People. For to us it did not seem that any of the various parties really *knew* anything for certain about the whole business."

"Dear, dear," the Doctor muttered as Chee-Chee ended. "The first religious strife-the first of so many. What a pity! —Just as though it mattered to any one what his neighbour believed so long as he himself led a sincere and useful life and was happy!"

· 17 ·

# WE HEAR OF "THE COUNCIL"

This expedition on the trail of the Whispering Vines proved to be one of the most fruitful and satisfactory of all our excursions.

When we finally arrived at the home of this species, we found it a very beautiful place. It was a rocky gulch hard by the jungle, where a dense curtain of creepers hung down into a sort of pocket precipice with a spring-fed pool at the bottom. In such a place you could imagine fairies dancing in the dusk, wild beasts of the forest sheltering, or outlaws making their headquarters.

With a squawk Polynesia flew up and settled in the hanging tendrils that draped the rock wall. Instantly we saw a general wave of movement go through the vines and a whispering noise broke out which could be plainly heard by any ears. Evidently the vines were somewhat disturbed at this invasion by a bird they did not know. Polynesia, a little upset herself, flew back to us at once.

"Shiver my timbers!" said she in a disgruntled mutter. "This country would give a body the creeps. Those vines actually moved and squirmed like snakes when I took a hold of them."

"They are not used to you, Polynesia," laughed the Doctor. "You probably scared them to death. Let us see if we can get into conversation with them."

Here the Doctor's experience with the Singing Trees came in very helpfully. I noticed as I watched him go to work with what small apparatus he had brought with him that he now seemed much surer of how to begin. And it was indeed a surprisingly short time before he was actually in conversation with them, as though he had almost been talking with them all his life.

Presently he turned to me and spoke almost the thought that was in my mind.

"Stubbins," he said, "the ease with which these plants answer me would almost make me think *they have spoken with a man before*! Look, I can actually make responses with the lips, like ordinary human speech."

He dropped the little contrivance he held in his hands and hissing softly through his teeth he gave out a sort of whispered cadence. It was a curious combination between some one humming a tune and hissing a

## 17. WE HEAR OF "THE COUNCIL"   277

conversational sentence.

Usually it had taken John Dolittle some hours, occasionally some days, to establish a communication with these strange almost human moon trees good enough to exchange ideas with them. But both Chee-Chee and I grunted with astonishment at the way they instantly responded to his whispered speech. Swinging their leafy tendrils around to meet the breeze at a certain angle, they instantly gave back a humming, hissing message that might have been a repetition of that made by the Doctor himself.

"They say they are glad to see us, Stubbins," he jerked out over his shoulder.

"Why, Doctor," I said, "this is marvellous! You got results right away. I never saw anything like it."

"They have spoken with a man before," he repeated. "Not a doubt of it. I can tell by the way they— Good gracious, what's this?"

He turned and found Chee-Chee tugging at his left sleeve. I have never seen the poor monkey so overcome with fright. He stuttered and jibbered but no intelligible sounds came through his chattering teeth.

"Why, Chee-Chee!" said the Doctor. "What is it? —What's wrong?"

"Look!"—was all he finally managed to gulp.

He pointed down to the margin of the pond lying at the foot of the cliff. We had scaled up to a shelf of rock to get nearer to the vines for convenience. Where the monkey now pointed there was clearly visible in the yellow sand of the pool's beach two enormous footprints such as we had seen by the shores of the lake.

"*The Moon Man*!" the Doctor whispered.—"Well, I was sure of it—that these vines had spoken with a man before. I wonder—"

"Sh!" Polynesia interrupted. "Don't let them see you looking. But when you get a chance glance up towards the left-hand shoulder of the gulch."

Both the Doctor and I behaved as though we were proceeding with our business of conversing with the vines. Then pretending I was scratching my ear I looked up in the direction the parrot had indicated. There I saw several birds. They were trying to keep themselves hidden among the leaves. But there was no doubt that they were there on the watch.

As we turned back to our work an enormous shadow passed over us, shutting off the light of the sun. We looked up, fearing as any one would, some attack or danger from the air. Slowly a giant moth of the same kind that had brought us to this mysterious world sailed across the heavens and disappeared.

A general silence fell over us all that must have lasted a good three minutes.

"Well," said the Doctor at length, "if this means that the Animal Kingdom has decided finally to make our acquaintance, so much the better. Those are the first birds we have seen—and that was the first insect—since our moth left us. Curious, to find the bird life so much smaller than the insect. However, I suppose they will let us know more when they are ready. Meantime we have plenty to do here. Have you a note book, Stubbins?"

"Yes, Doctor," said I. "I'm quite prepared whenever you are."

Thereupon the Doctor proceeded with his conversation with the Whispering Vines and fired off questions and answers so fast that I was kept more than busy booking what he said.

It was indeed, as I have told you, by far the most satisfactory inquiry we had made into the life of the Moon, animal or vegetable, up to that time. Because while these vines had not the almost human appearance of the Vanity Lilies, they did seem to be in far closer touch with the general life of the Moon. The Doctor asked them about this warfare which we had heard of from the last plants we had visited—the struggle that occurred when one species of plant wished for more room and had to push away its intruding neighbours. And it was then for the first time we heard about the Council.

"Oh," said they, "you mustn't get the idea that one species of plant is allowed to make war for its own benefit regardless of the lives or rights of others. Oh, dear, no! We folk of the Moon have long since got past that. There was a day when we had constant strife, species against species, plants against plants, birds against insects, and so on. But not any more."

"Well, how do you manage?" asked the Doctor, "when two different species want the same thing?"

"It's all arranged by the Council," said the vines.

"Er—excuse me," said the Doctor. "I don't quite understand. What council?"

"Well, you see," said the vines, "some hundreds of years ago—that is, of course, well within the memory of most of us, we—"

"Excuse me again," the Doctor interrupted. "Do you mean that most of the plants and insects and birds here have been living several centuries already?"

"Why, certainly," said the Whispering Vines.

"Some, of course, are older than others. But here on the Moon we consider a plant or a bird or a moth quite young if he has seen no more than two hundred years. And there are several trees, and a few members of the Animal Kingdom too, whose memories go back to over a thousand years."

"You don't say!" murmured the Doctor. "I realized, of course, that your lives were much longer than ours on the Earth. But I had no idea you went as far back as that. Goodness me! —Well, please go on."

"In the old days, then, before we instituted the Council," the vines continued, "there was a terrible lot of waste and slaughter. They tell of one time when a species of big lizard overran the whole Moon. They grew so enormous that they ate up almost all the green stuff there was. No tree or bush or plant got a chance to bring itself to seeding-time because as soon as it put out a leaf it was gobbled up by those hungry brutes. Then the rest of us got together to see what we could do."

"Er—pardon," said the Doctor. "But how do you mean, got together? You plants could not move, could you?"

"Oh, no," said the vines. "We couldn't move, But we could communicate with the rest—take part in conferences, as it were, by means of messengers—birds and insects, you know."

"How long ago was that?" asked the Doctor.—"I mean, for how long has the animal and vegetable world here been able to communicate with one another?"

"Precisely," said the vines, "we can't tell you. Of course, some sort of communication goes back a perfectly enormous long way, some hundreds of thousands of years. But it was not always as good as it is now. It has been improving all the time. Nowadays it would be impossible for anything of any importance at all to happen in our corner of the Moon without its being passed along through plants and trees and insects and birds to every other corner of our globe within a few moments. For instance, we have known almost every movement you and your party have made since you landed in our world."

"Dear me!" muttered the Doctor. "I had no idea. However, please proceed."

"Of course," they went on, "it was not always so. But after the institution of the Council communication and co-operation became much better and continued to grow until it reached its present stage."

· 18 ·

# THE PRESIDENT

The Whispering Vines then went on to tell the Doctor in greater detail of that institution which they had vaguely spoken of already, "The Council." This was apparently a committee or general government made up of members from both the Animal and Vegetable Kingdoms. Its main purpose was to regulate life on the Moon in such a way that there should be no more warfare. For example, if a certain kind of shrub wanted more room for expansion, and the territory it wished to take over was already occupied by, we'll say, bullrushes, it was not allowed to thrust out its neighbour without first submitting the case to the Council. Or if a certain kind of butterfly wished to feed upon the honey of some flower and was interfered with by a species of bee or beetle, again the argument had to be put to the vote of this all-powerful committee before any action could be taken.

This information explained a great deal which had heretofore puzzled us.

"You see, Stubbins," said the Doctor, "the great size of almost all life here, the development of intelligence in plant forms, and much more besides, could not possibly have come about if this regulation had not been in force. Our world could learn a lot from the Moon, Stubbins—the Moon, its own child whom it presumes to despise! We have no balancing or real protection of life. With us it is, and has always been, 'dog eat dog.'"

The Doctor shook his head and gazed off into space to where the globe of our mother Earth glowed dimly. Just so had I often seen the Moon from Puddleby by daylight.

"Yes," he repeated, his manner becoming of a sudden deeply serious, "our world that thinks itself so far advanced has not the wisdom, the foresight, Stubbins, which we have seen here. Fighting, gighting, fighting, always fighting!—So it goes on down there with us.... The 'survival of the fittest'! ... I've spent my whole life trying to help the animal, the so-called lower, forms of life. I don't mean I am complaining. Far from it. I've had a very good time getting in touch with the beasts and winning their friendship. If I had my life over again I'd do just the same thing. But often, so often, I have felt that in the end it was bound to be a losing game. It is this thing here, this Council of Life—of life adjustment—that could have saved the day and brought happiness to all."

"Yes, Doctor," said I, "but listen: compared with our world, they have no animal life here at all, so far as we've seen. Only insets and birds. They've no lions or tigers who have to hunt for deer and wild goats to get a living, have they?"

"True, Stubbins—probably true," said he. "But don't forget that that same warfare of species against species goes on in the Insect Kingdom as well as among the larger carnivora. In another million years from now some scientist may show that the war going on between Man and the House Fly to-day is the most important thing in current history.—And besides, who shall say what kind of a creature the tiger was before he took to a diet of meat?"

John Dolittle then turned back to the vines and asked some further questions. These were mostly about the Council; how it worked; of what it was composed; how often it met, etc. And the answers that they gave filled out a picture which we had already half guessed and half seen of Life on the Moon.

When I come to describe it I find myself wishing that I were a great poet, or at all events a great writer. For this moon-world was indeed a land of wondrous rest. Trees that sang; flowers that could see; butterflies and bees that conversed with one another and with the plants on which they fed, watched over by a parent council that guarded the interests of great and small, strong and weak, alike—the whole community presented a world of peace, goodwill and happiness which no words of mine could convey a fair idea of.

"One thing I don't quite understand," said the Doctor to the vines, "is how you manage about seeding. Don't some of the plants throw down too much seed and bring forth a larger crop than is desirable?"

"That," said the Whispering Vines, "is taken care of by the birds. They have orders to eat up all the seed except a certain quantity for each species of plant."

"Humph!" said the Doctor. "I hope I have not upset things for the Council. I did a little experimental planting myself when I first arrived here. I had brought several kinds of seed with me from the Earth and I wanted to see how they would do in this climate. So far, however, the seeds have not come up at all."

The vines swayed slightly with a rustling sound that might easily have been a titter of amusement.

"You have forgotten, Doctor," said they, "that news travels fast in the Moon. Your gardening experiments were seen and immediately reported to the Council. And after you had gone back to your camp every single seed that you had planted was carefully dug up by long-billed birds and destroyed. The Council is awfully particular about seeds. It has to be. If we got overrun by any plant, weed or shrub, all of our peaceful balance would be upset and goodness knows what might happen. Why, the President—"

The particular vines which were doing the talking were three large ones that hung close by the Doctor's shoulder. In a very sudden and curious manner they had broken off in the middle of what they were saying like a person who had let something slip out in conversation which had been better left unsaid. Instantly a tremendous excitement was visible throughout all the creepers that hung around the gulch. You never saw such swaying, writhing, twisting and agitation. With squawks of alarm a number of brightly coloured birds fluttered out of the curtain of leaves and flew away over the rocky shoulders above our heads.

"What's the matter? —What has happened, Doctor?" I asked as still more birds left the concealment of the creepers and disappeared in the distance.

"I've no idea, Stubbins," said he. "Some one has said a little too much, I fancy. Tell me," he asked, turning to the vines again:"Who is the President?"

"The president of the Council," they replied after a pause.

"Yes, that I understand," said the Doctor. "But what, who, is he?"

For a little there was no answer, while the excitement and agitation broke out with renewed confusion among the long tendrils that draped the rocky alcove. Evidently some warnings and remarks were being exchanged which we were not to understand.

At last the original vines which had acted as spokesmen in the conversation addressed John Dolittle again.

"We are sorry," they said, "but we have our orders. Certain things we have been forbidden to tell you."

"Who forbade you?" asked the Doctor.

But from then on not a single word would they answer. The Doctor made several attempts to get them talking again but without success. Finally we were compelled to give it up and return to camp—which we reached very late.

"I think," said Polynesia, as the Doctor, Chee-Chee and I set about preparing the vegetarian supper, "that we sort of upset Society in the Moon this afternoon. Gracious, I never saw such a land in my life! —And I've seen a few. I suppose that by now every bumble bee and weed on the whole globe is talking about the Whispering Vines and the slip they made in mentioning the President. *President*! Shiver my timbers! You'd think he were St. Peter himself! What are they making such a mystery about, I'd like to know?"

"We'll probably learn pretty soon now," said the Doctor, cutting into a huge melon-like fruit. "I have a feeling that they won't think it worth while to hold aloof from us much longer.—I hope not anyway."

"Me too," said Chee-Chee. "Frankly, this secrecy is beginning to get under my skin. I'd like to feel assured that we are going to be given a passage back to Puddleby. For a while, anyway, I've had enough of adventure."

"Oh, well, don't worry," said the Doctor. "I still feel convinced that we'll be taken care of. Whoever it was that got us up here did so with some good intention.

When I have done what it is that's wanted of me, arrangements will be made for putting us back on the Earth, never fear."

"Humph!" grunted Polynesia, who was cracking nuts on a limb above our heads. "I hope you're right. I'm none too sure, myself—No, none too sure."

· 19 ·

# THE MOON MAN

That night was, I think, the most disturbed one that we spent in the whole course of our stay on the Moon. Not one of us slept soundly or continuously. For one thing, our growth had proceeded at an alarming and prodigious rate; and what bedding we had (we slept in that mild climate with the blankets under us instead of over us) had become absurdly short and insufficient for our new figures. Knees and elbows spilled over the sides and got dreadfully sore on the hard earth. But besides that discomfort, we were again conscious throughout the whole night of mysterious noises and presences. Every one of us seemed to be uneasy in his mind. I remember waking up one time and hearing the Doctor, Chee-Chee and Polynesia all talking in their sleep at the same time.

Hollow-eyed and unrested we finally, at daybreak, crawled out of our various roosts and turned silently to the business of getting breakfast. That veteran campaigner

Polynesia was the first to pull herself together. She came back from examining the ground about the camp with a very serious look on her old face.

"Well," said she, "if there's any one in the Moon who *hasn't* been messing round our bunks while we slept I'd like to know who it is."

"Why?" asked the Doctor. "Anything unusual?"

"Come and see," said the parrot, and led the way out into the clearing that surrounded our bunks and baggage.

Well, we were accustomed to finding tracks around our home, but this which Polynesia showed us was certainly something quite out of the ordinary. For a belt of a hundred yards or more about our headquarters the earth and sand and mud was a mass of footprints. Strange insect tracks, the marks of enormous birds, and—most evident of all—numberless prints of that gigantic human foot which we had seen before.

"Tut, tut!" said the Doctor peevishly. "They don't do us any harm anyway. What does it matter if they come and look at us in our sleep? I'm not greatly interested, Polynesia. Let us take breakfast. A few extra tracks don't make much difference."

We sat down and started the meal.

But John Dolittle's prophecy that the Animal Kingdom would not delay much longer in getting in touch with us was surprisingly and suddenly fulfilled. I had a piece of yam smeared with honey half-way to my mouth when I became conscious of an enormous shadow soaring over me. I looked up and there was the giant moth who had brought us from Puddleby; I could hardly believe my eyes. With a graceful sweep of his gigantic wings he settled down beside me—a battleship beside a mouse—as though such exact and accurate landings were no more than a part of the ordinary day's work.

We had no time to remark on the moth's arrival before two or three more of the same kind suddenly swept up from nowhere, fanned the dust all over us with their giant wings and settled down beside their brother.

Next, various birds appeared. Some species among these we had already seen in the vines. But there were many we had not: enormous storks, geese, swans and several others. Half of them seemed little bigger than their own kind on the Earth. But others were unbelievably large and were coloured and shaped somewhat differently— though you could nearly always tell to what family they belonged.

Again more than one of us opened his mouth to say

something and then closed it as some new and stranger arrival made its appearance and joined the gathering. The bees were the next. I remembered then seeing different kinds on the Earth, though I had never made a study of them. Here they all came trooping, magnified into great terrible-looking monsters out of a dream: the big black bumble bee, the little yellow bumble bee, the common honey bee, the bright green, fast-flying, slender bee. And with them came all their cousins and relatives, though there never seemed to be more than two or three specimens of each kind.

I could see that poor Chee-Chee was simply scared out of his wits. And little wonder! Insects of this size gathering silently about one were surely enough to appal the stoutest heart. Yet to me they were not entirely terrible. Perhaps I was merely taking my cue from the Doctor who was clearly more interested than alarmed. But besides that, the manner of the creatures did not appear unfriendly. Serious and orderly, they seemed to be gathering according to a set plan; and I felt sure that very soon something was going to happen which would explain it all.

And sure enough, a few moments later, when the ground about our camp was literally one solid mass of giant insects and birds, we heard a tread. Usually a footfall in the open air makes little or no sound at all—though it must not be forgotten that we had found that sound of any kind travelled much more readily on the Moon than on the Earth. But this was something quite peculiar. Actually it shook the ground under us in a way that might have meant an earthquake. Yet somehow one *knew* it was a tread.

Chee-Chee ran to the Doctor and hid under his coat. Polynesia never moved, just sat there on her tree-branch, looking rather peeved and impatient but evidently interested. I followed the direction of her gaze with my own eyes, for I knew that her instinct was always a good guide. I found that she was watching the woods that surrounded the clearing where we had established our camp. Her beady little eyes were fixed immovably on a V-shaped cleft in the horizon of trees away to my left.

It is curious how in those important moments I always seemed to keep an eye on old Polynesia. I don't mean to say that I did not follow the Doctor and stand ready to take his orders. But whenever anything unusual or puzzling like this came up, especially a case where animals were concerned, it was my impulse to keep an eye on the old parrot to see how she was taking it.

Now I saw her cocking her head on one side—in a quite characteristic pose—looking upward towards the cleft in the forest wall. She was muttering something beneath her breath (probably in Swedish, her favourite swearing language), but I could not make out more than a low peevish murmur. Presently, watching with her, I thought I saw the trees sway. Then something large and round seemed to come in view above them in the cleft.

It was now growing dusk. It had taken, we suddenly realized, a whole day for the creatures to gather; and in our absorbed interest we had not missed our meals. One could not be certain of his vision, I noticed the Doctor suddenly half rise, spilling poor old Chee-Chee out upon the ground. The big round thing above the tree-tops grew bigger and higher; it swayed gently as it came forward and with it the forest swayed also, as grass moves when a cat stalks through it.

Any minute I was expecting the Doctor to say something. The creature approaching, whatever—whoever—it was, must clearly be so monstrous that everything we had met with on the Moon so far would dwindle into insignificance in comparison.

And still old Polynesia sat motionless on her limb muttering and spluttering like a fire-cracker on a damp night.

Very soon we could hear other sounds from the oncoming creature besides his earth-shaking footfall. Giant trees snapped and crackled beneath his tread like twigs under a mortal's foot. I confess that an ominous terror clutched at my heart too now. I could sympathize with poor Chee-Chee's timidity. Oddly enough though at this, the most terrifying moment in all our experience on the Moon, the monkey did not try to conceal himself. He was standing beside the Doctor fascinatedly watching the great shadow towering above the trees.

Onward, nearer, came the lumbering figure. Soon there was no mistaking its shape. It had cleared the woods now. The gathered insects and waiting birds were making way for it. Suddenly we realized that it was towering over us, quite near, its long arms hanging at its sides. *It was human*.

We had seen the Moon Man at last!

"Well, for pity's sake!" squawked Polynesia, breaking the awed silence. "You may be a frightfully important person here. But my goodness! It has taken you an awfully long time to come and call on us!"

Serious as the occasion was in all conscience, Polynesia's remarks, continued in an uninterrupted stream of annoyed criticism, finally gave me the giggles. And after I once got started I couldn't have kept a straight face if I had been promised a fortune.

The dusk had now settled down over the strange assembly. Starlight glowed weirdly in the eyes of the moths and birds that stood about us, like a lamp's flame reflected in the eyes of a cat. As I made another effort to stifle my silly titters I saw John Dolittle, the size of his figure looking perfectly absurd in comparison with the Moon Man's, rise to meet the giant who had come to visit us.

"I am glad to meet you—at last," said he in dignified well-bred English. A curious grunt of incomprehension was all that met his civility.

Then seeing that the Moon Man evidently did not follow his language, John Dolittle set to work to find some tongue that would be understandable to him. I suppose there never was, and probably never will be, any one who had the command of languages that the Doctor had. One by one he ran through most of the earthly human tongues that are used to-day or have been preserved from the past. None of them had the slightest effect upon the Moon Man. Turning to animal languages however, the Doctor met with slightly better results. A word here and there seemed to be understood.

## 19. THE MOON MAN

But it was when John Dolittle fell back on the languages of the Insect and Vegetable Kingdoms that the Moon Man at last began to wake up and show interest. With fixed gaze Chee-Chee, Polynesia and I watched the two figures as they wrestled with the problems of common speech. Minute after minute went by, hour after hour. Finally the Doctor made a signal to me behind his back and I knew that now he was really ready. I picked up my note book and pencil from the ground.

As I laid back a page in preparation for dictation there came a strange cry from Chee-Chee.

"Look! —*The right wrist*! —Look!"

We peered through the twilight.... Yes, there *was* something around the giant's wrist, but so tight that it was almost buried in the flesh. The Doctor touched it gently. But before he could say anything Chee-Chee's voice broke out again, his words cutting the stillness in a curious, hoarse, sharp whisper.

"*The blue stone beads*! —Don't you see them?... They don't fit him any more since he's grown a giant. But he's Otho Bludge the artist. That's the bracelet he got from Pippiteepa the grandmother of the Fairies!: —It is he, Doctor, Otho Bludge, who was blown off the Earth in the *Days Before There Was a Moon*!"

· 20 ·

# THE DOCTOR AND
# THE GIANT

"All right, Chee-Chee, all right," said the Doctor hurriedly. "Wait now. We'll see what we can find out. Don't get excited."

In spite of the Doctor's reassuring words, I could see that he himself was by this time quite a little agitated. And for that no one could blame him. After weeks in this weird world where naught but extraordinary things came up day after day we had been constantly wondering when we'd see the strange Human whose traces and influence were everywhere so evident. Now at last he had appeared.

I gazed up at the gigantic figure rearing away into the skies above our heads. With one of his feet he could easily have crushed the lot of us like so many cockroaches. Yet he, with the rest of the gathering, seemed not unfriendly to us, if a bit puzzled by our size. As for John Dolittle, he may have been a little upset by Chee-Chee's announcement, but he certainly wasn't scared. He at once set to work to get into touch with this strange creature who had called on us. And, as was usual with his experiments of this kind, the other side seemed more than willing to help.

The giant wore very little clothes. A garment somewhat similar to our own, made from the flexible bark and leaves we had discovered in the forest, covered his middle from the arm-pits down to the lower thighs. His hair was long and shaggy, falling almost to his shoulders. The Doctor measured up to a line somewhere near his ankle-bone. Apparently realizing that it was difficult for John Dolittle to talk with him at that range, the giant made a movement with his hand and at once the insects nearest to us rose and crawled away. In the space thus cleared the man-monster sat down to converse with his visitors from the Earth.

It was curious that after this I too no longer feared the enormous creature who looked like something from a fairy-tale or a nightmare. Stretching down a tremendous hand, he lifted the Doctor, as though he had been a doll, and set him upon his bare knee. From this height—at least thirty feet above my head—John Dolittle clambered still further up the giant's frame till he stood upon his shoulder.

Here he apparently had much greater success in making himself understood than he had had lower down. By standing on tip-toe he could just reach the Moon Man's ear. Presently descending to the knee again, he began calling to me.

"Stubbins—I say, Stubbins! Have you got a notebook handy?"

"Yes, Doctor. In my pocket. Do you want me to take dictation?"

"Please," he shouted back—for all the world like a foreman yelling orders from a high building. "Get this down. I have hardly established communication yet, but I want you to book some preliminary notes. Are you ready?"

As a matter of fact, the Doctor in his enthusiasm had misjudged how easy he'd find it to converse with the Moon Man. For a good hour I stood waiting with my pencil poised and no words for dictation were handed down. Finally the Doctor called to me that he would have to delay matters a little till he got in close touch with our giant visitor.

"Humph!" grunted Polynesia. "I don't see why he bothers. I never saw such an unattractive enormous brute.—Doesn't look as though he had the wits of a caterpillar anyway. And to think that it was this great lump of unintelligent mutton that has kept the Doctor—John Dolittle, M.D.—and the rest of us, hanging about till it suited him to call on us! —After sending for us, mind you! That's the part that rattles me!"

"Oh, but goodness!" muttered Chee-Chee, peering up at the towering figure in the dusk. "Think—*think* how old he is! That man was living when the Moon separated from the Earth—thousands, maybe millions, of years ago! Golly, what an age!"

"Yes, he's old enough to know better," snapped the parrot—"better manners anyway. Just because he's fat and overgrown is no reason why he should treat his guests with such outrageous rudeness."

"Oh, but come now, Polynesia," I said, "we must not forget that this is a human being who has been separated from his own kind for centuries and centuries. And even such civilization as he knew on the Earth, way back in those Stone Age days, was not, I imagine, anything to boast of. Pretty crude, I'll bet it was, the world then. The wonder is, to my way of thinking, that he has any mind at all—with no other humans to mingle with through all that countless time. I'm not surprised that John Dolittle finds it difficult to talk with him."

"Oh, well now, Tommy Stubbins," said she, "that may sound all very scientific and high-falutin. But just the same there's no denying that this overgrown booby was the one who got us up here. And the least he could have done was to see that we were properly received and cared for—instead of letting us fish for ourselves with no one to guide us or to put us on to the ropes. Very poor hospitality, I call it."

"You seem to forget, Polynesia," I said mildly, "that in spite of our small size, we may have seemed—as the Doctor said—quite as fearful to him and his world as he and his have been to us—even if he did arrange to get us here. Did you notice that he limped?"

"I did," said she, tossing her head. "He dragged his left foot after him with an odd gait. Pshaw! I'll bet that's what he got the Doctor up here for—rheumatism or a splinter in his toe. Still, what I *don't* understand is how he heard of John Dolittle, famous though he is, with no communication between his world and ours."

It was very interesting to me to watch the Doctor trying to talk with the Moon Man. I could not make the wildest guess at what sort of language it could be that they would finally hit upon. After all that time of separation from his fellows, how much could this strange

## 20. THE DOCTOR AND THE GIANT

creature remember of a mother tongue?

As a matter of fact, I did not find out that evening at all. The Doctor kept at his experiments, in his usual way, entirely forgetful of time or anything else. After I had watched for a while Chee-Chee's head nodding sleepily I finally dozed off myself.

When I awoke it was daylight. The Doctor was still engaged with the giant in his struggles to understand and be understood. However, I could see at once that he was encouraged. I shouted up to him that it was breakfast-time. He heard, nodded back to me and then apparently asked the giant to join us at our meal. I was surprised and delighted to see with what ease he managed to convey this idea to our big friend. For the Moon Man at once sat him down upon the ground near our tarpaulin which served as a table-cloth and gazed critically over the foodstuffs laid out. We offered him some of our famous yellow yam. At this he shook his head vigorously. Then with signs and grunts he proceeded to explain something to John Dolittle.

"He tells me, Stubbins," said the Doctor presently, "that the yellow yam is the principal cause of rapid growth. Everything in this world, it seems, tends towards size; but this particular food is the worst. He advises us to drop it—unless we want to grow as big as he is. He has been trying to get back to our size, apparently, for ever so long."

"Try him with some of the melon, Doctor," said Chee-Chee.

This, when offered to the Moon Man, was accepted gladly; and for a little we all munched in silence.

"How are you getting on with his language, Doctor?" I asked presently.

"Oh, so so," he grumbled. "It's odd—awfully strange. At first I supposed it would be something like most human languages, a variation of vocal sounds. And I tried for hours to get in touch with him along those lines. But it was only a few vague far-off memories that I could bring out. I was, of course, particularly interested to link up a connection with some earthly language. Finally I went on to the languages of the insects and the plants and found that he spoke all dialects, in both, perfectly. On the whole I am awfully pleased with my experiments. Even if I cannot link him up with some of our own dead languages, at least his superior knowledge of the insect and vegetable tongues will be of great value to me."

"Has he said anything so far about why he got you

up here?" asked Polynesia.

"Not as yet," said the Doctor. "But we've only just begun, you know. All in good time, Polynesia, all in good time."

· 21 ·
# HOW OTHO BLUDGE CAME TO THE MOON

The Doctor's warning to the parrot that perhaps we were just as terrifying to the Moon Man (in spite of his size) as he and his world were to us, proved to be quite true. After breakfast was over and I got out the usual note book for dictation it soon appeared that this giant, the dread President of the Council, was the mildest creature living. He let us crawl all over him and seemed quite pleased that we took so much interest in him. This did not appear to surprise the Doctor, who from the start had regarded him as a friend. But to Chee-Chee and myself, who had thought that he might gobble us up at any moment, it was, to say the least, a great relief. I will not set down here in detail that first talk between the Moon Man and the Doctor. It was very long and went into a great many matters of languages and natural history that might not be of great interest to the general reader. But here and there in my report of that conversation I may dictate it word for word, where such a course may seem necessary to give a clear picture of the ideas exchanged. For it was certainly an interview of great importance.

The Doctor began by questioning the giant on the history that Chee-Chee had told us as it had been handed down to him by his grandmother. Here the Moon Man's memory seemed very vague; but when prompted with details from the Monkeys' History, he occasionally responded and more than once agreed with the Doctor's statements or corrected them with a good deal of certainty and firmness.

I think I ought perhaps to say something here about the Moon Man's face. In the pale daylight of a lunar dawn it looked clever and intelligent enough, but not nearly so old as one would have expected. It is indeed hard to describe that face. It wasn't brutish and yet it had in it something quite foreign to the average human countenance as seen on the Earth. I imagine that his being separated from human kind for so long may have accounted for this. Beyond question it was an animal-like countenance and yet it was entirely free from anything like ferocity. If one could imagine a kindly animal who had used all his faculties in the furtherance of helpful and charitable ends one would have the nearest possible idea of the face of the Moon Man, as I saw it clearly for the first time when he took breakfast with us that morning.

In the strange tongues of insects and plants John Dolittle fired off question after question at our giant guest. Yes, he admitted, he probably was Otho Bludge, the prehistoric artist. This bracelet? —Yes, he wore it because some one... And then his memory failed him.... What some one?... Well anyway he remembered that it had first been worn by a woman before he had it. What matter, after all? It was long ago, terribly long. Was there anything else that we would like to know?

There was a question I myself wanted to ask. The night before, in my wanderings with Chee-Chee over the giant's huge body, I had discovered a disc or plate hanging to his belt. In the dusk then I had not been able to make out what it was. But this morning I got a better view of it: the most exquisite picture of a girl kneeling with a bow and arrow in her hands, carved upon a plate of reindeer horn. I asked the Doctor did he not want to question the Moon Man about it. We all guessed, of course, from Chee-Chee's story, what it was. But I thought it might prompt the giant's memory to things out of the past that would be of value to the Doctor. I even whispered to John Dolittle that the giant might be

## 21. HOW OTHO BLUDGE CAME TO THE MOON

persuaded to give it to us or barter it for something. Even I knew enough about museum relics to realize its tremendous value.

The Doctor indeed did speak of it to him. The giant raised it from his belt, where it hung by a slender thong of bark and gazed at it a while. A spark of recollection lit up his eyes for a moment Then, with a pathetic fumbling sort of gesture, he pressed it to his heart a moment while that odd fuddled look came over his countenance once more. The Doctor and I, I think, both felt we had been rather tactless and did not touch upon the subject again.

I have often been since—though I certainly was not at the time—amused at the way the Doctor took charge of the situation and raced all over this enormous creature as though he were some new kind of specimen to be labelled and docketed for a natural history museum. Yet he did it in such a way as not to give the slightest offence.

"Yes. Very good," said he. "We have now established you as Otho Bludge, the Stone Age artist, who was blown off the Earth when the Moon set herself up in the sky. But how about this Council? I understand you are president of it and can control its workings. Is that so?"

The great giant swung his enormous head round and

regarded for a moment the pigmy figure of the Doctor standing, just then, on his forearm.

"The Council?" said he dreamily. "Oh, ah, yes, to be sure, the Council.... Well, we had to establish that, you know. At one time it was nothing but war—war, war all the time. We saw that if we did not arrange a balance we would have an awful mess. Too many seeds. Plants spread like everything. Birds laid too many eggs. Bees swarmed too often. Terrible! —You've seen that down there on the Earth, I imagine, have you not?"

"Yes, yes, to be sure," said the Doctor. "Go on, please."

"Well, there isn't much more to that. We just made sure, by means of the Council, that there should be *no more warfare*"

"Humph!" the Doctor grunted. "But tell me: how is it you yourself have lived so long? No one knows how many years ago it is that the Moon broke away from the Earth. And your age, compared with the life of Man in our world, must be something staggering."

"Well, of course," said the Moon Man, "just how I got here is something that I have never been able to explain completely, even to myself. But why bother? Here I am. What recollections I have of that time are

## 21. HOW OTHO BLUDGE CAME TO THE MOON 313

awfully hazy. Let me see: when I came to myself I could hardly breathe. I remember that. The air—everything—was so different. But I was determined to survive. That, I think, is what must have saved me. I was *determined* to survive. This piece of land, I recollect, when it stopped swirling, was pretty barren. But it had the remnants of trees and plants which it had brought with it from the Earth. I lived on roots and all manner of stuff to begin with. Many a time I thought that I would have to perish. But I didn't—*because I was determined to survive*. And in the end I did. After a while plants began to grow; insects, which had come with the plants, flourished. Birds the same way—they, like me, were determined to survive. A new world was formed. Years after I realized that I was the one to steer and guide its destiny since I had—at that time anyway—more intelligence than the other forms of life. I saw what this fighting of kind against kind must lead to. So I formed the Council. Since then—oh, dear, how long ago! —vegetable and animal species have come to—Well, you see it here.... That's all. It's quite simple."

"Yes, yes," said the Doctor hurriedly. "I quite understand that—the necessities that led you to establish the Council.—And an exceedingly fine thing it is, in my opinion. We will come back to that later. In the meantime I am greatly puzzled as to how you came to hear of me—with no communication between your world and ours. Your moth came to Puddleby and asked me to accompany him back here. It was you who sent him, I presume?"

"Well, it was I and the Council who sent him," the Moon Man corrected. "As for the ways in which your reputation reached us, communication is, as you say, very rare between the two worlds. But it does occur once in a long while. Some disturbance takes place in your globe that throws particles so high that they get beyond the influence of earth gravity and come under the influence of our gravity. Then they are drawn to the Moon and stay here. I remember,' many centuries ago, a great whirlwind or some other form of rumpus in your world occurred which tossed shrubs and stones to such a height that they lost touch with the Earth altogether and finally landed here. And a great nuisance they were too. The shrubs seeded and spread like wildfire before we realized they had arrived and we had a terrible time getting them under control."

"That is most interesting," said the Doctor, glancing in my direction, as he translated, to make sure I

21. HOW OTHO BLUDGE CAME TO THE MOON    315

got the notes down in my book. "But please tell me of the occasion by which you first learned of me and decided you wanted me up here."

"That," said the Moon Man, "came about through something which was, I imagine, a volcanic eruption. From what I can make out, one of your big mountains down there suddenly blew its head off, after remaining quiet and peaceful for many years. It was an enormous and terribly powerful explosion and tons of earth and trees and stuff were fired off into space. Some of this material that started away in the direction of the Moon finally came within the influence of our attraction and was drawn to us. And, as you doubtless know, when earth or plants are shot away some animal life nearly always goes with it. In this case a bird, a kingfisher, in fact, who was building her nest in the banks of a mountain lake, was carried off. Several pieces of the earth landed on the Moon. Some, striking land, were smashed to dust and any animal life they carried—mostly insect of course—was destroyed. But the piece on which the kingfisher travelled fell into one of our lakes."

It was an astounding story and yet I believe it true. For how else could the Doctor's fame have reached the Moon? Of course any but a water bird would have been drowned because apparently the mass plunged down fifty feet below the surface, but the kingfisher at once came up and flew off for the shore. It was a marvel that she was alive. I imagine her trip through the dead belt had been made at such tremendous speed that she managed to escape suffocation without the artificial breathing devices which we had been compelled to use.

· 22 ·
# HOW THE MOON FOLK HEARD OF DOCTOR DOLITTLE

The bird the Moon Man had spoken of (it seems he had since been elected to the Council) was presently brought forward and introduced to the Doctor. He gave us some valuable information about his trip to the Moon and how he had since adapted himself to new conditions.

He admitted it was he who had told the Moon Folk about John Dolittle and his wonderful skill in treating sicknesses, of his great reputation among the birds, beasts and fishes of the Earth.

It was through this introduction also that we learned that the gathering about us was nothing less than a full assembly of the Council itself—with the exception, of course, of the Vegetable Kingdom, who could not come. That community was however represented by different creatures from the Insect and Bird Worlds who were there to see to it that its interests were properly looked after.

This was evidently a big day for the Moon People. After our interview with the kingfisher we could see that arguments were going on between different groups and parties all over the place. At times it looked like a political meeting of the rowdiest kind. These discussions the Doctor finally put down quite firmly by demanding of the Moon Man in a loud voice the reason for his being summoned here.

"After all," said he when some measure of quiet had been restored, "you must realize that I am a very busy man. I appreciate it as a great honour that I have been asked to come here. But I have duties and obligations to perform on the Earth which I have left. I presume that you asked me here for some special purpose. Won't you please let me know what it is?"

A silent pause spread over the chattering assembly. I glanced round the queer audience of birds and bugs who squatted, listening. The Doctor, quite apart from his demand for attention, had evidently touched upon a ticklish subject. Even the Moon Man himself seemed somewhat ill at ease.

"Well," he said at last, "the truth is we were sorely in need of a good physician. I myself have been plagued

## 22. HOW THE MOON FOLK HEARD OF DOCTOR DOLITTLE

by a bad pain in the foot. And then many of the bigger insects—the grasshoppers especially—have been in very poor health now for some time. From what the kingfisher told me, I felt you were the only one who could help us—that you—er—perhaps wouldn't mind if we got you up here where your skill was so sorely needed. Tell me now: you were not put out by the confidence we placed in you? We had no one in our own world who could help us. Therefore we agreed, in a special meeting of the Council, to send down and try to get you."

The Doctor made no reply.

"You must realize," the Moon Man went on, his voice dropping to a still more apologetic tone, "that this moth we sent took his life in his hand. We cast lots among the larger birds, moths, butterflies and other insects. It had to be one of our larger kinds. It was a long trip, requiring enormous staying power...."

The Moon Man spread out his giant hands in protest—a gesture very suggestive of the other world from which he originally came. The Doctor hastened to reassure him.

"Why, of course, of course," said he. "I—we— were most glad to come. In spite of the fact that I am always terribly busy down there, this was something so new and promising in natural history I laid every interest aside in my eagerness to get here. With the moth you sent the difficulty of language did not permit me to make the preparations I would have liked. But pray do not think that I have regretted coming. I would not have missed this experience for worlds. It is true I could have wished that you had seen your way to getting in touch with us sooner. But there—I imagine you too have your difficulties. I suppose you must be kept pretty busy."

"Busy?" said the Moon Man blankly. "Oh, no. I'm not busy. Life is very quiet and pleasant here.— Sometimes too quiet, we think. A session with the Council every now and then and a general inspection of the globe every so often: that is all I have to bother with. The reason I didn't come and see you sooner, to be quite honest, was because I was a bit scared. It was something so new, having human folks visit you from another world. There was no telling what you might turn out to be—what you might do. For another thing, I expected you to be alone. For weeks past I have had the birds and insects—and the plants too—send me reports of your movements and character. You see, I had relied solely on the statements of a kingfisher. No matter how kind and

## 22. HOW THE MOON FOLK HEARD OF DOCTOR DOLITTLE

helpful you had been to the creatures of your own world, it did not follow that you would be the same way inclined towards the Moon Folk. I am sorry if I did not appear properly hospitable. But you must make allowances. It—it was all so—so new."

"Oh, quite, quite," said the Doctor, again most anxious to make his host feel at ease. "Say no more, please, of that. I understand perfectly. There are a few points, however, on which I would like to have some light thrown. For one thing, we thought we saw smoke on the Moon, from Puddleby, shortly after your moth arrived. Can you tell us anything about that?"

"Why, of course," said the Moon Man quickly. "I did that. We were quite worried about the moth. As I told you, we felt kind of guilty about the risky job we had given him. It was Jamaro who finally drew the marked card in the lottery."

"Jamaro!" muttered the Doctor, slightly bewildered—"Lottery? —I—er—"

"The lottery to decide who should go," the Moon Man explained. "I told you: we drew lots. Jamaro Bumblelily was the moth who drew the ticket which gave the task to him."

"Oh, I see," said the Doctor—"Jamaro. Yes, yes.

You give your insects names in this land. Very natural and proper of course, where they are so large and take such an important part in the life and government of the community. You can no doubt tell all these insects one from another, even when they belong to the same species?"

"Certainly," said the Moon Man. "We have, I suppose, several hundreds of thousands of bees in the Moon. But I know each one by his first name, as well as his swarm, or family, name. Anyhow, to continue: it was then Jamaro Bumblelily who drew the ticket that gave him the job of going to the Earth after you. He was very sportsmanlike and never grumbled a bit. But we were naturally anxious. It is true that creatures had come, at rare intervals, from the Earth to our world. But so far none had gone from us to the Earth. We had only the vaguest idea of what your world would be like—from the descriptions of the kingfisher. And even in getting those we had been greatly handicapped by language. It had only been after days and weeks of work that we had been able to understand one another in the roughest way. So we had arranged with Jamaro Bumblelily that as soon as he landed he was to try and find some way to signal us to let us know he was all right. And we were to signal

## 22. HOW THE MOON FOLK HEARD OF DOCTOR DOLITTLE

back to him. It seems he made a bad landing and lay helpless in your garden for some days. For a long while we waited in great anxiety. We feared he must have perished in his heroic exploit. Then we thought that maybe if we signalled to him he would be encouraged and know that we were still expecting his return. So we set off the smoke smudge."

"Yes," said the Doctor. "I saw it, even if Jamaro didn't. But tell me: how did you manage to raise such an enormous smudge? It must have been as big as a mountain."

"True," said the Moon Man. "For twenty days before Jamaro's departure I and most of the larger birds and insects had gathered the Jing-jing bark from the forest."

"Gathered the *what*?" asked the Doctor.

"The Jing-jing bark," the Moon Man repeated. "It is a highly explosive bark from a certain tree we have here."

"But how did you light it?" asked the Doctor.

"By friction," said the Moon Man—"drilling a hard-wood stick into a soft-wood log. We had tons and tons of the bark piled in a barren rocky valley where it would be safe from firing the bush or jungle. We are always terrified of bush-fires here—our world is not large, you know. I set the pile off with a live ember which I carried on a slate. Then I sprang back behind a rock bluff to defend my eyes. The explosion was terrific and the smoke kept us all coughing for days before it finally cleared away."

· 23 ·

# THE MAN WHO MADE HIMSELF A KING

We were frequently reminded during this long conversation (it lasted over a full day and a half) that the strange crowd about us was the great Council itself. Questions every now and then were hurled at the Moon Man from the dimness of the rear. He was continually turning his head as messages and inquiries were carried across to him from mouth to mouth. Sometimes without consulting the Doctor further he would answer them himself in queer sounds and signs. It was quite evident that the Council was determined to keep in touch with any negotiations that were going on.

As for John Dolittle, there was so much that he wanted to find out it looked—in spite of his hurry to get back to the Earth—as though his queries would never end—which, in a first meeting between two worlds, is not after all to be wondered at.

"Can you remember," he asked, "when you first

felt the Moon steadying herself, how you got accustomed to the new conditions? We had on our arrival a perfectly terrible time, you know. Different air, different gravity, different hearing and the rest. Tell me: how did you manage?"

Frowning, the Moon Man passed his gigantic hand across his brow.

"Really—it's so long ago," he muttered. "As I told you, I nearly died, many times. Getting enough food to stay alive on kept me busy the first few months. Then when I was sure that that problem was solved I began to watch. Soon I saw that the birds and insects were faced with the same difficulties as I was. I searched the Moon globe from end to end. There were no others of my own kind here. I was the only man. I needed company badly. 'All right,' I said, 'I'll study the Insect and Bird Kingdoms.' The birds adapted themselves much quicker than I did to the new conditions. I soon found that they, being in the same boat as myself, were only too glad to co-operate with me in anything that would contribute to our common good. Of course I was careful to kill nothing. For one thing I had no desire to; and for another I realized that if, on such a little globe, I started to make enemies, I could not last long. From the beginning I had done my best to live and let live. With no other human to talk with I can't tell you how terribly, desperately lonely I felt. Then I decided I'd try to learn the language of the birds. Clearly they had a language. No one could listen to their warblings and not see that. For years I worked at it—often terribly discouraged at my poor progress. Finally—don't ask me when—I got to the point where I could whistle short conversations with them. Then came the insects—the birds helped me in that too. Then the plant languages. The bees started me. They knew all the dialects. And ... well ..."

"Go on," said the Doctor. The tone of his voice was calm and quiet, but I could see that he was deeply, intensely interested.

"Oh, dear me," sighed the Moon Man, almost petulantly, "my memory, you know, for dates as far back as that, is awfully poor. To-day it seems as though I had talked Heron and Geranium all my life. But just when it was, actually, that I reached the point where I could converse freely with the insects and plants, I couldn't give you the vaguest idea. I do know that it took me far, far longer to get in touch with the vegetable forms of life than it did with either the insects or the birds. I am afraid that our keeping count of time throughout has been pretty sketchy—certainly in our earlier history anyway. But then you must remember we were occupied with a great number of far more serious tasks. Recently—the last thousand years or so—we have been making an effort to keep a history and we can show you, I think, a pretty good record of most of the more important events within that time. The trouble is that nearly all of the dates you want are earlier than that."

"Well, never mind," said the Doctor. "We are getting on very well under the circumstances. I would like very much to see that record you speak of and will ask you to show it to me, if you will be so good, later."

He then entered into a long examination of the Moon Man (carefully avoiding all dates, periods and references to time) on a whole host of subjects. The majority of them were concerned with insect and plant evolution and he kept a strict eye on me to see that all questions and replies were jotted down in the note book. Gracious! What an unending list it seemed to my tired mind! How had the Moon Man first realized that the plants were anxious to talk and co-operate with him? What had led him to believe that the bees were in communication with the flowers they fed on? Which fruits and vegetables had he found were good for human food and how had he discovered their nutritious qualities without poisoning himself? etc., etc., etc. It went on for hours. I got most of it down, with very few mistakes, I think. But I know I was more than half asleep during the last hours of the interview.

The only trouble with most of it was this same old bugbear of time. After all these ages of living without human company the poor giant's mind had got to the point where it simply didn't *use* time. Even in this record of the last thousand years, which he had proudly told us was properly dated, we found, when he showed it to us, that an error of a century more or less meant very little.

This history had been carved in pictures and signs on the face of a wide flat rock. The workmanship of Otho the prehistoric artist showed up here to great advantage. While the carvings were not by any means to be compared with his masterpiece of the kneeling girl, they nevertheless had a dash and beauty of design that would arrest the attention of almost any one.

Nevertheless, despite the errors of time, both in his recollections and his graven history, we got down the best booking that we could in the circumstances. And with all its slips and gaps it was a most thrilling and exciting document. It was the story of a new world's evolution; of how a man, suddenly transported into space with nothing but what his two hands held at the moment of the catastrophe, had made himself the kindly monarch of a kingdom—a kingdom more wondrous than the wildest imaginings of the mortals he had left behind. For he was indeed a king, even if he called himself no more than the President of the Council. And what hardships and terrible difficulties he had overcome in doing it, only we could realize—we, who had come here with advantages and aids which he had never known.

Finally a lull did come in this long, long conversation between the Doctor and the Moon Man. And while I lay back and stretched my right hand, cramped from constant writing, Polynesia gave vent to a great deal which she had evidently had on her mind for some time.

"Well," she grunted, lifting her eyebrows, "what did I tell you, Tommy? Rheumatism! That's what the Doctor has come all this way for—*rheumatism*! I wouldn't mind it so much in the case of the Moon Man himself. Because he certainly is a man in a hundred. But *grasshoppers*! Think of it! —Think of bringing John Dolittle, M.D., billions of miles" (Polynesia's ideas on geographical measurement were a bit sketchy) "just to wait on a bunch of grasshoppers! I—"

But the remainder of her indignant speech got mixed up with some of her favourite Swedish swear words and the result was something that no one could make head or tail of.

Very soon this pause in the conversation between the Doctor and the Moon Man was filled up by a great deal of talking among the Council. Every member of that important parliament apparently wanted to know exactly what had been said and decided on and what new measures—if any—were to be put in force. We could see that the poor President was being kept very busy.

At length the Doctor turned once more to the giant and said:

"Well now, when would it be convenient for you and the insect patients to be examined? I shall be most happy to do everything possible for you all, but you must realize that I would like to get back to the Earth as soon as I conveniently can."

Before answering the Moon Man proceeded to consult his Council behind him. And, to judge from the length of the discussions that followed, he was meeting with quite a little criticism in whatever plans he was proposing. But finally he managed to quiet them; and addressing John Dolittle once more, he said:

"Thank you. If it will not inconvenience you, we will come to-morrow and have you minister to us. You have been very kind to come at all. I hope we will not seem too large an undertaking for you. At least, since you have approved of our system and government here, you will have the satisfaction of knowing that you are assisting us in a time of great need."

"Why, of course, of course," said the Doctor at once. "I shall be only too glad. That is what I am for, after all. I am a doctor, you know, a physician—even if I have become a naturalist in my later years. At what hour will you be ready for me?"

"At dawn," said the Moon Man. Even in these modern days ideas of time on the Moon seemed strangely simple. "We will wait on you at sunrise. Till then, pleasant dreams and good rest!"

· 24 ·

# DOCTOR DOLITTLE OPENS HIS SURGERY ON THE MOON

Even the garrulous Polynesia was too tired to talk much more that night. For all of us it had been a long and steady session, that interview, tense with excitement. The Moon Man and his Council had barely departed before every one of us was dozing off without a change of clothes or a bite to eat. I am sure that nothing on Earth—or Moon—could have disturbed our slumbers.

The daylight was just beginning to show when we were awakened. I am not certain who was the first to arouse himself (probably John Dolittle), but I do know that I was the first to get up.

What a strange sight! In the dim light hundreds, perhaps thousands, of gigantic insects, all invalids, stood about our camp staring at the tiny human physician who had come so far to cure their ailments. Some of these creatures we had not so far seen and never even suspected their presence on the Moon: caterpillars as long as a village street with gout in a dozen feet; immense beetles suffering from an affliction of the eyes; grasshoppers as tall as a three-storey house with crude bandages on their gawky joints; enormous birds with a wing held painfully in an odd position. The Doctor's home had become once more a clinic; and all the halt and lame of Moon Society had gathered at his door.

The great man, when I finally roused him, swallowed two or three gulps of melon, washed them down with a draft of honey and water, took off his coat and set to work.

Of course the poor little black bag, which had done such yeoman service for many years in many lands, was not equal to a demand like this. The first thing to run out was the supply of bandages. Chee-Chee and I tore up blankets and shirts to make more. Then the embrocation became exhausted; next the iodine and the rest of the antiseptics. But in his botanical studies of the trees and plants of this world the Doctor had observed and experimented with several things which he had found helpful in rheumatic conditions and other medical uses. Chee-Chee and Polynesia were despatched at once to find the herbs and roots and leaves that he wanted.

## 24. DOCTOR DOLITTLE OPENS HIS SURGERY ON THE MOON

For hours and hours he worked like a slave. It seemed as though the end of the line of patients would never be reached. But finally he did get the last of them fixed up and despatched. It was only then he realized that the Moon Man had let all the other sufferers come forward ahead of himself. Dusk was coming on. The Doctor peered round the great space about our camp. It was empty, save for a giant figure that squatted silent, motionless and alone, by the forest's edge.

"My goodness!" muttered the Doctor. "I had entirely forgotten him. And he never uttered a word. Well, no one can say he is selfish. That, I fancy, is why he rules here. I must see what is the matter with him at once."

John Dolittle hurried across the open space and questioned the giant. An enormous left leg was stretched out for his examination. Like a fly, the Doctor travelled rapidly up and down it, pinching and squeezing and testing here and there.

"More gout," he said at last with definite decision. "A bad enough case too. Now listen, Otho Bludge."

Then he lectured his big friend for a long time. Mostly it seemed about diet, but there was a great deal concerning anatomy, exercise, dropsy, and *starch* in it too.

At the end of it the Moon Man seemed quite a little impressed, much happier in his mind and a great deal more lively and hopeful. Finally, after thanking the Doctor at great length, he departed, while the ground shook again beneath his limping tread.

Once more we were all fagged out and desperately sleepy.

"Well," said the Doctor as he arranged his one remaining blanket on his bed, "I think that's about all we can do. To-morrow—or maybe the next day—we will, if all goes well, start back for Puddleby."

"*Sh*!" whispered Polynesia. "There's some one listening. I'm sure—over there behind those trees."

"Oh, pshaw!" said the Doctor. "No one could hear us at that range."

"Don't forget how sound travels on the Moon," warned the parrot.

"But my goodness!" said the Doctor. "They *know* we've got to go some time. We can't stay here for ever. Didn't I tell the President himself I had jobs to attend to on the Earth? If I felt they needed me badly enough I wouldn't mind staying quite a while yet. But there's Stubbins here. He came away without even telling his

## 24. DOCTOR DOLITTLE OPENS HIS SURGERY ON THE MOON

parents where he was going or how long it might be before he returned. I don't know what Jacob Stubbins may be thinking, or his good wife. Probably worried to death. I—"

"Sh! —*Sh*! —Will you be quiet?" whispered Polynesia again. "Didn't you hear that? I tell you there's some one listening—or I'm a Double Dutchman. Pipe down, for pity's sake. There are ears all round us. Go to sleep!"

We all took the old parrot's advice—only too willingly. And very soon every one of us was snoring.

This time we did not awaken early. We had no jobs to attend to and we took advantage of a chance to snooze away as long as we wished.

It was nearly midday again when we finally got stirring. We were in need of water for breakfast. Getting the water had always been Chee-Chee's job. This morning, however, the Doctor wanted him to hunt up a further supply of medicinal plants for his surgical work. I volunteered therefore to act as water-carrier.

With several vessels which we had made from gourds I started out for the forests.

I had once or twice performed this same office of emergency water-carrier before. I was therefore able on reaching the edge of the jungle to make straight for the place where we usually got our supplies.

I hadn't gone very far before Polynesia overtook me.

"Watch out, Tommy!" said she, in a mysterious whisper as she settled on my shoulder.

"Why?" I asked. "Is anything amiss?"

"I don't quite know," said she. "But I'm uneasy and I wanted to warn you. Listen: that whole crowd that came to be doctored yesterday, you know? Well, not one of them has shown up again since. Why?"

There was a pause.

"Well," said I presently, "I don't see any particular reason why they should. They got their medicine, their treatment. Why should they pester the Doctor further? It's a jolly good thing that some patients leave him alone after they are treated, isn't it?"

"True, true," said she. "Just the same their all staying away the next day looks fishy to me. They didn't *all* get treated. There's something in it. I feel it in my bones. And besides, I can't find the Moon Man himself. I've been hunting everywhere for him. He too has gone into hiding again, just the same as they all did when we first arrived here.... Well, look out! That's all. I must go back now. But keep your eyes open, Tommy. Good

## 24. DOCTOR DOLITTLE OPENS HIS SURGERY ON THE MOON

luck!"

I couldn't make head or tail of the parrot's warning and, greatly puzzled, I proceeded on my way to the pool to fill my water-pots.

There I found the Moon Man. It was a strange and sudden meeting. I had no warning of his presence till I was actually standing in the water filling the gourds. Then a movement of one of his feet revealed his immense form squatting in the concealment of the dense jungle. He rose to his feet as soon as he saw that I perceived him.

His expression was not unfriendly—just as usual, a kindly, calm half-smile. Yet I felt at once uneasy and a little terrified. Lame as he was, his speed and size made escape by running out of the question. He did not understand my language, nor I his. It was a lonely spot, deep in the woods. No cry for help would be likely to reach the Doctor's ears.

I was not left long in doubt as to his intentions. Stretching out his immense right hand, he lifted me out of the water as though I were a specimen of some flower he wanted for a collection. Then with enormous strides he carried me away through the forest. One step of his was half-an-hour's journey for me. And yet it seemed as though he put his feet down very softly, presumably in order that his usual thunderous tread should not be heard—or felt—by others.

At length he stopped. He had reached a wide clearing. Jamaro Bumblelily, the same moth that had brought us from the Earth, was waiting. The Moon Man set me down upon the giant insect's back. I heard the low rumble of his voice as he gave some final orders. I had been kidnapped.

## · 25 ·
# PUDDLEBY ONCE MORE

Never have I felt so utterly helpless in my life. While he spoke with the moth the giant held me down with his huge hand upon the insect's back. A cry, I thought, might still be worth attempting. I opened my mouth and bawled as hard as I could. Instantly the Moon Man's thumb came round and covered my face. He ceased speaking.

Soon I could feel from the stirring of the insect's legs that he was getting ready to fly. The Doctor could not reach me now in time even if he had heard my cry. The giant removed his hand and left me free as the moth broke into a run. On either side of me the great wings spread out, acres-wide, to breast the air. In one last mad effort I raced over the left wing and took a flying leap. I landed at the giant's waistline and clung for all I was worth, still yelling lustily for the Doctor. The Moon Man picked me off and set me back upon the moth. But as my hold at his waist was wrenched loose something ripped and came away in my hand. It was the masterpiece, the horn picture of Pippiteepa. In his anxiety to put me aboard Jamaro again, who was now racing over the ground at a terrible speed, he never noticed that I carried his treasure with me.

Nor indeed was I vastly concerned with it at the moment. My mind only contained one thought: I was being taken away from the Doctor. Apparently I was to be carried off alone and set back upon the Earth. As the moth's speed increased still further I heard a fluttering near my right ear. I turned my head. And there, thank goodness, was Polynesia flying along like a swallow! In a torrent of words she poured out her message. For once in her life she was too pressed for time to swear.

"Tommy! —They know the Doctor is worried about your staying away from your parents. I told him to be careful last night. They heard. They're afraid if you stay he'll want to leave too, to get you back. And—"

The moth's feet had left the ground and his nose was tilted upward to clear the tops of the trees that bordered the open space. The powerful rush of air, so familiar to me from my first voyage of this kind, was already beginning—and growing all the time. Flapping and beating, Polynesia put on her best speed and for a while longer managed to stay level with my giant airship.

"Don't worry, Tommy," she screeched. "I had an inkling of what the Moon Man had up his sleeve, though I couldn't find out where he was hiding. And I warned the Doctor. He gave me this last message for you in case they should try to ship you out: Look after the old lame horse in the stable. Give an eyes to the fruit trees. *And don't worry*! He'll find a way down all right, he says. Watch out for the second smoke signal." (Polynesia's voice was growing faint and she was already dropping behind) ... "Good-bye and good luck!"

I tried to shout an answer; but the rushing air stopped my breath and made me gasp. "Good-bye and good luck!"—It was the last I heard from the Moon.

I lowered myself down among the deep fur to avoid the pressure of the tearing wind. My groping hands touched something strange. It was the moon bells. The giant in sending me down to the Earth had thought of the needs of the human. I grabbed one of the big flowers and held it handy to plunge my face in. Bad times were coming, I knew when we must cross the Dead Belt. There was nothing more I could do for the present. I would lie still and take it easy till I reached Puddleby and the little house with the big garden.

Well, for the most part my journey back was not very different from out first voyage. If it was lonelier for me than had been the trip with the Doctor, I, at all events, had the comfort this time of knowing from experience that the journey *could* be performed by a human with safety.

But dear me, what a sad trip it was! In addition to my loneliness I had a terrible feeling of guilt. I was leaving the Doctor behind—the Doctor who had never abandoned me nor any friend in need. True, it was not my fault, as I assured myself over and over again. Yet I couldn't quite get rid of the idea that if I had only been a little more resourceful or quicker-witted this would not have happened. And how, *how* was I going to face Dab-Dab, Jip and the rest of them with the news that John Dolittle had been left in the Moon?

The journey seemed endlessly long. Some fruit also had been provided, I found, by the Moon Man; but as soon as we approached the Dead Belt I felt too seasick to eat and remained so for the rest of the voyage.

At last the motion abated enough to let me sit up and take observations. We were quite close to the Earth. I could see it shining cheerfully in the sun and the sight of it warmed my heart. I had not realized till then how homesick I had been for weeks past.

The moth landed me on Salisbury Plain. While not familiar with the district, I knew the spire of Salisbury Cathedral from pictures. And the sight of it across this flat characteristic country told me where I was. Apparently it was very early morning, though I had no idea of the exact hour.

The heavier air and gravity of the Earth took a good deal of getting used to after the very different conditions of the Moon. Feeling like nothing so much as a ton-weight of misery, I clambered down from the moth's back and took stock of my surroundings.

Morning mists were rolling and breaking over this flat piece of my native Earth. From higher up it had seemed so sunny and homelike and friendly. Down here on closer acquaintance it didn't seem attractive at all.

Presently when the mists broke a little, I saw, not far off, a road. A man was walking along it. A farm labourer, no doubt, going to his work. How small he seemed! Perhaps he was a dwarf. With a sudden longing for human company, I decided to speak to him. I lunged heavily forward (the trial of the disturbing journey and the unfamiliar balance of earth gravity together made me reel like a drunken man) and when I had come within twenty paces I hailed him. The results were astonishing to say the least. He turned at the sound of my voice. His face went white as a sheet. Then he bolted like a rabbit and was gone into the mist.

I stood in the road down which he had disappeared. And suddenly it came over me what I was and how I must have looked. I had not measured myself recently on the Moon, but I did so soon after my return to the Earth. My height was nine feet nine inches and my waist measurement fifty-one inches and a half. I was dressed in a home-made suit of bark and leaves. My shoes and leggings were made of root-fibre and my hair was long enough to touch my shoulders.

No wonder the poor farm hand suddenly confronted by such an apparition on the wilds of Salisbury Plain had bolted! Suddenly I thought of Jamaro Bumblelily again. I would try to give him a message for the Doctor. If the moth could not understand me, I'd write something for him to carry back. I set out in search. But I never saw him again. Whether the mists misled me in direction or whether he had already departed moonwards again I never found out.

So, here I was, a giant dressed like a scarecrow, no

money in my pockets—no earthly possessions beyond a piece of reindeer horn, with a prehistoric picture carved on it. And then I realized, of course, that the farm labourer's reception of me would be what I would meet with everywhere. It was a long way from Salisbury to Puddleby, that I knew. I must have coach-fare; I must have food.

I tramped along the road a while thinking. I came in sight of a farm-house. The appetizing smell of frying bacon reached me. I was terribly hungry. It was worth trying. I strode up to the door and knocked gently. A woman opened it. She gave one scream at sight of me and slammed the door in my face. A moment later a man threw open a window and levelled a shot-gun at me.

"Get off the place," he snarled—"Quick! Or I'll blow your ugly head off."

More miserable than ever I wandered on down the road. What was to become of me? There was no one to whom I could tell the truth. For who would believe my story? But I must get to Puddleby. I admitted I was not particularly keen to do that—to face the Dolittle household with the news. And yet I must. Even without the Doctor's last message about the old horse and the fruit trees, and the rest, it was my job—to do my best to take his place while he was away. And then my parents—poor folk! I fear I had forgotten them in my misery. And would even they recognize me now?

Then of a sudden I came upon a caravan of gipsies. They were camped in a thicket of gorse by the side of the road and I had not seen them as I approached.

They too were cooking breakfast and more savoury smells tantalized my empty stomach. It is rather strange that the gipsies were the only people I met who were not afraid of me. They all came out of the wagons and gathered about me gaping; but they were interested, not scared. Soon I was invited to sit down and eat. The head of the party, an old man, told me they were going on to a county fair and would be glad to have me come with them.

I agreed with thanks. Any sort of friendship which would save me from an outcast lot was something to be jumped at. I found out later that the old gipsy's idea was to hire me off (at a commission) to a circus as a giant.

But as a matter of fact, that lot also I was glad to accept when the time came. I had to have money. I could not appear in Puddleby like a scarecrow. I needed clothes, I needed coach-fare, and I needed food to live on.

The circus proprietor—when I was introduced by

my friend the gipsy—turned out to be quite a decent fellow. He wanted to book me up for a year's engagement. But I, of course, refused. He suggested six months. Still I shook my head. My own idea was the shortest possible length of time which would earn me enough money to get back to Puddleby looking decent. I guessed from the circus man's eagerness that he wanted me in his show at almost any cost and for almost any length of time. Finally after much argument we agreed upon a month.

Then came the question of clothes. At this point I was very cautious. He at first wanted me to keep my hair long and wear little more than a loin-cloth. I was to be a "Missing Link from Mars" or something of the sort. I told him I didn't want to be anything of the kind (though his notion was much nearer to the truth than he knew). His next idea for me was "The Giant Cowboy from the Pampas." For this I was to wear an enormous sun-hat, woolly trousers, pistols galore, and spurs with rowels like saucers. That didn't appeal to me either very much as a Sunday suit to show to Puddleby.

Finally, as I realized more fully how keen the showman was to have me, I thought I would try to arrange my own terms.

"Look here, Sir," I said: "I have no desire to appear

something I am not. I am a scientist, an explorer, returned from foreign parts. My great growth is a result of the climates I have been through and the diet I have had to live on. I will not deceive the public by masquerading as a Missing Link or Western Cowboy. Give me a decent suit of black such as a man of learning would wear. And I will guarantee to tell your audiences tales of travel—true tales—such as they have never imagined in their wildest dreams. But I will not sign on for more than a month. That is my last word. Is it a bargain?"

Well, it was. He finally agreed to all my terms. My wages were to be three shillings a day. My clothes were to be my own property when I had concluded my engagement. I was to have a bed and a wagon to myself. My hours for public appearance were strictly laid down and the rest of my time was to be my own.

It was not hard work. I went on show from ten to twelve in the morning, from three to five in the afternoon, and from eight to ten at night. A tailor was produced who fitted my enormous frame with a decent-looking suit. A barber was summoned to cut my hair. During my show hours I signed my autograph to pictures of myself which the circus proprietor had printed in great numbers. They were sold at threepence apiece. Twice a day I told the gaping crowds of holiday folk the story of my travels. But I never spoke of the Moon. I called it just a "foreign land"—which indeed was true enough.

At last the day of my release came. My contract was ended, and with three pounds fifteen shillings in my pocket, and a good suit of clothes upon my back, I was free to go where I wished. I took the first coach in the direction of Puddleby. Of course many changes had to be made and I was compelled to stop the night at one point before I could make connections for my native town.

On the way, because of my great size, I was stared and gaped at by all who saw me. But I did not mind it so much now. I knew that at least I was not a terrifying sight.

On reaching Puddleby at last, I decided I would call on my parents first, before I went to the Doctor's house. This may have been just a putting off of the evil hour. But anyway, I had the good excuse that I should put an end to my parents' anxiety.

I found them just the same as they had always been—very glad to see me, eager for news of where I had gone and what I had done. I was astonished, however, that they had taken my unannounced departure so calmly—that is, I *was* astonished until it came out that, having heard that the Doctor also had mysteriously disappeared, they had not been nearly so worried as they might have been. Such was their faith in the great man, like the confidence that all placed in him. If *he* had gone and taken me with him, then everything was surely all right.

I was glad too that they recognized me despite my unnatural size. Indeed, I think they took a sort of pride in that I had, like Cæsar, "grown so great." We sat in front of the fire and I told them all of our adventures as well as I could remember them.

It seemed strange that they, simple people though they were, accepted my preposterous story of a journey to the Moon with no vestige of doubt or disbelief. I feared there were no other humans in the world—outside of Matthew Mugg, who would so receive my statement. They asked me when I expected the Doctor's return. I told them what Polynesia had said of the second smoke signal by which John Dolittle planned to notify me of his departure from the Moon. But I had to admit I felt none too sure of his escape from a land where his services were so urgently demanded. Then when I almost broke down, accusing myself of abandoning the Doctor, they both comforted me with assurances that I could not have done more than I had.

Finally my mother insisted that I stay the night at

## 25. PUDDLEBY ONCE MORE

their house and not attempt to notify the Dolittle household until the morrow. I was clearly overtired and worn out, she said. So, still willing to put off the evil hour, I persuaded myself that I *was* tired and turned in.

The next day I sought out Matthew Mugg, the Cats'-meat-Man. I merely wanted his support when I should present myself at "the little house with the big garden." But it took me two hours to answer all the questions he fired at me about the Moon and our voyage.

At last I did get to the Doctor's house. My hand had hardly touched the gate-latch before I was surrounded by them all. Too-Too the vigilant sentinel had probably been on duty ever since we left and one hoot from him brought the whole family into the front garden like a fire alarm. A thousand exclamations and remarks about my increased growth and changed appearance filled the air. But there never was a doubt in their minds as to who I was.

And then suddenly a strange silence fell over them all when they saw that I had returned alone. Surrounded by them I entered the house and went to the kitchen. And there by the fireside, where the great man himself has so often sat and told us tales, I related the whole story of our visit to the Moon.

At the end they were nearly all in tears, Gub-Gub

howling out loud.

"We'll never see him again!" he wailed. "They'll never let him go. Oh, Tommy, how *could* you have left him?"

"Oh, be quiet!" snapped Jip. "He couldn't help it. He was kidnapped. Didn't he tell you? Don't worry. We'll watch for the smoke signal. John Dolittle will come back to us, never fear. Remember he has Polynesia with him."

"Aye!" squeaked the white mouse. "She'll find a way."

"*I* am not worried," sniffed Dab-Dab, brushing away her tears with one wing, and swatting some flies off the bread-board with the other. "But it's sort of lonely here without him."

"Tut-tut!" grunted Too-Too. "Of course he'll come back!"

There was a tapping at the window.

"Cheapside," said Dab-Dab. "Let him in, Tommy."

I lifted the sash and the cockney sparrow fluttered in and took his place upon the kitchen table, where he fell to picking up what bread-crumbs had been left after the housekeeper's careful "clearing away." Too-Too told him the situation in a couple of sentences.

"Why, bless my heart!" said the sparrow. "Why all these long faces? John Dolittle stuck in the Moon! — Preposterous notion! —*Pre*-posterous, I tell you. You couldn't get that man stuck nowhere. My word, Dab-Dab! When you clear away you don't leave much fodder behind, do you? Any mice what live in your 'ouse shouldn't 'ave no difficulty keepin' their figures."

Well, it was done. And I was glad to be back in the old house. I knew it was only a question of time before I would regain a normal size on a normal diet. Meanwhile here I would not have to see anyone I did not want to.

And so I settled down to pruning the fruit-trees, caring for the comfort of the old horse in the stable and generally trying to take the Doctor's place as best I could. And night after night as the year wore on Jip, Too-Too and I would sit out, two at a time, while the Moon was visible, to watch for the smoke signal. Often when we returned to the house with the daylight, discouraged and unhappy, Jip would rub his head against my leg and say:

"Don't worry, Tommy. He'll come back. Remember he has Polynesia with him. Between them they will find a way."

**(THE END)**

# 后　记

　　2015年8月末，我来到了美国加州，在一所当地高中念十年级。从熟悉的家乡来到一个完全陌生的国度，繁重紧张的功课、好朋友的缺失都让我感到了巨大的压力和不适，特别是晚上做完了功课后更觉得疲倦和无聊，于是看书成了我唯一的消遣。10月的一天，我又一次翻开了那本已经看过好几遍的《杜立德医生航海奇遇记》，忽然想去找找杜立德医生的其他故事看看。我在网上找了好久，终于在澳大利亚古腾堡计划（该计划致力于将各种文学作品电子化）的官网上找到了这本配有原版插画的 *Doctor Dolittle On The Moon*，令我非常惊喜。要知道我可是杜立德医生迷，国内出版的所有关于杜立德医生的小说我几乎全部都看过，可是对这本小说我竟然一无所知。于是，我津津有味地看了起来，不到一个星期就全部看完了，之后生怕因为语言问题漏掉了什么有趣的细节，我又认认真真地看了两遍。看着看着，我心底里突然冒出了一个念头:既然没有发现在国内有这本书的中译本,那我为什么不能尝试一下把它翻译成中文呢?(其实当时国内有中译本 只是自己没有发现,此为后话。)这样国内那些和我一样热爱杜立德医生的伙伴们不是又有一本精彩的小说可以看了吗?

于是,从那天起,每天晚上做完了功课,我都会挤出时间来翻译几段文字,少则二三十分钟,多则一小时,双休日还会花更多的时间来翻译。说来也怪,自从开始这项翻译工作后,原本单调枯燥的生活好像变得充实有趣起来。每次一打开电脑,看到那个和善睿智的小个子医生带着那些可爱的小动物们在未知的世界里探险,我的心也跟着兴奋起来,觉得自己也已经化身为其中一员,一起在探索月球上的种种奥秘。这每晚的半个多小时也因此成了我一天中最轻松快乐的时光。

这样陆陆续续地从 2015 年 10 月到次年 6 月,我终于完成了这部小说翻译的第一稿,接着又利用暑假时间完成了第二稿和第三稿,最终在 2016 年的 9 月全部完工。

在翻译过程中,我碰到的最大困难是好多时候发现自己中文的词穷理亏——无法用精确的中文准确表达出原著句子确切的含义,同时为了避免词语的枯燥,必须用不同的中文词汇表达相近的英文含义。另外,原著作者喜用大段大段的从句,这对我的英语理解水平也提出了新的挑战。虽然我已经竭尽全力,但是由于水平有限,书中一定有不少的不足甚至谬误,希望读者们能多多指正。因为不管是英文还是中文学习,对我来说都是任重而道远。

我特别想说的是,通过翻译这本小说,不仅让我的英文水平和中文水平都有了长足的进步,也帮助我渡过了初到美国那段紧张慌乱和孤单寂寞的时光,让我的心能够沉静下来,专注而执着地去完成一件自己喜欢的事。所以,从这个意义上来说,我应该特别感谢《杜立德医生在月球》这本书。

最后,我还要特别感谢上海文汇出版社的竺振榕老师为本书的出版所做的工作,也特别感谢王建幸老师为本书所配的插图。

盛正茂
2017 年 3 月

# AFTERWORD

I came to the United States, or, precisely, to California, in late August 2015, and began attending a local high school. As the familiarity of home was suddenly replaced by the strangeness of a new environment , I felt some pressure and discomfort at first, feelings only strengthened by school workloads and an early lack of friendship.

After completing my homework, nighttime became particularly boring and exhausting to me, and reading turned out to be the only relaxation. One day in October, again I took out of my bookshelf *The Voyages of Doctor Dolittle*, a book I had read repetitively. While enjoying it, I grew more curious to the other Doctor Dolittle novels, and it took me some time before finally discovering a copy of *Doctor Dolittle on the Moon* with original illustrations on Gutenberg Australia. Even though I had read substantially on Doctor Dolittle, this is a book I had never heard of.

Delighted, I finished the book in a week, then I re-read it twice just in case that I had missed any interesting details during the first course. And a thought appeared: since I found no Chinese translation of this book (Actually there are, i just did not find them), why cannot I do it myself and enable more Chinese readers to learn about these fascinating stories?

Every weekday since that night I spent time ranging from twenty minutes to, occasionally, an hour (more time was devoted on weekends), on translation, and it became a very exciting leisure for me. Every time I turned on the laptop and saw the friendly, wise Doctor with his animal friends traveling in an unknown world, my mind grew wild and looked forward to being a member of such great adventures.

In June 2016, the first draft was completed, and during the summer break I reviewed and revised it twice, finally finishing the entire process by September.

I also encountered several problems and difficulties in the process, among them are the failure to choose the Chinese term that best fits the original English expression of Hugh Lofting and the struggle to use various wordings for a same meaning, avoiding repetitiveness. Furthermore, the author's habit of building long, complicated sentences also proved to be challenging for me at that time. Thus, despite the efforts I put into it, the translation would inevitably contain some irregularities, even mistakes, and I would be thankful if any readers would generously indicate to me those problems. For me, there is still a long way to go for both English and Chinese study.

Finally, I would like to thank this book, *Doctor Dolittle on the Moon*, itself, since while reading and translating it, my understanding for both languages deepened. It also enabled me to put time and efforts into something I truly love, and accompanied me through the first confusing months spent on this new, unfamiliar land.

Also, I have to sincerely thank Ms. Zhenrong Zhu of Shanghai Wenhui Publishing House for the publication of this book and Mr. Jianxing Wang for his illustrations in the book.

**Zhengmao Sheng**
In March 2017

**图书在版编目(CIP)数据**

杜立德医生在月球 / (美) 休·罗夫丁著;盛正茂译. —上海:文汇出版社,2017.5
ISBN 978-7-5496-2148-4

Ⅰ.①杜… Ⅱ.①休… ②盛… Ⅲ.①童话—美国—现代 Ⅳ.①I712.88

中国版本图书馆CIP数据核字(2017)第130219号

## 杜立德医生在月球

[美] 休·罗夫丁 / 著
盛正茂(Zhengmao Sheng) / 译

责任编辑 / 竺振榕
插　　图 / 王建幸
封面装帧 / 张　晋

出版发行 / 文汇出版社
　　　　　上海市威海路755号
　　　　　(邮政编码 200041)
经　　销 / 全国新华书店
排　　版 / 南京展望文化发展有限公司
印刷装订 / 上海宝山译文印刷厂
版　　次 / 2017年5月第1版
印　　次 / 2017年5月第1次印刷
开　　本 / 787×1092　1/32
字　　数 / 200千字
印　　张 / 11.75

ISBN 978-7-5496-2148-4
定　　价 / 35.00元